Jobella:
A Story of Loss and Redemption

D.L. Stalnaker

WESTBOW
PRESS
A DIVISION OF THOMAS NELSON

WestBow Press books may be ordered through booksellers or by contacting:

WestBow Press
A Division of Thomas Nelson
1663 Liberty Drive
Bloomington, IN 47403
www.westbowpress.com
1-(866) 928-1240

ISBN: 978-1-4908-0139-1 (sc)
ISBN: 978-1-4908-0140-7 (hc)
ISBN: 978-1-4908-0138-4 (e)

Library of Congress Control Number: 2013912351

Printed in the United States of America.

WestBow Press rev. date: 07/16/2013

Dedicated to my family . . .

<u>Milton</u>, my husband of forty-one years who has stuck with me all this time and put up with my long hours at the computer when I should have been cleaning the house and cooking, especially now that I'm retired.

<u>My Daughters, Laura and her family, and Kara,</u> Thank you for your support. You all are truly special to me, each in your own way.

<u>My brothers and sisters,</u> who have always believed in me and encouraged me when I decided to write.

<u>My Dad and Mom,</u> Dad because he was an inspiration to me because he also didn't start writing until he retired and was able to publish several books on his own and my Mom because she was a rock to all of us. Our family misses you and we will see you again in Heaven one day.

And most of all I want to thank my God. You have been the inspiration for this book and all those that I hope will follow. Without you, we are nothing and our words are meaningless, blown about in the wind and falling nowhere.

Acknowledgments:

All scriptures quoted are from the
King James Version of the Bible

The story of Jobella is loosely based on
the Old Testament book of Job.

Disclaimer:

Table of Contents

Prologue

And the Lord said unto Satan. Whence comest thou? Then Satan answered the Lord, and said from going to and fro in the earth, and from walking up and down in it. And the Lord said unto Satan. Hast Thou considered my servant Job, that there is none like him in the earth, a perfect and upright man, one that feareth God and escheweth evil? Then Satan answered the Lord and said, doth Job fear God for naught? Hast not thou made a hedge about him and about his house, and about all that he hath on every side? Thou hast blessed the work of his hands and his substance is increased in the land. But put forth thine hand now, and touch all that he hath and he will curse thee to thy face. And the Lord said unto Satan, behold, all that he hath is in thy power; only upon himself put not forth thine hand. So Satan went forth from the presence of the Lord.

Job 1:7-12

It has been a very long one and a half years since the first time I saw this courtroom, but it seems like forever. Nothing has changed much since that day. As I sit waiting, I take in all of the sights and sounds of it. It is a beautiful room for a courtroom, with its mahogany furniture, hunter green walls, and white marble floors. Behind the judges desk there are two stained glass windows. On the right side, the window shows the Ten Commandments, and on the left side is Lady Justice with her scales held high. This is one courtroom that has made the decision to keep the Ten Commandments on display even though the popular trend now is to remove them or any part of God from public offices. It would be too costly to replace such a magnificent rendering in stained glass.

This is the third time I've been in this courtroom. Hopefully it will be my last time at least on this side of the desk in the position of someone seeking justice for my family and myself. The next time I come, hopefully it will be with a law degree in hand, representing someone else who needs help as much I have. Because of the kindness and professionalism of my lawyer, Abigail "Abby" Freeman, I decided to become a lawyer myself, with an emphasis in family law.

Today is the hearing that will determine if I will be granted the custody of my twin younger brother and sister, Joshua and Joanna. They will be four years old now. They have lived in foster care for the last year and a half. I've heard they are close to their foster parents and have started in pre-school and have made a lot of new friends. They may have forgotten all about their mom, dad and me after this length of time. They say you don't remember much of what you knew before starting school, but I hope they at least remember me and what I did was for their own good, and that I loved them so much. I want them to come home and live with my new husband and me. I hope they will be willing to leave their foster home, if everything goes in my favor, that is.

I've overcome a great deal of heartache and pain since mom and dad were killed, but now it's time to move on with my life. I look at my trembling hands and will them to be still. I twist the bright gold ring on my left hand and remember that at least all of life isn't dark, and hopeless, and there are things left that are worth fighting for. To bring Josh and Joanie home to live with my new family and me would be worth every bit of it.

I turn and smile at my new husband, and my new mom and dad (for that is how I'll always think of them) sitting in the audience, and supporting me all the way. He gives me a thumbs up sign, and smiles back at me. I know he wants this for me as much as I do.

I'm sitting at the large wooden desk doodling on the yellow pad in front of me, when I hear loud clicking of heels on the marble floor. I turn, and see Abigail coming towards me with a determination to get this done. Abigail has been my lawyer and mentor over the past two years, and has been a very dear friend during my trials, both literally and personally.

"Well, good morning, Jobella, are you ready for this new adventure?" she asked, smiling, as she sat down. "This is the day you've been waiting for, let's hope it turns out the way you've pictured it.

"I hope so. I'm really anxious to see my brother and sister again. I hope they recognize me. It seems like a lifetime ago I sent them away to live in foster care. You don't think that they will hate me for that, do you? I want them to know I want the best for them, always."

"Give them more credit than that. I'm sure they will not only remember you, but have long since forgiven you. I'm sure they know what you did for them was for their safety, and well-being.

"Hear ye, hear ye, please rise. The Honorable Judge Norman Peterson presiding, please rise for his Honor." I hear the bailiff announce as the judge nears his desk.

I sit back down and start doodling again on the yellow note pad in front of me. My lawyer looked at me as I watched the children being led in by their foster mother and father. I wanted to run to them, and hug them, and never let them go.

It has been so long since Josh and Joanie had been placed in foster care. They look so grown up now. It breaks my heart to think of the times that we didn't get to share in the last one and a half years, like their first day of pre-school, holidays, plays, and programs at school and church they would have been in and of course the heartaches they would have had, knowing that their older sister gave them away, and not fully understanding why their mommy, and daddy, and older sister were gone.

My thoughts drifted back unbidden to the nightmare that started one and a half years ago. The tears threatened to race down my cheeks, as I thought about how wonderful my life once was, and how at the time, everything was going so great for me, and then it all changed in those horrible moments, and nothing would ever be the same again. I prayed silently for strength that whatever happened today would close this horrible chapter in my life, and my family would be reunited.

My thoughts continued, as I remembered the sadness in the twin's eyes as they said goodbye to our mom and dad. Joanie put her favorite teddy bear in the grave so they wouldn't be so lonely for her, and would remember her, when she saw them again in heaven. Josh tried to be a little man and not cry, as he took the little shovel and threw dirt on the grave.

It must have hurt them dearly when I took them to the police station a few days later. They must have thought they did something wrong, when I left them and walked away without looking back, because I didn't want them to see me crying.

Looking back at everything now, I realize I could have made better decisions, but in my own grief, I know I didn't think things through. I was young, confused, and impulsive, and I thought I knew what was best. I have learned so much in the last year and a half, and I have grown so much in that short of a time. What really happened to me a little more than a year ago? What could I have done differently? Was God testing my character? And most important, am I ready for this next step in being a mother figure to my younger brother and sister? Will Joanie and Josh want to come home with me? Will the judge overlook my troubled past, and deem me fit to be a mother?

Chapter 1

"Jobella, dear, could you do a huge favor for me today? Your dad and I are hosting the Bible study group at our house tonight and we have a ton of cooking and cleaning to do. Would you mind taking your brother and sister to the sitter on your way to school and picking them up on your way home this evening?"

"Sure, Mom. You know how much I love driving our new BMW. Besides, it really isn't a problem. It's on my way, but do remember, I have a student council meeting after school and a pep rally after that for our basketball game this weekend. It's our final game! So I will be a little late in picking them up."

"That's all right. That will give me even more time to finish my chores. Just make sure Mrs. Griffith knows you'll be an hour or so late. You are a real angel, Jobella. I don't know what I'd ever do without you!"

"You'd think of something, I'm sure." I laughed.

"Your dad's getting off at noon today, and he will be here to help me clean and move furniture. I love having our friends from church over, but between you and me, I'm glad we only do this once a year!"

"Aw, you know you like being the center of attention and showing off our beautiful home. Don't deny it." I smiled and gave her a big hug. "You're the best mom I ever had!"

"I'm the only mom you ever had." She laughed, and then she called up the stairs. "Joshua and Joanna Jordan, I need you down here right this minute. You need to eat your breakfast and get ready to go to the sitters. Jobella is taking you, and she needs to get to school!"

The twins came running down the stairs into the arms of Mom, laughing and excited about their day.

"Come on, kiddos. Let's get out of Mommy's hair for a little while." I said after they finished their breakfast.

As I started to go out the door with the twins I turned to Mom. "Goodbye, Mom. Have a fun day working and sweating for your party tonight. I love you!"

The twins ran to their mother and gave her big hugs. "We love you too, Mommy," they said in unison.

As I backed out of the neighborhood, I looked around at the beauty of it. We lived in a well-maintained upper middle class neighborhood of old Victorian homes that had been remodeled and updated to look new. Everyone had beautiful gardens, and well-kept lawns. It was very pleasant, and I felt quite fortunate to live in this wonderful neighborhood. I thought: *When I go to heaven, I hope my mansion looks like one of these. It is so peaceful here and everyone knows everyone else and it is a true community of friends.*

We were very fortunate my mom didn't have to work, and it was especially nice to be able to come home and have her there to greet us. Sometimes she would send the twins to day care when she did her volunteer work. She was very involved in the activities of the church and would often go to visit shut-ins, bring them food, and just be there for them if they needed anything. She believed it was our station in life to do what we could to ease the problems of the less fortunate. She always instilled in us the belief that we were to take care of others if we had the ability to do so.

My dad, Kevin, was the CEO of one of the largest plants in Clairmonte. He was a deacon in the church and a Sunday school teacher for the young men's class. He was a good role model for all who knew him and I was proud to call him my dad. He truly was someone I could look up to.

Mom and I sang in the choir and worked in the nursery once a month. I enjoyed spending time with my church family. We were very close to all of them. Sometimes I think people might have been a little jealous of my family. We were, by most standards, well to do and God had blessed us with good health, money, and a lot of close friends. Life was very idyllic for us. But then, why shouldn't God be good to us? Look at everything we did for him.

Mrs. Griffith was standing at the door of her home as I drove up to drop off the kids.

"Hi, Jobella. How come you're bringing the little ones today?"

"Good morning, Mrs. Griffith. I'm just dropping them off for Mom and Dad on my way to school. I'll be by to get them around 4:30 or 5:00. I have meetings after school. Mom and Dad are having a Bible class study and fellowship tonight at our house, and they need to get everything ready.

"Josh and Joanna, you be good for Mrs. Griffith, you hear?" I asked, shaking my finger at them.

I gave them both hugs and kisses, turned them over to the sitter's care, and continued on my way to school. As I approached the school, I saw my three best friends, Billie, Eliza, and Zoe, walking together, laughing.

"Hey, you gonna give us a ride in that fancy car?" Billie called out. Billie was the most outspoken and outgoing of my three friends. She was one of the cheerleaders for our team. She was exuberant and beautiful, the kind of girl that all the guys were crazy about.

"Sure, hop in. Just be careful, and don't tear the seats or mess it up."

"You can't tear leather." Eliza laughed. Eliza was the sensible one. She and I were probably the closest of my three friends. We were both planning on going to Duke in the fall and hoped to be roommates. She was the secretary of the senior class. I was the president, so we spent a lot of time together, planning projects for our school.

"How much damage can we do in two blocks?" added Zoe. Zoe was the oddball of the group. She always wore dark clothes and nail polish. She also wore too much make up and her hair was jet black. She was the very picture of a Goth girl. She looked dark and fearsome but she was sweet and would give the shirt off her back if you asked for it. She claimed to be a Christian, but judging by her appearance you had to wonder. Still, she was a good friend, and I wouldn't trade her for the world.

"How come you've got the car today?" Eliza asked.

"I had to take my little brother and sister to the sitters for Mom."

"I'll bet you argued and fussed about how abused you were the whole way here, right?" laughed Billie. "You're such a dutiful daughter. I'll bet you couldn't wait to show off this fancy car. You're such a little princess in your shiny new carriage. Hey speaking of carriages, are you and Steve going to the ball this Saturday, Cinderella?"

"If you mean the prom, no. Steve is going to be a preacher and he doesn't go in for dances and such. He doesn't think that dancing is honorable to God."

"Girl, you seriously need a new boyfriend. You've been hanging out with him for too long! You two sound like an old married couple already. Loosen up, and have some fun already! And besides where in the Bible does it command you not to dance?" asked Zoe.

"I'm not sure, but I know it can lead to more unclean acts, and some dancing just looks sinful."

"Whatever," replied Zoe. "That's just all in your mind!"

"Let's just agree to disagree on that one, okay? I wouldn't want to go anywhere without Steve and if he doesn't want to go, we just won't go."

"I know it's your life, but you'll be missing out on a lot of fun!" Billie added.

Steve and I had been dating since the beginning of high school. He graduated before me and was currently in college, working toward a degree in theology. We go to the same church and are active in the youth ministry. We've gone on several mission trips through the church, and I believe that Steve may eventually decide go into missions. That would suit me just fine. I would follow him to the ends of the earth if that's what the Lord wants us to do.

"Well, guys, here we are at good ole East Clairmonte High. I'll see you later."

"Hey, how about a ride home?" asked Zoe for the three of them.

"Can't do it today, unless you want to wait around for me until after my meetings, and then I have to get the twins."

"That's okay, we don't want to wait that long. Even if it does mean that we get to ride in your fancy car," sighed Eliza as she rolled her eyes.

"Can't you miss your meetings just this once? Puh-lease?" asked Billie.

"You know little Miss Perfect can't miss anything," said Zoe with a laugh. "She might mess up her scholarship to Duke, and then Eliza would have to find another roommate!"

"We're only kidding," added Billie. "We'll see you later."

I had been friends with the three girls ever since we were in grade school. We were so close that everyone called us the three musketeers plus one. That one, of course, was me, because I was different from my friends. They all went to my church, but they weren't as active as

I was and some people had doubts about whether or not they were even Christians at all. Some of their actions were a little suspect.

As I settled down into my classes for the day I began to have an eerie feeling that wouldn't go away. I felt as if a heavy cloud hung over me, the kind of thing that you read about, kind of like ESP or telepathy. I felt like something was going to happen. I had trouble concentrating and that wasn't like me. I made straight A's in school, and I was always alert in classes. Maybe I was just worried about finals or graduation. I tried to pass it off and put more effort into what the teacher was saying. As the bell rang I got up slowly and dragged myself to the last class of the day.

My steps were slower than usual. *Great, I must be coming down with something,* I told myself. *That's all I need right now.'*

As I sat in my homeroom at the end of the day, I was trying to do some homework, when an announcement came over the loud speaker. "Jobella Jordan, you're needed in the guidance office immediately," It blared.

"Oh Jobella, what did you do? Little Miss Perfect did something wrong." I heard an obnoxious voice call out from the back of the room.

The teacher let me be excused, and as I walked out of the room, other students were whispering conspiracy theories all around me. I felt my heart pounding in my chest. I wasn't use to being called to the principal's office.

I was surprised when I got to the office to see a police officer standing next to a grim appearing principal. The guidance counselor, and her secretary were sitting on the sofa in her office, and they looked as though they had been crying.

"Jobella, please come and sit with me, dear." My guidance counselor said as she patted the sofa beside her, in her office.

"What's going on? What happened? Is it the car? I tried to be careful with it. Did something happen to it?"

"No dear," she said through her tears, "It's something much worse, Jobella. You'd better sit down now."

I lowered down onto the sofa between the secretary and the guidance counselor. Then I looked from the policeman, to the principal, trying to read their eyes. They looked deeply troubled, and I knew it was bad.

The principal spoke first: "It's nothing that you did, or did not do, Ms. Jordan, it's your parents. They were in a fire today. Your house caught on fire in a freak electrical accident, and the firemen couldn't get your parents out before they were badly injured. Your house is also gone. I'm so very sorry, I know how close you were to your folks."

"NO! NO! This can't be happening! This isn't happening! You're lying to me! This is only a bad dream. God wouldn't do this to us!"

I looked at the secretary, but when I saw the tears in her eyes, and her nod, I totally broke down, my body weak with crying. When I finally calmed down, I looked up at the police officer and saw the pity in his eyes. I asked him if he would mind taking me to the hospital to see my parents. I didn't think I'd be able to drive in my present state. I was too upset.

"I need to get my things from my locker, and I'll be ready to go." I told the officer.

"I'll meet you in the front of the building. I'll be standing beside the squad car." Replied the officer.

When I got to my locker, my friends were waiting on me. They paused, when they saw that I had been crying.

"What happened to you? Girl, are you in trouble?" Billie asked.

"There was a fire at my house, and my parents are in the hospital. I'm leaving now with the policeman. I'll let you know the details later, as soon as I find out something.

"Oh my gosh!" Eliza gasped. "Let us know if we can do anything."

I thanked them, and got into the squad car with the policeman. On the way to the hospital, I suddenly remembered Josh and Joanna. "I told my brother and sister I'd pick them up at the sitters after school."

We'll drop by and get them after you go to the hospital. Give me your sitter's number, and I'll give her a call, to let her know you'll be late. I'll stay with you as long as it takes, and then we'll go by the school, and you can get your car, and then you can pick up the kids."

"Thank you so much for your kindness, officer. I would appreciate that."

As we were going to the hospital, we passed the shell of what use to be my home. There were still a few firemen at the scene. I was shocked at how much of my house was gone. I started weeping again, as I thought about my Mom and Dad, and how frightened they must have been as they tried to escape the inferno, and I know they were frantically trying to save our home, and all our belongings. Our once beautiful, comfortable home was gone forever.

When we finally arrived at the emergency room, I began to panic. I could feel my heart racing, and I could barely breathe. I thought I was going to faint. When I finally did catch my breath, I started to scream. "Where are they? What have you done with them? I want to see my Mom and Dad."

The receptionist answered "Calm down, you'll frighten the other patients. Where are you looking for?"

"My parents, Gabrielle and Kevin Jordan!"

"Please have a seat. I'll get the nurse assigned to them." Answered the grim looking receptionist. Then she announced over the PA system. "Would the nurse taking care of the burns in room seven, please come to the lobby?"

I sat down next to the policeman. He put his arm around me to comfort me while I waited for what seemed like hours, even though in reality it was just a few minutes.

The nurse came out to see me, along with the doctor. "Are you Jobella Jordan?"

"I am. Are my parents going to be okay?"

"I need for you to come to my office. Please follow me."

He looked sad, and I knew whatever he had to tell me wasn't good. I thought I even saw tears in his eyes.

As we sat in his office, he was quiet for a moment. Then came the news that I was reluctant to hear, the news that would change my life forever.

"Jobella, I knew your father and mother for quite a while. I've even been out with them on several occasions. They were truly wonderful people, and it upsets me to give you this news, Jobella, your mother and father died on the way to the hospital. We tried everything we could do to save them, but they were burned over ninety percent of their bodies. There was nothing we could do."

"Can I go and see them?"

"We've already sent them to the morgue. You will have to go, and identify them of course, but keep in mind, I can't prepare you for what you are going to see, their faces are okay, but the rest of their bodies have major burns on them. Try to remember them, and how they looked before the fire, and thank the Lord, that he carried them on home so they would no longer have to suffer."

The nurse hugged her. "I'm so sorry, I knew your parents from church. They were wonderful people. This has really been hard for all of us."

The doctor walked with me down to the morgue. It was the longest walk of my life. I wanted to turn back with every step. I didn't want to see mom and dad that way, but I knew I had to, just like I knew I would have to face an unknown future.

I looked at my mom and dad. The coroner only let see their faces. They looked peaceful. It was as if they had seen the faces of angels as they died. I took a strange comfort in that, but seeing the reality of their death was terribly hard on me, even though I knew they had gone home to be with Jesus.

"Could I see the hospital chaplain?

"Actually, your pastor is here. Would you rather see him?" asked the doctor. "When he heard who was in the fire, he came straight here, and then decided to wait until you arrived."

"Yes sir, I would like to see him now."

"If you wish, you can go down to the hospital chapel, I will send him there. It is the third door on the left, down that hall." He said as he pointed in the direction of the chapel.

As I started down the hall, I met up with the officer who brought me in.

"Do you want me to go with you until the pastor comes?" He asked.

"No, thank you, I would like to be by myself for a little while."

I walked slowly to the front of the chapel, and knelt to pray. As Pastor Stewart came in, I was pleading with God. "Why did you take my Mom and Dad away from me? What have I done to deserve this? I try to do your will. Did I do something wrong? Did they do something wrong? Why are you punishing us?"

I heard a familiar voice behind me. "God is not punishing you or your family. God doesn't take away our loved ones for anything we might have done wrong.

"Oh, Pastor Stewart," I sobbed as he cradled me in his arms, "why did this happen to us?"

"This wasn't your fault. God loves you, and wants to be there for you through your sadness. Bad things often happen because sin was allowed to come into the world through the work of Satan. It started in the Garden of Eden, and it still continues. Sometimes Satan does evil things to God's people, to try to turn them away from God. How you react to these evil times will show how much faith you truly have in God. God will comfort you, and will show you what you need, to overcome this tragedy. You need to put your faith in God."

"Where was God when my house burned down? Why couldn't he send his angels to protect Mom and Dad? He's done that before to other people. Why didn't he help us?"

"I don't know all the answers, but I do know God loves you, and has a will for your life, and you will need to trust him to work through this with you."

"I'm having a lot of trouble believing in a loving God now, and that he would allow Satan to do this to good people, like my family. Mom and Dad did a lot of things for the church. They were the most faithful Christians I knew. Why would he allow this to happen to them?"

"I really don't know, but I do know that your mom and dad loved God and served him faithfully, and now they are in heaven with Jesus, and they will never suffer again. I know that isn't much comfort to you now, but someday you'll be with them again."

"What about now? Josh, Joanie, and I are on our own now. We will be suffering the rest of our lives without our mom and dad." I pushed away from, and ran out of the chapel, crying.

Chapter 2

The police officer was waiting for me at the front door of the ER. We were quiet on the ride back to the high school. I was deep in thought, as my mind was processing everything that had happened to me in the last two hours. When we got back to the school parking lot, I thanked him for all his kindness, as I stepped out of the patrol car.

"Are you going to be alright to drive now? He asked.

"I think so. I really need to get my brother and sister. The baby sitter must be frantic wondering where I am."

"I called her and let her know what happened. She's expecting you to come by later. She said it was okay, and she wasn't going to charge you anything for today."

As I drove to the sitter's house, I was trying to think about how I should tell the twins about our mom and dad. It was hard enough for me to work through it. How will they feel when they find out their only source of love and security is gone. The weight of responsibility was just too much for me. The twins are going to need me more than ever now. I need to be strong for them. 'I don't want this responsibility'. I thought to myself. 'What happens when I go away to college? Will I even be able to go now? I could feel the tears starting anew as I thought about everything. *'Stop it, Jobella. Don't let them see you cry. You have to be strong for them.'* I scolded myself. When I picked them up, Mrs. Griffith saw that I was distressed. My face was red and puffy, and my make up smeared, from all my crying.

"Are you all right?" Mrs. Griffith asked. "The policeman that called said you were at the hospital and you would be late getting the kids, but he didn't tell me what happened."

"Mom and Dad were killed today! Our house burned down, and the firemen couldn't get them out in time. I just came from the hospital. I'm sorry I'm late picking them up. Where are they now?" I cried, as I looked frantically around the room, and didn't see them.

I was interrupted when they came in from outside to greet me. "'Bella, 'Bella." They called together, out of breath as they ran into the house, from the playground out back. "Are you going to take us home now?"

"I didn't say anything to the kids. I thought it best to come from you." Mrs. Griffith said.

"Thank you." I said, as I hugged them both tightly. I didn't ever want to let them go. I was very protective of them, especially now. They were all I had left of our family.

As they went off to get their backpacks, and their art project from today, I spoke quietly to Mrs. Griffith.

"My goodness, what are you going to do now? Where are you, and the kids going to go?" The sitter asked as she pulled me aside.

"Oh my gosh, I didn't even think about the fact that there was no where to go!"

Then the sitter suddenly remembered the emergency contact number on the twins application form. "I understand that you have an aunt and uncle that live on the other side of town. I can give you their number, if you'd like."

"I forgot about them. It's been years since I talked to them. I guess I don't have much of a choice, do I? They're the only ones left, and I don't want to impose on my friends' families. I suppose they will want to know what happened anyway. Aunt Ruth was my Mom's sister. I'll give her a call on my cell phone. I don't know if they'll even remember me. I was a little girl when Aunt Ruth and Mom quit talking. I hope they'll take us in. We really don't have anywhere else to go."

My Aunt Ruth lived on the south side of town. She and my mother had a falling out several years ago after my grandparents were killed in a car wreck. They had all been Christians, but Aunt Ruth blamed God for the wreck, and their subsequent deaths, and never reconciled with my mother over it. She got mixed up with the wrong kind of crowd after that, and married a man she met in a bar, and they didn't live quite so 'happily ever after'. My mom and dad continued serving in the church after the accident, their faith never wavering. I was five years old at the time of the accident. Mom and Dad raised me in a Christian home, and that's all I ever knew. Sure, they had heartaches over what happened to grandma and grandpa, but they didn't blame God, and I didn't either. Mom's strength has always been in the church. Socially and economically my parents thrived, and we became one of the richest families in Clairmonte. My aunt wasn't so lucky. She became extremely bitter against my family, and didn't want anything else to do with us, because she felt that she couldn't live up to our standards.

I didn't want to go to her house to live, even temporarily, but I didn't see any other choice. I didn't want to impose on my friends, and it wouldn't look right if Steve's family took me in, even if he was my boyfriend, and his parents were okay with it. I had too much pride to look for handouts from my friends.

It had been years since I'd seen my aunt and I could hardly remember her at all except for the things Mom and Dad said about her and Uncle Bud. My Mom actually wanted to go, and visit her a few times, but Dad stopped her. He didn't feel that she would be safe driving in that part of town.

I guessed I would just have to take my chances until something better came along. I'd make other arrangements as soon as I could. Maybe after I graduate, I can find a job, and move into an apartment with the twins. I had to keep telling myself things would be better eventually, and maybe the picture wasn't quite as bleak as I thought it would be.

I dialed my aunt's phone number. "Aunt Ruth, this is Jobella Jordan, you know, Gabrielle's daughter. Something terrible has happened."

"I haven't heard from your mom, dad, or you in a 'coons' age! What's goin' on that you are calling me now for?"

I had to stifle the sobs that threatened to choke me. "Mom and dad were killed today in our house fire. Our home was totally destroyed, as well. Josh, Joanna and I have nowhere to go. We were wondering if you would let us stay at your house, until we figure out what to do. We will try not to impose on you any longer than we need to, if you're willing."

"Don't you mean, any longer than you have to?" she asked. "Oh, I'm sorry if I'm being rude, too bad 'bout your loss though. Yes, you can stay here. Your mom and I haven't been very close, but that doesn't give me the right to treat you children badly. You can stay as long as ya' need to. I didn't hear 'bout the fire, and your parents, but why should the cops call us? It ain't like we're the next of kin or somethin'. I did hear the fire trucks earlier today. I was wondering what happened, and lookie here, it involved me after all. Come on over whenever you want. We live at 148th South Street. It's not as fancy as what you're accustomed to, but it'll be a roof over your head, and I guess you'll be needin' that."

"Thank you, Aunt Ruth. We are leaving the sitters now. We'll be there in a little while." I thanked Mrs. Griffith, and told her I didn't know if, or when we'd be back.

My cell phone rang as soon as I hung up with my aunt. It was my boyfriend, Steve. "Hi, I heard what happened. Are you all right? Can I do anything?"

"My parent's are dead, and our house, and everything we owned are gone! Am I supposed to be all right? I'm sorry. I'm just so upset right now. The twins, and I are on my way over to my aunt's house right now. Could you meet me there? I really need to see you. I'll give you instructions how to get there."

After picking up Joanna and Josh at the daycare, and talking with Steven, I headed to my aunt's house. After I passed my neighborhood, and the burnt shell of our house, I headed to the south side of town, where my aunt lived. I wasn't quite prepared for how bad it really was where she lived. The homes were noticeably older, and more run down, than I was use to. There were homeless people hanging out, and begging for money, and teenagers were standing around, outside of seedy looking restaurants, and video stores, smoking, drinking, and using drugs. I began to wonder why I decided to do this, and not try to see if any of my friends could take us in. *'What's done is done'* I sighed. *'It's probably better not to impose on my friends either'*.

My cell phone started to ring again, and as I answered, I heard Steve's voice. "I'm on my way, are you sure you want to do this? This neighborhood doesn't look so hot."

"I know, I'm not looking forward to seeing her either, she doesn't sound very nice. You'd better wait outside, and let us have a few minutes with her, before you come to the door. I'm sure we're enough of a shock to her, without adding a boyfriend to the mix."

"Well at least you won't have to be there long, since you'll be going to college in a couple of months."

"That is, if I even get to go to college now. I don't know what I'll do without my parent's financial, and emotional support helping me prepare to go. I'm at a total loss of what I need to do."

"Your friends, and I will help you, and you always have God. Let him help you find your way through this. He'll work out the details. Just trust him."

"I wish I had your faith, Steve. I'll see you in a few minutes. We're here at her house now."

I parked my car in front of my aunt's house. I felt a little intimidated by my surroundings, as I stepped out of the car. I let the twins out, and they clung to me, as we walked to the door.

"'Bella, why are we here? Why are we not going home? Where are Mommy and Daddy?" They cried.

When they saw the tears in my eyes, they knew there was no more home, and their Mommy and Daddy were gone.

My heart was breaking, as I told them again about what happened.

When my aunt opened the door, she was wearing a dirty bathrobe, smoking a cigarette, and drinking a beer. I looked past her into the living room behind her. An open box of cold pizza was sitting on the coffee table, and clutter was everywhere. The television was turned on to her favorite soap opera. I thought I would vomit at the smell of the garbage, and stale cigarette smoke in the air.

Joanna tugged at my slacks, and whispered. "'Bella, I don't like it here."

"Well, well, well, you must be Jobella! You look just like your mama when she was your age except for the red hair, and these precious little darlin's must be Joanna and Joshua. They look just like you, when you were their age. Your mom sent us an announcement, when they were born. I believe that is actually the last time I heard from her."

As I glanced around the room, the sight of empty beer cans, ashtrays full of cigarette butts, and other garbage lying about, nauseated me. The kitchen counters were covered with dirty dishes, and flies were everywhere. I tried not to look too shocked at her bad housekeeping.

I stammered, and hoped my revulsion wasn't too transparent, when I greeted her. "It's good to see you again, Aunt Ruth." I lied. "Where's Uncle Bud?"

"My old man is still at work. Sometimes he comes home late. He likes to stop at the bar with a few of his work buddies on the way home. It's a good thing. That will give us a few minutes to get reacquainted before he gets here. Sorry for the looks of the place. I wasn't expecting any company, least of all my long lost relatives. I'll bet your mom was a wonderful housekeeper, not like me."

"It's alright, we'll get use to it. I can help you clean, if you want me to. It is very kind of you to accept us on short notice like this. I'm sorry to intrude on you this way, Aunt Ruth, but I didn't know what else to do or where to go."

"Aw, that's perfectly alright, anything for my dear departed sister, that I haven't seen in ages." She sneered.

I couldn't help but be aware of the sarcasm in her voice. "Look, this isn't easy for us either, you know. I wouldn't have bothered you, if I could make other plans. I know how busy you are, and what an inconvenience we must be."

"I'm just messin' with ya'. Come on in. My home is yours, for as long as ya' need it."

As soon as I entered the house, my cell phone rang again. It was my boyfriend. He was about to be here. I was sure looking forward to see him. I needed an intrusion in this uncomfortable interchange.

My aunt interrupted our conversation on the phone. "Ya' know when the funeral's goin' to be yet? Have ya' made any plans?"

"Steve, please get here soon, I need you!" I cried, hanging up my phone.

I turned to my aunt, as I put away my phone. "Aunt Ruth, to answer your question, no, I haven't made any plans yet. They just died this afternoon. I haven't had time to pull myself together, let alone, make funeral arrangements. I haven't really thought about all that yet!"

"Well, you'd better. The morgue isn't gonna' keep them bodies forever. The hospital is gonna' need to know where to send them."

"I'm sorry." I cried. "I'm just too upset to think about all that right now, okay?"

The doorbell rang and it was Steve. "Thank goodness, you're here! I think I need to go somewhere, and clear my mind."

As I was hugging him, my aunt said, "We'll who is this, Jobella? I didn't know ya' had a boyfriend. How 'bout introducing me to this good looking fella'."

"This is Steve, my fiancé. Steve, this is my Aunt Ruth. She's my Mom's sister."

"I'm pleased to make your acquaintance. Your fiancé, huh? Have you two set a date?"

"No, not for a couple of years. I'd love to chat, but we'd better go. I'm here to take Jobella out for a bit. We'll probably go to our pastor's house, so we can start making plans for the funeral. Is that alright with you?" He winked at me, as he asked the last question.

"Just don't be gone too long. Your Uncle Bud will be here soon, and he'll be wondering why I have two little rug rats running around."

"Thanks for coming by, Steve." I said as we were walking out to his car. The twins wanted to go too, but we needed some time to be alone, and I promised to get them something while I was out, if they were good. After we were in the car, he held me, and I started to cry again.

"I'm so sorry, honey. Will you be okay?" He asked.

"Better, now that you're here. I don't know about having to deal with this aunt of mine. Her life style is so totally different than ours. I know what I believe in, but how will they affect the kids? Oh, Steve, what am I going to do?" I sobbed.

"Let's go see the pastor, maybe he can help us work things out."

"Okay, I don't know how much help he'll be. He may not want to see me again today. I'm afraid I ran out on him at the hospital, while he was trying to console me."

"I'm sure he doesn't think anything about it. We do need to talk with him about what the next steps should be in the burial arrangements."

As Steve and I walked toward the parsonage, I worried about my brother and sister. I didn't trust my aunt and uncle, but unfortunately I had no choice. None was given to me. I had no other relatives to leave them with. I would be going to college soon, but the twins would be stuck there without me. I worried about whether they would still be able to go to church, or if they would forbid them to go, or think us foolish for worshipping a God they didn't believe in.

Steve interrupted my thoughts. "I'm not too sure about that aunt of yours. Her life style is too foreign to what you are use to. You've never lived in a dump like that."

"I'm worried about that too. I do hope she'll at least let us continue going to church."

"You mean, you don't think she will allow you to go?"

"She's not a Christian, and one of the things her and mom had a falling out about, was religion."

"Don't take this the wrong way, but I wish we could get married right away, and I could take you, and the twins away from her influence."

"Much as I'd love to do that, we did make a promise to our parents that we would wait until we have a couple of years of college behind us, and we could afford to live on our own. I wouldn't dare back down on a promise I made to my mom and dad, especially now."

"I know. I would want to be able to support us, as well. Who knows, maybe by your living your Christian life around them, and showing them what a positive person you are, maybe you can lead them back to Christ."

"That's a laugh. She has a hardened heart toward religion. She was raised in a Christian home same as my Mom, but when grandma and grandpa were killed in a wreck, she blamed God, and quit going to church. She's been running away from God for a long time.

"With God all things are possible, don't forget."

"All except saving my parents from the fire, that is." I answered bitterly.

When we arrived at Pastor Stewart's house, Steve asked me "Well here we are, you want me to go in with you?"

"Of course, I need all the support I can get, and I can't think of anyone else I'd rather lean on, than you." I smiled.

Pastor Stewart greeted us at the door, and led us into his office. "Would either of you like a soda or a glass of tea?"

"Tea would be nice, thank you."

As Mrs. Stewart went for the tea, I apologized. "I'm sorry I ran out on you today at the hospital when you were only trying to help me."

"Think nothing of it, I probably would've done the same thing." He gave me a big hug, and comforted me. "Please have a seat, and tell me what I can do to help."

"As my aunt so '*lovingly*' put it, we need to be making plans for the funeral, and what happens to me, Josh, and Joanie after everything is done."

"She is right about needing to let the hospital know about the funeral plans. I believe I can help you with that. It's unpleasant to think about those things, but the hospital will need to know where to send them. That part is easy. Your parents and I had a talk a few months back about what to do in case something happened to them. Maybe God gave them a premonition about their death. In any case, they told me that they filed their will with the lawyers, and they chose Hill and Sons to prepare their bodies for burial. I can go with you, if you like, when you are ready to choose their coffins, and grave markers. Don't worry about the money. They had a portion of their savings set aside for that. Their bank accounts were to be turned over to you, so you will be able to pay their expenses with that. They wanted me to perform the service at the church, and then to be buried in our cemetery next to the church. As far as to plans about you, and the twins, they were less specific about that. Since your aunt and uncle are the only living relatives close by, I guess staying with them would be the only option I can come up with, at least until the will is read. Can you think of any alternatives to that?"

"No, I don't know of anyone else. It isn't good, but unfortunately, they are all we have."

"Well maybe it won't be so bad once you get to know each other. I understand that you haven't seen one another in several years."

"That's right, and I now know why. They are nothing like my parents. My first impression wasn't a good one. Aunt Ruth appears to be lazy, and her house is a mess! I hadn't met Uncle Bud yet. She said he was in a bar, drinking with his friends. That can't be good. I'm afraid of the kind of influence they'll have on the kids."

"Jobella, you need to keep your integrity in all this. You are a Christian. You will need to continue your walk with the Lord. Don't let your aunt and uncle influence you into denying your faith. You will need to be strong, and you will need to continue to encourage Josh and Joanie in their faith. They will need your guidance and example in all of this, and who knows, it may be your example, that could guide your aunt and uncle towards becoming Christians."

"That's what Steve said, but I'll be gone in August when I leave for college. How will I trust them to watch over them, then?"

"It will be then, that you will have to pray all the harder. Ask God to watch over them and to keep them safe, and then have faith that he will answer your prayers. You will continue to be the biggest influence in the children's lives, even when they don't have you around. You need to continue in your plans for school. Your life isn't over, and you will need to continue to prepare to take care of them."

"Thanks, Pastor Stewart, I'll try to remember."

"Mind if I pray before you leave?" He asked, and continued. "Lord, guide these young people during this time of need. Keep them safe, and grounded in faith. Let no harm come to them, and help them to make choices that would be honoring to you. Give them strength during these hard times, and help them to remember that you are in control, even now. Help them to remember that their parents are safe with you now for eternity, and that someday they will be reunited in your perfect heaven. In Jesus name, amen."

After we prayed, we got up to leave. "Thank you for your help. I'll try to be strong, and do what I have to do. We'll be in touch soon about the funeral arrangements."

The following days were a blur, as the pastor, Steven, and I, prepared for my parent's funeral. It was heartbreaking, but it was also a time for drawing my old comfortable life to a close, and moving on to a not so comfortable future. My aunt and uncle were pleasant enough during our time of mourning, and tried not to bother me, when the children and I wanted to be left alone. I had to miss a couple of days of school, but through my grief, I wouldn't have been able to concentrate, anyways. I still had another week until finals, and I was hoping my teachers would understand, and let me take my tests late, and still be able to graduate with my friends. I went by the shell of our house on the way back from the funeral, to my aunt's house. I sat down in the middle of what use to be my bedroom, and I cried uncontrollably. I didn't even care that I was covered in ashes. "*How appropriate*" I said through my tears. Then I glanced over to where my bedside table used to be, and found my Bible covered with soot. Other than being dirty, and slightly damp from the firemen's hoses, it was still intact. Inside the front cover, I found a picture of my family. It was the last one we had made for our church directory. We were all there, smiling, and with love and hope in our eyes. This is how I always wanted to remember them. I placed the picture back into the Bible, and in my despair, I made my way back to my aunt's house clutching my Bible, saddened, but ready to begin my new life.

Chapter 3

For days following the funeral, I went through the motions of trying to keep my life together. My church, and school friends had been very supportive. The funeral was beautiful, for a funeral that is. My parents had a lot of friends, and most of them were there. My aunt and uncle stood silently beside us. I glanced at my aunt, and thought I saw tears in her eyes. Underneath that rough exterior, my aunt might just have a tender heart, after all. Most of my friends were there, as well as Steven, and his family. Pastor Stewart gave an eloquent speech about my Mom and Dad, and it brought fresh tears to many eyes. It was especially hard for me, when they lowered them into their graves.

My friends got together in the next few days to give some toys to the children, and clothes, and toiletries for all three of us. I had some money in the bank for my college fund, and my parents still had some money left in their checking, that I was able to use for necessities. I bought a few things for us, that the others didn't provide. I had to be careful with the money, and use it as little as possible. I didn't want it to be depleted before I was able to go college. Still the children had needs, and I'm sure that my aunt and uncle couldn't afford what they needed, and wouldn't willingly give anything to them.

We had tolerated living with my aunt and uncle, at least for the most part, of the first two weeks. Everything was all right if they kept to themselves, and we ignored their frequent arguments. Uncle Bud came home most nights drunk and belligerent. The children were frightened of him when he had been drinking. They weren't use to adults acting this way in their idyllic former lives. They often ran to their rooms and hid from him when he came home drunk.

I returned to school on the Monday following the funeral. I hated leaving the twins at my aunt's home without me being there. I would have liked to take them to a sitter, but I didn't have the money for that.

"How's life with the wicked aunt and uncle?" asked Billie.

"I'm not so sure." I replied, not laughing at her joke. "She said she'd take care of them, but I'm not convinced that it's in their best interest. Still, at the moment they do seem to be somewhat sympathetic, but who knows what they'll be like later."

"Well, I for one, wish you luck!" Billie added as we arrived at our classroom.

On Thursday, we all went to see Judge Peterson for the first time. The Jordan's lawyer, Mrs. Freeman, was to read their will. My aunt and uncle were in the room along with us. The lawyer wanted them there, as well. I was uneasy being seen with them in the judges' chambers. I was afraid they would cause a scene. I didn't know how much would be left, after the fire had destroyed everything. I didn't think there would be anything left to be disputed about. I was surprised to learn that my mom and dad had invested, and saved over five million dollars. That money was to be transferred to trust funds for each one of us in equal amounts, and could be cashed in when we turned twenty-one, went to college, or married. It was also stated in the will that if our aunt and uncle would be willing to raise us kids in the event of their premature death they could received ten percent of their total money at the time the younger children reached their twenty-first birthday, that is, if they were still under their care. Uncle Bud did some quick figuring, that would be five hundred grand, he'd get in eighteen years. Not a bad deal, considering my family's estrangement.

Of course uncle Bud didn't disappoint me. He was his same obnoxious self. "Why should we have to wait until the brats, excuse me, the children get that old before we get any money. What are we going to use to take care of them in the meantime? It takes money to raise kids, you know, and I don't make that much."

The lawyer replied "There is a clause, Mr. Spencer, that you can borrow up to ten percent of the total, that is due you, once you accept the children into your home. However, if the children were to leave your care for any reason, the money you borrowed, would become payable in full, on the day they are off your premises. Again, uncle Bud figured out that he could get around forty to fifty thousand dollars a year, borrowed against the total amount.

"I don't quite understand all that legal jargon, but I guess all that sounds okay."

After leaving the courthouse, we went back to their house. For a few days, at least, they treated us kind enough.

The next Saturday, I went to the nursing home as I usually did every week, before the fire happened. I had let the administrator know I would be there around 1:00. I felt that by going, and doing some of my routine things like my volunteer work with the residents, I would feel better. Besides, it got me out of the house for a little while. Somehow, the residents found out what happened. My guess was when I wasn't there the past Saturday, some of the staff might have told them what happened. Also, I forgot all about today being my eighteenth birthday. When I entered the dining area, I saw that they had laid out a whole birthday spread, and all the residents had made me cards for my birthday, as well as sympathy cards. I was overwhelmed by their kindness and love. They all showed up to comfort, and honor me. I now know why I loved them so much. They were all the grandparents I never knew.

My heart was light as I went back to my aunt's house, but I wasn't prepared for what I was about to see. My brother and sister were sitting in a corner with fresh tears streaming down their faces. My aunt was sitting on the sofa ignoring them.

"What happened to you guys? Why are you crying?"

"You brats had better be quiet if ya' know what's good for ya'," yelled Aunt Ruth

"Bella, we were crying, and she wouldn't let us have any lunch until we stopped. We're hungry!" cried Joanie.

"Is this true Aunt Ruth?"

"They have to quit snibbling. It's time they get over everything, and move on with their lives."

"They're just kids! You can't expect them to behave like adults! I still cry too. Are you going to starve me too? Come on kids. Let's go to McDonalds, I'll get something for you to eat."

"You'd better be back before your Uncle Bud gets home, young lady! He won't like you overriding our discipline." Yelled my aunt, as I grabbed their hands, and ran out the door.

"'Bella, we want to go home. They are too mean to us." Josh said as they reached the car.

"We can't go home, our house burned down, there's nothing there any more. Mommy and Daddy went to be with Jesus, remember?"

"Can we go see our house, 'Bella?" Asked Joanie.

"I guess so, if you don't see it for yourself, you probably won't believe me."

The three of us passed the site of our burned down house on the way to McDonalds. The city building crew was already at work, bulldozing what was left of our beautiful home.

"Can you build us a new house, 'Bella, when you and Steve get married?" asked Josh.

"Can it be like our old house, and can we have our own rooms, 'Bella?" chimed in Joanna.

"That may be a little while off, but we'll try. Maybe we can build one just like our old house, only better." I promised.

"Yeah!" they both exclaimed, at the same time.

That night I helped my brother and sister with their baths, and got them ready for bed. What I saw as I was undressing them, angered me to the depth of my soul. Joshua had bright red whelps on his back and buttocks, and Joanna had bruises on both her arms and legs.

"What happened?" I asked them. I could hardly speak, I was so angry.

"Uncle Bud spanked me with his belt." Replied Josh. "He said, if we didn't stop crying, he was going to give us something to cry about."

"Had he been drinking when he did this?' I asked, even though it didn't make a difference.

"I think so, he smelled king of funny when he was yelling at me." Offered Josh.

"Aunt Ruth grabbed my arms, and shook me." Joanie said, and then added, "like this!" she grabbed my arms and shook me.

"I have to do something about this. I'm going to report them to the police. I will not have them abusing you. We may have to be separated for a while, but they are not going to hurt you again. As soon as I'm on my own, and have a job, I'll try to get custody of you two, and you all can come back, and live with me, okay?"

The thoughts of being separated from the twins, even for a day, tore at my heart, but I knew what I had to do for their own good. We stole out of the house after everyone was asleep. I had packed a small bag for each of them, and with an extreme amount of heaviness in my heart, we left for the police station.

When we arrived there, they had the doctor on call examine them. When the extent of the bruises became apparent, the doctor said they were consistent with abuse. Once that was determined, they called in a social worker. While we were waiting, the officer took my statement. I explained everything that happened, and the children collaborated with what I told them. I also told them about everything that happened over the last two weeks. It was decided that the twins would be better off put in foster care until I could take over the care of them, and be legally responsible to take care of their needs. The paperwork was then filled out for them to become wards of the state. As they were taken away, I tried not to cry in front of them. They hugged me tight and begged me not to go, and then the social worker gently took their hands, and led them away.

The tears came, as I drove back to my aunt's house. I dreaded the confrontation that was sure to come.

Aunt Ruth was at the door when I arrived. "Where have you been, and where are the kids?" she yelled.

"I took them away from you and Uncle Bud, so you can't hurt them anymore. You didn't want them to start with, and I'll see to it that you won't get one red cent of my parent's money!" I yelled back.

Uncle Bud came into the room, when he heard me. "Well, you'd just better find yourself another place to stay too, Missy! You and the brats have been nothing trouble for us, since you moved in here. We got along just fine until we started fighting over how to take care of you, and your bratty brother and sister!"

"Tomorrow, while I'm at school, I'll check with a few of my friends, to see if I can stay with them until I go to college. Maybe somebody can find it in their hearts to let me stay with them for two months."

"Take all of your things with you when you go, I don't want to have to see you again." Uncle Bud said.

"That's fine with me, I don't want to come back here, either."

I ran to my bedroom, and slammed the door. I spent the rest of the day in there, I didn't even go out to get something to eat.

As I was packing my bags, I heard my cell phone ring. It was Steve.

"Hi, are you going to go to the youth meeting after church tonight?" he asked.

"Oh my gosh, I forgot that it is Sunday! Steve, I'm really upset right now," I cried, "my brother and sister are gone. I took them to the police station during the night because they were being physically abused, and now they are being sent to foster homes. I'm planning on leaving in the morning, as well. I'm packing up right now, but maybe I could sneak away for a little while. It would probably do me some good to go to church, and to let Pastor Stewart know what's happening. I don't want my aunt and uncle to see me leave, though."

"I'll park about a block away, and you can meet me outside of your bedroom window. We'll take the back way. I'll meet you around seven-thirty."

"Okay, seven-thirty outside my bedroom window. I'll see you then." I repeated.

What I didn't know, while we were talking, Uncle Bud was listening through the door, and heard our plans.

"What are ya' listening to you old fool? Why did you have to go and whip up on them kids anyway?" Aunt Ruth asked Uncle Bud.

"Don't blame me, woman. You are as much at fault as I am. You were shaking that girl trying to make her stop crying, and made them go without eating until they stopped. They will probably throw us in the jail for this, if not under it! You'd better make up something good before they decide to try and find us. All I can say is, good riddance to the lot of them, but she's not going anywhere until I get through with her.

"Missy, you get out here right now!" He yelled, pounding on the door. "I want to speak with you now!"

I heard him yell. I became very afraid, and didn't answer him. I kept the door locked, and hid in the closet until it was time for Steve to come.

Chapter 4

'And the Lord said unto Satan. Hast thou considered my servant Job, that there is none like him in the earth, a perfect and upright man, one that feareth God, and escheweth evil? And still he holdeth fast his integrity, although thou movest me against him, to destroy him without cause. And Satan answered the Lord, and said, skin for skin, all that a man hath will he give for his life. But put forth thine hand now, and touch his bone and his flesh, and he will curse thee to thy face. And the Lord said unto Satan, behold he is in thine hand; but save his life'. Job 2:3-6.

The sky was already getting dark, when Steve came to get me. I climbed through the window, and we headed towards his car. We took the back alleys hoping that my aunt and uncle wouldn't see us leave. In hindsight, I realized that this probably wasn't such a good idea, but I didn't think about the dangers that were there, at the time. The backyards and alleyways in that neighborhood looked even more ominous at night. I thought I heard footsteps behind us, and my heart began racing. We started running as fast as we could. As we ran, I turned my ankle on the root of a tree and fell. Steve was a few steps ahead of me, and when he heard me fall, he turned around, and came back to help me up. Then he saw a large man with a ski mask on, grabbing me, and tearing off my clothes.

"Help me, Steve!" I yelled.

Steve was yelling as he came back to help me. "Get away from her! Leave her alone!

"You stay out of this punk!" He yelled back. He grabbed Steve, and started beating him up. After he knocked him down, he kicked him several times and hit him in the head with a rock. When he was through, Steve was lying on the ground, and wasn't moving. His face was bruised and blood was streaming from his mouth and nose.

I screamed when I saw what he had done to Steve. then he turned on me.

He overcame me, and as he held me down he tore off my blouse, and bra, and used them it to bind my hands, and gag me. He pushed me against the tree roots, and hit me several times. When I could no longer fight him off, he tore off my underwear, and raped me.

"Don't worry, missy, I'm not going to kill you, but when I'm through, you're going to wish I did."

I tried to grab the ski mask off of him with my bound hands, but didn't have any luck in doing that. In the end it didn't matter if I saw him, I knew who he was. I could tell by his build, his voice, and the stench of alcohol on his breath.

As he got up to run away, he threw his ski mask over the fence. I managed to pull the blouse loose that was binding my hands, with my teeth, and I wrapped my torn clothes around my body. I crawled over to Steve, and cradled his head in my arms. He wouldn't wake up, and he was barely breathing. I felt like I was going to faint from the trauma, and seeing Steve like that. I needed to be strong for him, and I prayed to God to spare us. Suddenly I remembered my cell phone and called 911.

The ambulance, and police came right away, but it seemed like an eternity before they got there. Onlookers started gathering around but no one did anything to help us.

When the rescue workers put the heart monitor on Steve, his heart rate was rapid and weak. I heard them say it was a sign that he was bleeding internally. His blood pressure, and oxygen levels were low as well, and his breaths were shallow. They knew from his vital signs that he would have to be treated immediately, or his outcome would be poor, and he could possibly lose his life. After their initial examination they felt that he may have some intracranial bleeding.

While they were working on Steve, another EMT looked at me and saw to my wounds. My wounds were superficial and not life threatening, but because of being raped, they took me to the emergency room along with Steve. I held his hand the whole way to the hospital, but he didn't even know I was there. Still I felt that by holding his hand, he could somehow sense that I wasn't going to give up on him.

As we pulled up to the door of the ER, Steve's parents met us as we were being wheeled in. I was being carried in on a stretcher as well.

His parents stayed with us until we could be seen. "What happened?" Mrs. James asked.

As I fell into her arms, I started crying. "I'm so sorry, Mrs. James, we were attacked. I was so scared. He beat Steve up, and then he came after me. Steve was hurt really bad."

'Oh God, please let him be okay!' I plead silently with God.

"Mr. James, he came to get me to take me to church. We went through the backyard of my aunt's house to get to his car so they wouldn't see us leave. I think it was my uncle who attacked us. He must have followed us back there. He was probably trying to get even with me for taking the twins away from them, and getting them put in foster care."

The police had already called the James's and briefed them on what happened, before they got to the hospital. His parents had already given their consent to do a CT scan, so they immediately took him to radiology to do that. They also gave their consent to do emergency surgery if needed.

The CT scan showed what was expected. He had some internal bleeding not only in his brain but also in his abdominal cavity. They took him to the OR and immediately did surgery to stop the bleeding, and clean out the clots that had formed. He went through the surgery okay, but only time would tell what damage was done to his brain, and if he would ever return to consciousness.

In the meantime, I was seen in one of the ED rooms. Steve's mom and dad waited in the waiting room until they were done with me and then they went to the OR waiting room to wait out Steve's surgery.

The doctor and nurse were with me, and did a thorough head to toe examination. They cleaned and dressed my wounds, and put me in a hospital gown before examining me for my rape injuries, as well as my wounds from being beat up. They bagged my clothes for evidence. I had a lot of bruising, and bleeding from being raped. It was painful when they used the rape kit to get samples. There was also blood under my fingernails from where I scratched my attacker, and so they scraped under them as well for DNA evidence. I'm sure they would find some of Steve's blood as well on my clothes from where I held his head and hand. It was very humiliating to be so thoroughly examined by the doctors, nurses, and crime lab people, but I knew that I was going to have to endure even more than this before this incident could be put behind me. The doctor ordered a pill for me to prevent me from getting pregnant, and he also gave me a sedative. After the crime lab collected the blood, semen, and hairs found on me the nurses were allowed to clean me up. The doctor wanted to keep me in the hospital for a few days until I healed from my physical wounds.

The police waited just outside the exam room because they wanted to talk with me as soon as the doctors, and nurses were through with me. When they saw that I was being transferred to a room they followed me there to question me. They didn't want to talk with me in front of the staff.

The nurse told them not to stay long because the sedative would be taking effect soon, and I needed my rest.

"Aren't you the lady that came into the station during the night, last night, with your brother and sister?" One of the officers asked.

"Yes, my aunt and uncle were abusing them."

"That's right. Do you think that this attack is related to that? I understand that you think that your uncle did this to you. How can you be sure, if you didn't get a good look at this face?" added the investigator.

"Because I recognized his voice, and I know my uncle had been drinking before he came home tonight. The man that did this to me had the same smell on his breath as my uncle, and he was the same build. I heard him, and my aunt arguing outside my room before I left. He and my aunt were arguing about my taking the kids to the station. He was very angry. I heard him refer to me as 'missy'. The same thing he said tonight when he was attacking me."

"Why do you think that he was angry enough to do this to you?"

"He and my aunt were going to get part of our inheritance for taking care of the three of us until we reached twenty-one. Because I took the children to the police station last night and they were taken by the social worker to live somewhere else, they won't get any of the money."

"Sounds like he had a means, opportunity, and a motive to do this. I believe we have our suspect. Even if he were to be found innocent on this charge, which he won't be, I'm sure, we can get him for abuse of a minor on all of them. Now let's let this young lady get some rest. We have a job to do before the trail gets cold."

After they left, I began to get extremely drowsy, but the nightmares didn't stop. The effect of the sedative made my dreams even more vivid than normal. I dreamed of the attack, and the twins were trying to come to me, but were being held back, and I wasn't able to reach them. I also dreamed of Steve, I kept trying to wake him up, but no matter what I did, I couldn't make him move. I saw him lying in a casket in a grave. Everyone was staring at me, and blaming me for his death. I woke up screaming. The nurse heard me and came back with another dose of the sedative.

They decided to keep me for a few days, for the healing of my body, as well as to protect me from my uncle. They thought that a few extra days of rest would be good for me, but they didn't anticipate what would happen next . . . .

Chapter 5

The nursing assistant walked into my room to bring me my breakfast tray the next morning. She dropped it in horror when she saw me. During the night I had found a pair of disposable suture cutters in the trash. I felt something crawling on my skin during the night, like I was covered with insects or something. I took the cutters, and kept scratching my skin with them. I was covered with scratches and bleeding everywhere when they found me the next morning. I had felt the 'bugs' crawling in my hair, as well, and I cut off my hair to get rid of 'them'. I kept scratching myself until I was in so much pain, that the itching finally stopped. When I saw how much I was bleeding, I wrapped a sheet around me but the blood soaked all the way through it. I must have looked awful to the aide because when she saw me, she screamed, and the nurse came running into the room and, immediately called the doctor.

When he came to see me, he too, was shocked. He ordered a complete blood count and a toxin screen to be done immediately. I had lost a lot of blood and he was concerned also that the medication

I had been given, might have caused me to do this to myself. I'm not so sure it was only the medication, because what I really wanted to do was just die, and I thought that if I lost enough blood, maybe that would happen.

After the lab technician left, the nurse and nursing assistant cleaned me up, and dressed my more serious wounds. Dr. Anderson walked in about a half hour later with the lab results.

"Jobella, your lab work shows you lost quite a bit of blood from your wounds from the attack and where you hurt yourself by scratching at your skin. You also have an elevated white count, which means you have some kind of infection, probably from the wounds from last night. You also might have had a reaction to the sedative, or the morning after pill, we gave you in the ER. I'm going to keep you in the hospital, and give you some IV antibiotics, and also a blood transfusion. In the meantime, I don't want you to injure yourself anymore, or I'm going to have to restrain your hands.

"Dr. Anderson, I don't want to live any longer. Everything is gone. My parents died, but you already know about that. My brother and sister were sent to a foster home yesterday, and I don't even know if I'll ever see them again. My fiancé is in ICU, and he may not make it, and if he does, he may never be the same again because of the brain damage. My future in-laws, I'm sure, blame me for the attack, and may never forgive me, and my aunt and uncle, don't even get me started on them. So doctor, I don't really feel like I have anything else to live for."

"I was good friends with your parents, and I know how proud they were of you. You were their life. I don't think they would want you to give up like this. You did the right thing by your brother and sister. I'm sure they will be put together with a very nice couple that will treat them as their own children, at least until you are able to care for them yourself. Yes, and I'm not going to lie about Steven. He is still in a coma, but we have every hope that he will wake up. We haven't given up on him, and neither should you. He's stable, and the fact that he made it through the night without getting worse is encouraging. I still believe in miracles, Jobella, don't you? Besides, you still have your life. God spared you because he still has a job for you to do. You can still give others your love. Your brother and sister will need you one day as well, and when Steven wakes up, I have a feeling you'll be the first person he will ask about. How will he feel if something were to happen to you? What will the twins do if you're gone?"

"I still believe in God, but I don't know if I still believe in miracles. God has deserted me. I have served him all my life, and so has my family, and he took them all away from me. Even my dignity is gone. No doctor, I don't feel like I have anything left. No one will love me anymore. How will my boyfriend feel when he finds out I'm not even a virgin anymore? I feel like damaged goods. He may even be repulsed by the sight of me. Why don't you just leave me alone, and let me die?"

"Jobella, I feel that we may need to keep you a little longer than we originally planned. Because of what you just said, and did here today, it's obvious that you are a danger to yourself. We will keep you on this unit for a couple more days to allow your wounds to heal, but I am going to have some mitts put on your hands so that you cannot scratch yourself anymore, and I'm going to recommend that you be placed on the behavioral health unit until you are no longer a danger to yourself. I contacted a psychiatrist friend of mine to come and see you. He is a Christian as well, and he won't try to do anything that is against our principles."

As we were talking, the aide brought in another breakfast tray.

"Take that away! I'm not hungry!" I yelled at her.

"Leave it, she may change her mind." Commanded the doctor.

"Why can't you just leave me alone?"

"Now, what kind of a doctor, or even a friend, would I be, if I let you continue to harm yourself?"

Dr. Habersham walked through the door, just as Dr. Anderson was getting ready to leave. "Why here's the good doctor now." Dr. Anderson stated. I'll leave you two to get acquainted. I'll see you later, Ms. Jordan."

"Hi, I'm Dr. Habersham." He said as he shook my hand. "You must be Ms. Jordan. I understand you have been going through a really bad time for the last few weeks. I've looked over your chart. You've suffered through more than most of us do in a whole lifetime. I'm here to see if we might be able to turn the corner now, and go to the other side of your ordeal, and make sure the rest of you life is a lot better."

I stared blankly at him as if he weren't even there. "Whatever."

"You didn't get all those scratches in your attack, did you?" observed Dr. Habersham.

"No, I didn't. I did this to myself."

"How would you like it, if I can see about letting you go down to the ICU, to see your boyfriend."

"Can I? Is he awake now?"

"No, he's not awake, but they've taken him off the vent, and he's breathing on his own. You can talk to him. They say that even people in a coma can hear what you say. Maybe you can give him some kind words of encouragement, and help bring him around. But before I let you go, I want you to eat something first"

"I knew there was a catch. Okay, I'll eat, but I've heard rumors about this hospital food."

"Don't believe everything you heard. It's actually a lot worse." He almost got a smile out of me with that joke, almost.

After breakfast I was wheeled down to the ICU. Steve's parents were sitting outside the waiting room. I tried to hide my face from them. I knew how bad I must have looked with my cropped hair and scratches. I knew I looked bad, even without looking in the mirror. I had on a hospital gown, and they put a knitted cap on my head to cover my hair. I hoped they wouldn't recognize me, but they did.

"Hello, Jobella, how are you doing today?" asked Mrs. James. She hugged me loosely as if she was only doing it out of pity or maybe because she thought she might hurt me because of my injuries. I know they had to blame me for the state that Steve was in. I know I blamed myself.

"Isn't it obvious? I'm sorry, I'm just a little down right now, well, actually, a lot down. How's Steve today? Have you been here all night? The doctor said I could visit for a few minutes. I hope you don't mind."

"It's fine with us. You know we care deeply about you. You are practically a daughter to us already, as a matter of fact, if I would have thought of it sooner, we would have had you, and the twins come to stay with us. None of this would have happened if you had been with us. We don't blame any of this on you. We just want you to know that."

"Thank you, Mrs. James, I was worried that you would. I love Steve. You know that I do. I'm so sorry that he was hurt. He was only trying to protect me."

When they wheeled me into his cubicle in the ICU, all the tubes still attached to him was frightening to me. He had IV's, a heart monitor, catheter, and even a drain from his side, and a bandaged head. His face was badly bruised and swollen. I had no idea that he would look this bad.

As I rolled in closer to him, I kissed him on the forehead, and tears began to flood my eyes. "Hi Steve, I love you, and I'm so sorry this happened to you. I shouldn't have let you come last night. I should have known my aunt and uncle would try something like this. If you can hear me, I want you to know that I will try to get better. I won't be able to see you for a while, but I'll be praying for us both. The doctor is going to put me in the psychiatric unit for a while until I can get my head together. If you see God while you are in your coma, tell him I still love him, and I don't blame him, anymore. Steve, something bad happened to me after you were knocked out.

I hope you will still love me, and will still want me to be your wife when you find out, after you get better."

As I left the ICU I turned again to Mrs. James, "Please come and visit me sometime. It looks like I'm going to be here a while too. I'm being transferred to the behavioral health unit on the ninth floor. I love you, and Mr. James. I'll be praying for all of you."

They watched sadly as I was wheeled off the unit, and back to my room. They turned their thoughts back to their son lying in the ICU, and wondered what I had said to him.

Later that day I was taken to the psychiatric unit, where I would spend the next several months.

Chapter 6

The night that Steve and I were attacked, the police and crime scene investigators were searching the area for evidence that would put my uncle, if he were the perpetrator, away for a long time, first for child abuse and now for rape, and attempted murder. With these added charges, he would be put in jail possibly for the rest of his sorry life. They sectioned off the crime scene, and found the ski mask on the other side of the fence in the neighbors yard. They found blood from the grassy area under the tree where Steve and I were attacked. All of the evidence was sent to the crime lab to test for DNA.

Back at the police station they looked for any prior reports on him, and found that he had been arrested several times for driving while intoxicated, and being a public nuisance. They had a record of his fingerprints, due to the former arrests, but they didn't have a sample of his DNA to compare with the DNA collected at the crime scene. They would need to get samples from his home. They obtained a temporary warrant from Judge Peterson to go inside the home to get something that they could get his DNA from. He was more than willing to give them one because of the previous encounter with him during the will reading.

When they got there, no one was home. The door was unlocked, and the lights were still on. They found his razor, and a comb that contained a few hairs, and bagged them for evidence, and then before they left, they found several cigarette butts in the ashtray and one of those was still burning, they gathered that my aunt and uncle couldn't have been gone long. They took the butts for evidence. Between all of these items, they would be able to find many epithelial cells they could use. After gathering all of those things, they looked through the laundry hamper and found some underwear, a shirt, and towels with blood on them. They took those and bagged them as well to determine if they had Steve's and my blood on them.

It seems Mr. "Bud" Spencer was pretty sloppy for a rapist, and would be murderer. He hadn't even tried to hide the evidence. He either wasn't very smart, or very experienced. It was probably the first time he ever committed this bad of a crime.

Because it looked as though they had fled in a hurry, and there was recent activity at the house, they decided to set up a roadblock around the county. From the DUI records they found the make and model of the car he was driving. They also found that he had an expired driver's license.

Within hours, they found him and his wife driving out of town. They were picked up on the interstate. Someone had called in a 911 stating that someone was speeding and swerving all over the road. They had a hunch that it might be them. When they followed up on that call, they found them going over the speed limit, and driving recklessly, and it didn't take the highway patrol long to run them off the road. They made the arrest on the spot, and took them to the police station after they cuffed them, and read them their Miranda Rights.

While they were there at the police station, the labs were completed. The DNA tests confirmed what we already suspected. Steven and I were attacked, and almost killed by my uncle.

"Bud, what have you done?" cried Ruth, as they were arresting him for rape, attempted murder, and child abuse. "She is our niece, and he was her boyfriend. What kind of monster, are you?"

"Shut up, woman! Who do you think you are, condemning me? You were just as abusive, and degrading, as I had ever been. She's your blood kin, and you had no compassion for any of them either. You didn't even care that your sister, their mother, was killed. You are not so high and mighty yourself, so don't play the innocent one to me!"

"But Jobella and Steven are innocent victims. You had no right to do that to them! You are a fool, and an abusive drunken coward, and you make me sick!"

They took Bud away and put him in a holding cell until they could bring formal charges against him. They wanted to talk with Ruth alone, to see what she would tell them.

They began to interrogate her: "Can you tell us what you remember about what led up to the incident tonight? Keep in mind that you don't have to tell us anything you don't want to, since you'd be a witness implicating your husband in a crime, but anything you can tell us about tonight would be most helpful. You can have a lawyer present if you wish, but you're not under arrest at this time." The investigator stated.

"I don't mind telling you anything because I am sick and tired of his ways. You can do with him what you will. It all started last night when Jobella brought the twins here to the station. When Bud found out, he was furious. He didn't realize that Jobella would take action after he whipped the kids, when he was disciplining them yesterday. They wouldn't stop crying. I know I was angry with them as well, and I made them sit in a corner. I guess I grabbed them too hard when I jerked them, so I will take partial blame for that. Later tonight, when he found out that she snuck out of the house without telling us he was furious, but said he was going after her to apologize. How foolish I was to have thought that he was telling the truth.

When he came back, he said he couldn't find her, and wanted us to go look for her together. He went into the bathroom to wash up a little because when he came back the first time, he was dirty. He said he tripped over something, and cut his hand and that is why he had some blood on him. I thought we were going to look for her when we got in the car. Then he started driving like a crazy person, swerving everywhere, and speeding. I was actually relieved when the cops pulled us over. I was afraid we were going to get in a wreck and be killed. He was all over the road. I knew Bud was a low life, but I never dreamed he had it in him to do the type of crime he's being accused of."

After they finished talking with her, they let her go. It was obvious to them, that she had no part in the attack, and knew nothing of his plans to degrade and hurt their niece, and her boyfriend. They told her to stay in the city, and that she could be put under house arrest, if she tried to leave the area.

She promised she wouldn't go anywhere, and she had nowhere to go anyway. Then she offered to help in any way they needed her.

After she left the police station, she decided to stop by the hospital on the way home to see me, and to apologize to me.

When she walked into the room, I glared at her. "What are you doing here? I don't want to see you, or that monster of a husband of yours ever again!"

"Please, let me explain." She said quietly. "I had no idea that this happened. You have to believe me. The police just arrested your uncle. He can't hurt you, or the twins ever again. I'll see to that! I don't ever want to be around him again, either. I know you don't believe me, but I am sorry, Jobella. I'm sorry for everything. I didn't want this to happen to you, the twins, and your boyfriend. I'm sorry for Gabrielle, and Kevin dying. I still loved my sister, even if I didn't show it. I wish I could have been part of your lives. I would've enjoyed watching you kids grow up since I didn't have any of my own. I guess after we had a parting of the ways, I was jealous because she had so much, and I had nothing. Our feud started out with your grandma and grandpa getting killed in that wreck, but it continued, because I envied her so much. I envied the fact that she had a nice home, and a loving, successful husband, and beautiful children. Look at me. I'm a has been. I married a low life, and now I'm stuck with him. He put me down so much that I too, believed that I was worthless, and had no prospects of bettering my life. I finally quit being in contact with Gabrielle, because I didn't want her to see what I had become. I'm ashamed of myself, Jobella, and I'm ashamed for him, but it was a cycle I couldn't break once I was swallowed in. I had nowhere else to go. I would've taken care of you kids like you deserved, but I was afraid to show you all affection because I was afraid of Bud. Please, find it in your heart to forgive me."

"You have hurt me, and the twins. You physically abused them, and mentally you abused all of us by withholding care when you knew we were hurting. This past month was the most horrible experience of our lives, and you acted like you didn't even care! Now that Uncle Bud has been thrown in jail, you think you can come in here, and act like the abused one, and that I can forgive you just like that? I don't think so. Look at me. My life is totally shattered. I don't even care if I live or die! Maybe if I survive all of this, maybe one day I will find it in my heart to forgive you, but not today. Today, I can only loathe you, and your husband for what he has done to my family, and me! I just want you to leave, now!"

Ruth turned, and walked slowly out the door. What did she expect, that Jobella was going to forgive her like nothing happened? She didn't blame her for not forgiving her, but a little light at the end of the tunnel would have been nice. Sure Jobella had a terrible, horrific month, but she had a terrible ten years, starting with the lost of her own parents, and now the loss of her sister, and her only living relatives hating her. *I could've used a little compassion myself. I lost everything as well, I just didn't realize how much until just now.'* She said to herself.

As she was about to leave the hospital, a thought came into her mind. She remembered something she had forgotten about so long ago, and instead on heading for the door, she walked down the long dark hallway to the chapel.

I tossed and turned all that night. I couldn't stop thinking about my aunt, and wondered, was I too harsh with her? Maybe she was deserving of my forgiveness. Why did I treat her that way? Has my spirit become hardened' with everything that happened to me? The old me would have found it in my heart to forgive her, but the new me was cynical and unforgiving. I felt I had to be hard, if I was going to survive this ordeal, and keep from hurting anymore.

As I was mulling over these new foreign feelings I had, sleep had finally claimed me when the sedative that the nurse gave me finally took effect.

The next morning the nursing assistant came in and opened my blinds. "Time to rise and shine, Ms. Jordan. We'll be getting you ready for your transfer after breakfast."

The sun was shining brightly, and the glare hurt my eyes. I had to cover my head. "Why do you have to be so cheerful?"

"I just do of course, it's a beautiful day, and you are going to get well, and be your old self again." She replied.

"Just how do you know my old self?" I asked.

"I use to go to your church. My little boy was in your Sunday school class, remember? He was always coming home with stories that you told to him. He loved you. I have faith that God will get you back on your feet again because I know he wants to use you."

"That's easy for you to say. You haven't been through what I have."

"How do you know? Maybe I've been exactly through what you have. I've had problems too, but God brought me out of all of them. He's got his angels watching over you, I'm sure of it!"

"Yah, right!"

After breakfast I picked up the few possessions I had, including my Bible, and was I wheeled up to the behavioral health unit, where I would spend the next six months.

"You're going to like it on that unit, Jobella. It's bright and cheerful." She said as she was taking me to unit. "It's almost impossible to be sad there. The nurse's will take real good care of you too. They have a lot of activities to keep your mind off your problems."

"I thought the idea was to face your problems and deal with them."

"We'll, yes that too." She sighed.

As the nursing assistant rolled me to my new room, I passed visitors and other patients in the hallways and elevators. I saw people, but I looked straight through them. A month ago I would have been the one cheering them up through my volunteer service. I felt like everyone was staring at me, and wondering why I was being rolled through the halls, covered with scratches, and sporting a poorly done haircut. Did they guess that I had been raped, and tried to commit suicide, after losing everything that I loved? I could feel their pity all the way down to my bones. I looked like a freak now with my cut up face, and chopped hair. I covered my head with the blanket in my lap, silently begging them to quit staring at me. *'This isn't me,'* I thought. *'This is only my shell. The real Jobella has left the building, never to return again.'*

The aide was right. The mental health unit was a bright and cheerful place. It was a kind of slap in the face, however, if you are depressed, and want to wallow in that depression. Right now I felt more comfortable in my depression, than I did in the cheery atmosphere. The nurses and aides all greeted me as I rolled in. It was okay so far, but I could tell they were talking about me in whispers, as I passed by them. I was rolled into the day room where there were other poor pathetic creatures, wandering around like zombies either walking aimlessly, shuffling their feet, or sitting in front of the TV, pretending they were interested in what was going on. I know the nurse that brought me down was giving report to the psych nurse because they glanced at me, and looked away quickly when they saw me looking at them. They didn't want me to know they were talking about me.

After my nurse left to go back to her floor, my new nurse came to the day room, and escorted me to my room, to get me settled in. I looked around my room. It was very sparse. It contained only a bed, a bedside table, and a chair. There were no curtains or blinds. The window was opaque Plexiglas. In other words, there was nothing in there that could be used to harm myself. If I wanted to look outside, watch television, or listen to music, I had to go to the common day room. It kind of reminded me of jail rooms that I've seen on television. There was no way that I could escape, or hurt myself. In the top drawer of the bedside table there was only a Bible that was placed there by the Gideons. The only other books on the unit were in the small library next to the day room. The Bible looked like the ones I saw at the nursing home. At least I had that to comfort me, and if I got too bored, it would be something I could read. My worn out Bible that I salvaged from the fire was placed in storage along with my clothes that the laundry had cleaned for me after the police were through with them. All my things that I had in the world could fill one small box. That was just plain sad.

I had the room to myself, which was okay by me. I didn't want company anyway, and if I wanted to be alone, I could go to my room. The nurse left me to settle in, which didn't take long since I didn't have anything. All I had was the clothes on my back, which was basically a hospital gown and robe. And the clothes I had when I was admitted. My toiletries were those given to me in my admission pack. Everything else I owned in the world, what little there was, was still at my aunt's house. They brought me a muumuu to put on. It was a loose baggy dress with no waist. It hung on me like a tent. It was bright and colorful, and it was better than the open-backed hospital gown I had on. It was comfortable, but in no way glamorous. All the other ladies were wearing them as well, so at least I didn't look out of place. *"At least we can all look pathetic together."* I sighed.

For the first week, I wasn't allowed to have any visitors. That was the policy of the unit. They wanted the patients to concentrate on getting well, by centering them on their own thoughts, without outside influences. I also needed the time to get accustomed to the routine of the unit, and the medications that were prescribed to me. Thank God, I wouldn't be seen by anyone other than the doctors, nurses, and other patients. I would be sheltered from that embarrassment at least for a little while.

I didn't want to do anything for the first week. I was pretty well sedated, and the time just seemed to drag by. I became even more depressed when I thought of my friends getting ready to graduate without me. I wondered if they even thought about me lying here.

Steve and I should have been getting all excited for this weekend, instead of our suffering in this place. I stared at the four walls around me. They were as stark as my life. I refused to eat or drink anything, and I didn't want to leave my room to mingle with anyone. I just wanted to be left alone. The other patients all had their own problems, and I sure didn't want to listen to them because I knew if I heard them, I would internalize their stories along with my own, and put me in an even greater depression.

Dr. Habersham came by to see me daily, and tried to talk with me, and see how I was doing. He also reassessed my wounds, and changed the dressings where needed.

"I'm a little concerned about you Ms. Jordan." He said one day when he came in. "Your wounds aren't healing very well. I heard that you haven't been eating, and you are doing nothing to help yourself get better. The medicine won't help if you won't allow it to, and you need good nutrition to help with your healing. I also heard that you aren't interacting with the others. I'm going to have you start with occupational and recreational therapy, just to give you something to do, and give you the opportunity to be creative, and to be with others. I'm also going to increase your antidepressants. If you don't start eating, I'm going to have to put in a central line to give you nourishment that way. Is that how you really want it to be? I'm not going to stand by, and watch you kill yourself."

"I guess I'll try a little harder, I promise. I hate needles. Please don't put any IVs in me!" I cried. "I still don't care if I live or not, but I'll try to do what you say."

"Good, we'll get you started on something today, okay?"

He turned to the nurse standing by him. "Make sure she eats most of her food. Start monitoring her intake and output. She looks like she lost some weight and I'm concerned about that. I don't want her getting anorexic. Her wounds will never heal properly if she doesn't eat."

At lunchtime I went to the unit dining room with the rest of the patients. The television was on, and as I was picking at my food, the noon news came into view. I ignored it for the most part until my heard my name.

"Sam Spencer, better known by his nickname 'Bud' was arrested a week ago for his attack on Jobella Jordan and Steven James. He came up for his hearing this morning and was formally indicted for the brutal rape of Miss Jordan, and attempted murder of Mr. James. The victims are still hospitalized with Mr. James still in critical but stable condition. Ms. Jordan is the daughter of Kevin and Gabrielle Jordan, who was fatally injured in their house fire two weeks ago. Mr. Spencer is not eligible to be released on bond due to the brutality of this attack and past arrests on his record." Blurted out the reporter.

When the nurse heard the news story, she went to the television to change the channel, but not fast enough for me, and the other patients to hear it. I wanted to go crawl in a corner and hide. I just knew everyone was looking at me now. Now they all knew what happened to me. I couldn't be more humiliated. I ran from the dayroom to the shelter of my room, and curled up in a ball.

It did bring a certain amount of relief to me, to know that my uncle was behind bars. He wouldn't be able to attack me, or the twins, or my boyfriend anymore. The certainty that my uncle had been caught brought about a deep satisfaction, and a sense of revenge to me. However displaced my feelings were, it was first emotion, other than numbness and depression, I felt during the first week of my hospitalization.

The days passed slowly, and each day was the same as the day before. After breakfast I went to my first art class. I was encouraged to draw what I felt. Black was my favorite color these days, and emptiness is what I felt so I drew a big black circle with a figure of a girl falling into it. After art class they had a counseling session with me, and we discussed my picture. After my individual session, we had group therapy. I hated group therapy because I didn't want to discuss my problems with everyone, and I certainly didn't want to hear everyone else's. No ones problems were as bad as mine, but I was sure they would have a lot to say about me, after hearing the news on the television.

After the therapy session, and lunch, I retired to my room, curled up, and wrapped the blanket around me like a cocoon. I stayed there until supper, when the nurse came, and made me get up. After supper, I was forced to stay in the dayroom until bedtime. No one was allowed in his or her own rooms. That was the time the staff went to each room, to clean and change bed linens and towels. They wanted patients to intermingle by playing games or watching television together.

Weeks went by without hearing any more about the trial. Had uncle Bud really been caught and arraigned, or was it just my imagination brought on by my medications. I should have heard something else by now. Surely they wouldn't keep me from hearing about his fate.

I was in my room working on a crossword puzzle, when the nurse came in, and told me I had a phone call at the nurse's station. It was a Mrs. Freeman.

"Hello Ms. Jordan, remember me? I'm Abigail Freeman." Said the voice on the other end of the line. I'm the lawyer who represented your parents, in the reading of their will several weeks back."

"Yes, I remember you. Why are you calling me now?"

"If you're willing, I would like to represent you in your uncle's trial. I know you don't have much money at this time, but I would be willing to work with you on that, possibly on a pro bono basis. I would like to see him put behind bars for the rest of his life. I'm pretty sure that's what you would like as well. I feel we have a real good case against him, but they would like to hear testimony from you, the victim. They want you to tell them what happened during the attack. We are also going to charge him with child abuse against your brother and sister at the same time, and we want you to give us the story on that as well. Do you feel you are strong enough to get up in court and testify against him?"

"But I thought he was already in jail?"

"He has been arrested, but he still has to go to trial. We need your testimony to convict him, and put him away for good."

"I'm not sure they will let me out of here long enough to do that. If they will let me, I think I can. I would like nothing better that to see him put away for the rest of his sorry life. I don't know what I'd wear though. The only clothes I have are these ugly muumuus that they gave us here, not to mention the fact that I look awful. I still have scars from where I cut myself, and my hair is still at all different lengths and scraggily looking. I wouldn't want anyone to see me like this."

"We'll, you would get the jury's sympathy, that's for sure." She smiled. "But I think we may be able to do something to fix you up. You must be getting better, you care about how others see you."

"You're not trying to cheer me up or anything like that, are you?" I smiled.

"I wouldn't dream of trying to make you feel better about yourself, you might get the big head." She laughed.

"I already spoke to the nurse and she is going to let me take you out for an afternoon prior to the trial, to go shopping. I'll get back to you when a date is set. You take care of yourself, and do everything the doctors and nurses tell you to do, okay? I'd love to chat a little more, but I have to meet with another client in a few minutes."

"It is good to talk with you again, Mrs. Freeman."

"Please, you can call me Abby. We'll get together soon, I promise. Bye for now."

Chapter 7

'Now when Job's three friends heard of all this evil that was come upon him, they came everyone from his own place; Eliphaz the Temanite, and Bildad the Shuhite, and Zophar the Naamathite; for they had an appointment together to come to mourn with him and to comfort him. And they lifted up their eyes afar off, and knew him not.' Job 2:11-12a.

Several more weeks came and went before I heard from Abby again. I withdrew back into myself again and I became more depressed. I stayed in my room most of the time now, and huddled in the corner wrapped in my blanket. I wanted to stay in my cocoon away from the cares of the world. I was just about to take a nap when the nurse came to my door.

"You have a visitor in the lobby. Do you want me to send her in?" asked the nurse.

I thought that Abby was here to see me to take me to the mall or visit. I was disappointed when I found out it wasn't her. It was my friend, Eliza.

"Oh, it's just you." I said flatly.

"Is that any way to greet a friend? I'm so sorry I disappointed you!"

"Sorry, I thought you were my lawyer. What are you doing here, and why haven't you been by here to see me before this? I thought you were my friend."

"Well, ah, I have been kind of busy. You know I started college, and it's been taking up a lot of my time. I tried to see you right after it happened, but they wouldn't let me come in. They said you couldn't have visitors."

"No visitors, was just for the first week. Why didn't you see me after that?"

"I'm so sorry, I didn't know. I guess I didn't want to see you feeling so bad. I figured you wouldn't want to see anyone either, then for the next few weeks my Mom and I were getting me ready to leave for school. I guess I just forgot about everything else. We're having fall break this week so I thought I'd drop by and see you. How are you feeling by the way? You really don't look so hot. What happened to your hair? You don't even look like yourself, and you're so thin! Don't they feed you here?"

"Did you come to just scrutinize me, and my looks, or did you come to visit me, because if you came to try to make me feel better, you're doing a lousy job of it!"

"What is up with you? You've always been the one to encourage other people. You've always been there whenever anyone had problems, including me. Maybe now I want to help you. When other people needed help, you gave them advice. That is why you were always so popular. You always had an answer for everything. Everyone liked you. Now that you have problems, don't be so quick to shut people out. You obviously aren't capable of helping yourself.

Look at you. You're so pathetic! Why don't you try to encourage yourself? Are you even listening to those who are trying to help you? Are you even praying to God, and listening for his answers?"

"I know God is real, and he loves me, but right now I feel so far away from him. I think that he has abandoned me. I wish I had never been born. I wish I never had a brother, and a sister, and a family to lose. Why couldn't God just have left my soul in heaven instead of putting it in a human body eighteen years ago? Why was I born to a family who loved me, and expected so much from me? It was really hard to live up to everyone's expectations of being a 'perfect' example to others.

"Will you listen to yourself? Snap out of it. Get on with your life! Sure you've had some serious problems. Do you honestly think you are the only one with problems? Other people have troubles also. We are all dealt certain things that happen to us in our lives. God knows our problems. He wants to help us. He wants to help you. You've always been the one to cheer others up, but now that you have suffered you can't handle it. Maybe you've been too sheltered. Life's been too easy for you. Did you think that by being good that you were immune to troubles? Did you think God would somehow spare you? God punishes everybody, trust me. Goodness knows, I've had my share of problems. The Bible says that everyone is a sinner. I guess this is just your turn to be punished."

Jobella hung her head. "You don't have to tell me about being a sinner. I know I'm not perfect. Maybe I haven't always shown it, but I've had plenty of evil thoughts. Even now when I heard about my uncle being in jail, I wished he were dead. I don't think I can face him when we go to trial. God wants us to forgive those who sin against us, but I can't forgive him. I've murdered him in my heart, and that is the same as killing him in God's eyes. When my aunt came to see me, to ask my forgiveness, I turned her away. I couldn't even forgive her. Yes I am a sinner, but I don't believe God turned his hand from me, even though I deserved it."

"The Bible says that you reap what you sow. God sometimes even destroys those who aren't doing His will. He just takes them out of this world. Maybe it's not something you've done. Maybe your parents did something that displeased him. Maybe he meant for this to happen to them just at this time. Maybe something was about to happen with them that God didn't approve of. He knows everything that's going to happen, you know. Maybe he wanted to remove them from that situation, so they wouldn't sin."

"That's totally unfair for you to say that. My parents were good people. They would've made the right choice between right and wrong. You don't know what you're talking about! Don't you dare talk about my parents that way! God wouldn't have allowed them to die for any reason like that. Who do you think you are to talk about any of this to me? Look at the times I helped you when you were in trouble. How I covered up for you when you were doing something wrong. Like the night you spent with your boyfriend. I told your mom that you were with me. Look at all the times I lied for you. Maybe God is punishing me for helping you! Maybe it's your fault that all this is happening."

"That's unfair. Don't turn this around, and blame me for your troubles. I didn't force you to cover up for me. You could've chosen to tell the truth."

"That's what friends do for each other. I mean, stick their necks out for them, to protect them. I think that you had better go now. I'm getting tired, and it will be my supper soon, and I need to rest. I know you were only trying to help, but you really didn't make me feel any better. Please go now. I hope you do well in college."

The next day Mrs. Freeman did come to see me. The nurse told her to wait while she checked on me. I had a set back after seeing my 'so called' friend and I didn't really want any visitors today. But since it was Abby, I said I would see her, and to give me a few minutes to get dressed.

Abby was shocked when she saw me. I had become thin and pale, and my hair was a mess and uncombed. I had dark circles under my eyes, and still had a few scars on my face from my self-mutilation. I know she was trying to hide her shock as she talked with me. I could see it in her face. The last time she had seen me was at the reading of the will several weeks ago, and I looked more normal then.

The only clothes I had to put on to visit with her, were the skirt and blouse I wore the night of my attack. They hung loosely on me now. I had to wear a belt to hold my skirt up around my waist and my blouse just hung off my shoulders. I didn't have any make-up to wear. They took everything from me when I came to the hospital and put it all in storage.

"Well, do you feel up to going out shopping today? Asked Abby.

"Yeh, I guess. I'm not much ready to see the world looking like this though." I sighed.

The nurse handed me a brush to try to calm my unruly hair.

"Try not to get too excited!" Replied my lawyer, smiling. "This should be a fun day for you."

"I was excited about seeing you before my friend Eliza came to see me yesterday. She really brought me down. She blamed me for what happened to my parents, and said that God was punishing me for my sins, and that is why it happened."

"You didn't believe that, did you?"

"She sounded pretty convincing and she even quoted scriptures. Who would've thought that? I didn't know she even knew any scriptures. She never even paid attention to the preacher in church."

"The devil also quoted the scriptures to Jesus, but that didn't make him a saint, remember that. Consider the source, and don't worry about her today. Not to change the subject, or anything but what happened to that hair of yours?" she frowned.

"That is a long story. It was a self-inflicted hairstyle. I did it the same day I tried to rearrange my face." I smiled at my own morbid joke. My hair grew out a few inches but it was uneven and being in here, I didn't really care what it looked like.

It did feel wonderful to be getting out of my hospital room for the afternoon. As Abby and I drove to the mall, I told her all about what happened when we were attacked, and the days I spent in the hospital afterwards. I told her about my aunt coming to see me, and to apologize to me, and how I was afraid of her.

"Have you heard anything more about Steven from his parents?" I asked her, hoping she had some good news to tell me."

"From what I understand, Steve is still in the ICU, but they are considering moving him to an intermediate care, or a skilled nursing facility. He is still in a coma, but he is stable, and breathing on his own. If and when he wakes up, they can start him on an intensive therapy program. They are becoming more hopeful that he will survive, but they can't tell at this point if there will be any long-term problems. By the way, Mr. and Mrs. James will be at the trial, as well, to testify on behalf of their son."

I had been sheltered at the center for about slx months, and this was the first time I was able to leave. The world felt strange and foreign to me. It was the first part of November, and the holidays were just around the corner. In the mall, I passed some old school mates that were hanging out. I could feel their eyes glaring at me as I walked by them with my lawyer. I could tell they didn't recognize me, but I could hear their whispers. I must have looked a sight to those who did recognize me. If they didn't know me, all the better. I could do without their pity. The mall was already being decorated for Christmas, and they were erecting the Santa's workshop. The sights did little to cheer me, as a matter of fact it made me more depressed than ever. It reminded me of the times we brought the twins to see Santa, and then go shopping for our presents for each other. As I thought of the twins, I wondered how they were doing, and if they were excited about the Christmas season, or if they too, were depressed along with me, knowing they wouldn't be home with Mommy, Daddy, and me this Christmas.

While we were at the mall, Mrs. Freeman helped me pick out a suit of clothes to wear in court, as well as a couple of changes of casual clothes. It was the first time in months that I looked in a mirror at myself. I had lost at least twenty pounds since I entered the hospital. I was shocked at how pale I was, and how bad my skin looked. My hair was uneven and sticking out in all the wrong places.

"I really look bad, don't I? No wonder everyone is staring at me."

"I didn't see anyone looking at you. Besides when we get through with you, you will look like a million dollars, and then everyone will stare at you because you will be so beautiful."

"Maybe you'd better not have me looking too good, you know you want the jury to pity me. Isn't that right?" I smiled.

After we finished shopping for clothes, Abby surprised me. We headed toward the beauty salon for a makeover. I was going to get my hair styled, and then a facial, and manicure. After the makeover, I looked in the mirror, and couldn't believe the transformation! I looked like the 'old' Jobella, but only better! My hair was cut short in a pixie style. It had been so uneven they had to take a lot off, but it really looked cute and stylish. My body and face still looked anorexic, but the makeup did wonders covering my scars, and the dark circles under my eyes. My new clothes flattered my too thin body. We went on to buy the make up, and hair products they used, but Abby would have to take those things with her because I wouldn't be allowed keep them on the ward with me.

Abby smiled, as she looked me over. "Now people will be looking at you, and wonder who the supermodel is that I'm representing!"

"This is just a surface transformation. My heart is still as heavy as ever. I do thank you for trying though. It did help, and I do feel a little better. It was good to get out for the afternoon."

"Unfortunately, I do have to take you back." She frowned.

The snow started to lightly fall on our way back to the hospital. I put on the jacket we had just bought. I was thankful for the warmth it gave me. I didn't realize how cold it had gotten until this moment. On the way back we stopped at Starbucks and got a hot drink. The heat from the coffee cup felt good on my cold hands.

"Can I go to the intermediate care unit to see Steve before I go back to my floor?"

"I guess so, as long as we don't stay too long, I told your nurse that I would have you back by supper.

Nothing much had changed with Steve. He was lying in his bed still attached to a heart and brain waves monitor, and he was receiving nutrition through a peg tube into his stomach. He looked so peaceful. His wounds had healed, and the swelling had gone down. He looked as though he was just lying there asleep. I took his hand and held it to my face. I was surprised by how smooth it felt against my skin. I kissed his hand, laid it across his chest, and then bent over to kiss him on his forehead. I envied him not knowing what was going on. I wished I could crawl in beside him, and hold him, and let the world go by us, and not have to be a part of it.

"Steve, I love you, please get well soon for me. I miss you so much." I sobbed, laying my head on his chest.

Abby poked her head in the door. "Ms. Jordan, we need to go now."

As I was leaving, I looked back at Steve. I thought I saw his hand move, as though he was saying goodbye. I stared at him not quite believing it, but hoping I would see it move again. Unfortunately, that was all I saw as I stared back at him. I walked away with my head hung low, and tears in my eyes. Heaven only knows when I would see him again.

When we got back to my unit, I saw the rest of the patients getting ready for supper. I gave my new clothes to the nurse manager to put away until I needed them. I begged them to allow me to keep my new jacket. It was leather with fur lining, and it was very soothing just to hold it. In the end, they did let me keep it, but at my own risk of someone taking it. I would fight anyone if they tried.

After supper, the staff started pulling out the boxes of Christmas decorations. I sat in the dayroom, and watched them laughing, and singing carols while they were putting the Christmas ornaments on the tree. When they finished trimming the tree, they started throwing tinsel on each other and laughing. I should have been happy watching this joyous scene. I had a wonderful outing, and was able to see my boyfriend, and I made a new friend of my lawyer, but all I could do was think about the things that were taken from me, my family, my boyfriend, and my future. As I sat there, I stared off into another world, and I thought about Christmas's past. I held my knees to my chest, and rested my chin on them, feeling sadder than ever.

I became withdrawn into myself again, and thought of a happier time the year before. I thought about when I was a volunteer at the nursing home. I was the one putting up the tree, and decorating it along with the residents. How the residents cheered and clapped their hands when it was finished. The tree was beautiful with all the handmade ornaments they made. After all the decorations were up, they sang Christmas carols, and we had cookies and punch. What a happy time that was. At home that evening, Josh and Joanie helped Mom, Dad and I put up our own tree. The twins wrapped the garland around their necks and started dancing. They were pretending to be snow fairies. How we all laughed at them. They did look otherworldly with their little pixie-like faces above the white snowy looking decorations. It would be so nice to go back to that time, and start the next year over without all the sadness that was to come.

I wondered if the twins were thinking of me right now while they were putting the decorations on their foster parent's tree. Would they be helping make the Christmas cookies, and making a mess while they were doing it, like they did at home? Would they be enjoying hot cocoa, and eating those cookies, and eagerly anticipating Santa Claus to come on Christmas Eve? Were they missing their Mommy, Daddy, and me?

Chapter 8

That night, as I was lying in my bed, a million thoughts flowed through my mind. The feelings I felt in the last few days, the sadness of my loss, the image I saw as I looked in the mirrors at the mall, my skin scarred, pale and drawn, the joy of getting new clothes, and getting a makeover, and the uncomfortable feelings of getting out back into the world, and then there were the memories of past Christmas's. I also thought about everything Eliza said to me, and how it made me feel to be accused of being the one to blame for my parent's death. Where was God in all this? Why did he desert me? Why could I not feel the love of God comforting me? I tried to pray but God felt too far away to hear my prayers. I loved God, but I could no longer pray effectively since my world fell apart. I just didn't feel God loved me anymore.

"Oh God!" I cried out. "Where are you? My grief is so heavy I can hardly bear it! God, why are you doing this to me? Why won't you just take me on home now so I can be with my mom and dad? I'm afraid after all the problems I am having now that I will never get my brother and sister back. Who would give the custody of small children to someone with mental problems? I don't even know if Steve will ever get better. I love him, but what if he becomes an invalid? I don't know if I would be able to handle that. Why should I hope when everything seems lost to me now? The only hope I have is that heaven is waiting for me. I can't even help myself anymore. I just don't have the strength. I thought Eliza would've found it in her heart to at least have pity on me, but her words were strong, and she blamed me for my problems. The words she spoke to me have brought back my feelings of guilt. Please take those feelings away, Lord. It is a hard thing for me to understand. I found no comfort in her heart, as she spoke to me. Help me to understand why all these things are happening to me. Lord, am I wrong to want to have peace in my soul? Bring me back into righteousness with you. I know my days are short on this earth, and we don't know when our end will be, but let me not live in anguish the rest of my life. Help me to find a purpose for my being, and for why all this happened. Lord my days are lonely, and my nights are full of the things that happened, and of days that may never show me kindness, and happiness again. Lord, why are you punishing me, and allowing all these things to happen to me so that I no longer like myself and wish myself dead? You are so mighty and powerful, and you know everything. Why do you even bother about us lowly humans? Why torment us so that we have to find forgiveness with you, or live in shame all our days? I am terrified to go to sleep at night because of my dreams. Lord, please take away these night terrors, and let me sleep, and be at peace."

Sleep did at last find me after I prayed, but my heart did not find the peace I so greatly desired.

The next morning brought an unusually warm December day. It would be Christmas in three weeks but the day was pleasant enough to go outside on the courtyard deck outside the dayroom. While I was sitting at the picnic table my friend Billie passed by.

"Hi, I was just visiting my sister in the hospital. She had a baby yesterday."

"That's nice, are they okay?"

"Sure, do you believe that I'm an aunt now?"

"That's hard to believe. What's going on with you these days?

"Remember my boyfriend, Danny? We're getting married on Valentine's Day not this coming one, but the next year! Isn't it romantic? See my engagement ring?"

"Wow, you are full of surprises! Congratulations!"

"Were you ever able to take your finals and graduate?" She asked.

"No, in case you haven't noticed, I've been a little down on my luck lately. I was attacked the night before I was to take my finals, remember? After that, I haven't had time to give it much thought, being in here, and all. Maybe someday when this is all over, I will be able to finish school." I sighed.

"I'm sorry, I didn't think about all this. I talked with Eliza the other day. She said she came by to see you."

"I'm afraid I didn't have a very good visit with her. I kind of put her off. I know she was only trying to help me, but I'm not a very good friend these days. I had the feeling she blamed me for everything. Apparently she believed, if I, or my family pleased God a little more, none of this would have happened."

"I don't think she really meant it that way. Even if you did do something wrong, I don't think God would have punished you. But still, to be on the safe side you should pray to God to have him cast away any sins that you may have committed. If you seek God, and beg him to forgive your sins and lead a good life, surely he will answer you, and make things right again. I believe he will make you well, and everything will be great again for you just like it was before all this happened. You had eighteen years of a near perfect existence, that's eighteen more years than most people have. You've been very lucky. God blessed you and your family. If you continue to blame God for what happened, you are a hypocrite, and your hope will die. If you don't trust God to get you through this, you will fail. God won't forget a perfect person, and he won't allow evil people to succeed. Jobella, you were the closest thing to a perfect person I had ever known, and it really bothers me to see you so down on yourself."

"Yes, I know I have had a great life. I've been lucky in the past. Now everything is gone. How can anyone say that it was God who allowed me to have lived a charmed life? I don't know. Maybe it was just luck of the draw, or maybe my parents did this for us, and God had nothing to do with it at all. There are a lot of bad people, and people who do not claim God as real, and they are just as successful as my parents were, and their children had it made as well as me, or better. God is so powerful and wise and he oversees the whole universe. Why would he care about my problems? How can I talk with him? Who am I to be able to communicate with this all-powerful being? He is allowing all this to happen to me. If I'm such an insignificant person, why is he letting Satan destroy me? I tried to pray to him last night, but I got the feeling that my prayers stopped at the ceiling. I didn't feel the compassion that I once felt from him."

"Sometimes God answers in ways we don't understand." Replied Billie. "He won't allow you to keep on suffering. You will get better. I'm sure he heard your prayer last night. We can't rely on how we feel. We don't often get an immediate answer from God. Sometimes we have to go through trials, to teach us how to have faith. If everything were perfect all the time, we would have no need for God. We'd be able to do everything on our own. God wants us to depend on him because he loves us and we are his children. He doesn't care what we can do for him. He only wants us to love him, and allow him to work out his plan for our lives."

"I feel like my life is over. It ended before it began. I don't even know what to ask God for right now. What good would it do? Things are what they are, and what time I do have left is spent in this place doing mundane things like watching TV, reading magazines, or talking with the other patients. My life is just slipping away through my fingers. I should be out there getting my high school diploma, and being in college right now. It's not fair to be stuck here with no foreseeable way out. I'm weary now. I'm sorry to complain to you about all my problems. I know you just came here for a visit. I promise that I will pray again to God, and pray for his forgiveness, and ask him why he is doing this to me. God is so mighty, and he rules over everything in nature, he holds the world and stars in his hands. Why should he even consider me? Why would he send Satan to test me? I speak with God, and ask him why, but why would I believe that he even listens to me? I can't reason with God. I can't beg his forgiveness for something when I'm not even sure of what I'm guilty of. If I say I'm innocent and have done nothing wrong, I speak lies. God knows my heart and knows that I have sin in my heart. So how can I ever be justified with him? I am afraid of my sadness. I'm afraid I will never be happy again and God will not bless me ever again. I don't have the strength to overcome my sin on my own. I don't have the strength to make everything right again. I'm afraid of God. If this is a test, I have failed miserably. Maybe he will continue to test me, and I won't have the capacity, or the willingness to face another trial. I don't want to continue to fear God like that."

After the visit was over, Billie left with a promise that she would continue to pray for me, and ask God to intercede for me.

Before I got ready for supper, I went to my room to be by myself, and commune with God. "Lord, I am so tired, I don't have the strength to fight you any more. Please remove my fear and self-hate. Lord, you know I am a sinner, but I tried to do the best I could. You've made my family and me, and everything that is in the world. You have done this to me. You gave me everything and now you've taken it all away. Why Lord, why are you torturing me like this? If you are so wise and wonderful, and you have my life in your hands, why do you continue to test me? If you are causing my misery, just leave me alone a little while, and let me find some peace."

Chapter 9

The week following my visit with Billie, the preliminary hearing for the trial of my uncle Bud began. I wouldn't have to testify against him at this trial, but Mrs. Freeman wanted me there so the judge could see me, and my reaction to his plea. She wanted him so see how devastated James's parents, and I were after the 'incident'. It was the same courtroom where my parent's will was read, and Judge Peterson, who was present at the reading of the will, would also be the judge for this trial. Steve's parent's sat next to me in the visitor stands and his mom held my hand as they brought Sam 'Uncle Bud' Spencer into the room. He was wearing the customary orange jumpsuit, and his hands and feet were in shackles. He was clean-shaven, and neater in appearance than I remembered, but I had a hard time getting over not seeing him in a ski mask, attacking me. I've had so many nightmares since the attack, and I was unable to forget even the smallest detail. I was angry with him, and afraid, but I tried not showing it. I didn't want him to gloat over my being uncomfortable at the sight of him. Steve's mom cried, and

71

his dad's countenance gave way to his anger. Their son was still in the intermediate care unit showing some signs of improvement on his long way to recovery, but they wanted to see Sam dead for what they did to him.

"Hear ye, hear ye." Called the bailiff. "The Honorable Judge Franklin Peterson residing. All stand."

The judge made his way into the courtroom and took his seat at the front podium and we all sat down.

"Will the attorneys for the plaintiff, and defendant approach the bench?" He ordered.

The attorneys rose and went to his bench. "Has any plea agreement been made on behalf of the defendant?"

"No, your honor." Ms. Freeman said to the judge for both the attorneys.

"Will the defendant please rise? In the first count, assault and battery with intent to inflict serious injury, how do you plead?"

"Not guilty."

"On the second count, battery and rape in the first degree, how do you plead?"

"Not guilty."

"On the third count, child abuse to two minor children in your care, how do you plead?"

"Not guilty."

"My client wants to plead 'not guilty' on all counts, your honor, by reason of mental defect." Said Mr. Rosen, Bud's attorney.

"Mr. Spencer," said the judge. "Do you concur with your attorney?"

"I do, your honor."

"By pleading not guilty, it automatically means a trial by jury to either prove, or disprove your guilt. If a jury comes back finding you guilty you will be subject to disciplinary measures up to, and including life imprisonment, do you understand this?"

"I do, your honor."

"We will begin your trial tomorrow morning at 9:00 am. Anyone arriving after that time will be in contempt of court. A jury has been selected for the entire trial, and will be sequestered for the remainder of it due to the seriousness of the accusations. Attorneys, please have your witnesses, and exhibits in order by the opening arguments. Thank you."

After the gavel sounded everyone left. I glared at my uncle as he was escorted out of the courtroom. I despised the sight of him, and dreaded having to see him for the next few days until the trial was over.

"This is going to be harder than I imagined, Mrs. Freeman. Do you think I'll be able to handle it? What if his lawyer gets him off because he was drunk when it happened?"

After we left, Mrs. Freeman pulled the James's, and me to a quiet corner. "I personally don't think he stands a chance. The defense lawyer has to have some kind of a defense when there is so much evidence against him. It's a pretty weak argument, and we have got a lot more ammunition than he does, so don't worry, you'll do fine. Between all of us, we'll have him nailed to that jail cell for the rest of his sorry life!"

As we were leaving, Steve's mom and dad gave me a big hug. They told me that when I was well enough, I could come, and stay with them until I was ready for college, and even then I could consider their home, to be mine. They said that Steve was gaining some improvement everyday, and that the doctors thought that he might come fully out of his coma at any time. The EEG showed increased brain activity and the doctors were elated.

That night I tossed and turned, and in my night terrors I saw my uncle coming after me. In my nightmare I looked for Steve but he wasn't there. The twins were standing next to my aunt and they were watching me being attacked. I tried to scream but nothing came out. I woke up and the night nurse came in to see what was wrong. She said I yelled out. When I told her about my dream, she gave me a sedative and tried to help me back to sleep by staying with me and talking to me.

The day of the trial had come at last. After breakfast, I bathed and, dressed in the same outfit I wore the day before. Abby came at eight-thirty to get me and took me to the courthouse. I wasn't looking forward to a full day of sitting, and listening as the lawyers brought forth evidence, and testimony of those who had investigated the attack. It would be like living it all over again. I dreaded getting up, and giving my testimony on the attack, as well as talking about the abuse of my brother and sister. I really dreaded the cross examination of the defense lawyer questioning me like I wasn't the victim, and only the person bent on putting his client in jail. He would make it look like it was entirely all my fault for driving my uncle to drink and his mental breakdown.

I sat quietly next to Steve's parents at the plaintiff's table as the lawyers made their opening statements.

Abby was first to give her opening statement. "I'm here to represent the plaintiffs: Mr. and Mrs. Nathaniel James are the parents of Steven David James, and will be representing him in this trial. Jobella Leanne Jordan will be representing herself, and the minor children, Joshua Robert Jordan and Joanna Rene Jordan, who are not present at this time. I intend to show that Mr. Sam Spencer also known as Bud Spencer, knowingly, and with premeditation, along with his wife abused the minor children resulting in their removal from the home of Mr. and Mrs. Spencer and later that same day Mr. Spencer acted alone in following, and assaulting Ms. Jordan and Mr. James, resulting in Mr. James being hospitalized and remaining in a coma these past six months. Ms. Jordan was raped, battered, and has suffered psychological, and physical harm since the attack. She is currently hospitalized for depression but was able to be released for only the trial. She, and the minor children had just lost their parents and home in a house fire two weeks prior to these attacks. Mr. James is Ms. Jordan's fiancé. Mrs. Spencer pled no contest in her part of the abuse on the children, and reached a plea agreement to cooperate in convicting Mr. Spencer. She is on probation, and is doing community service in lieu of jail time. We have the testimony of the plaintiffs, and other witnesses, as well as evidence from the crime scene, to present to this court. We will prove beyond a shadow of a doubt that the defendant is guilty of all these crimes, your honor. Thank you."

As she went back to her table, the lawyer for Uncle Bud came over to address the jury. "I want to introduce you to Mr. Sam Spencer. Mr. Spencer is accused of all these crimes, and yes the evidence is very one sided against him, but you need to listen to all the evidence that is provided, both pro and con to determine that if he were not drunk, would he have done this crime. Or did he even do this crime? Can you say without a shadow of a doubt, that he was even guilty? What is the real story here? You will have to sort out the evidence. How would you, or a family member react under similar circumstances? Could Sam here even be capable of committing the crimes that he is accused of? Could someone else be the culprit in some of this? You be the judge. I intend to show that if Mr. Spencer is guilty, he was so heavily under the influence of alcohol, that he was mentally and physically incapable of doing those things he's accused of. Thank you, your honor."

After the statements were read, there was a low murmuring in the courtroom. The judge struck his gavel to bring the court back in order.

Ms. Freeman, would you please call your first witness?" asked the judge.

"I would like to call Jobella Jordan to the stand."

After I reached the stand, I was sworn in. "Jobella Leanne Jordan, do you swear to tell the truth, the whole truth and nothing but the truth so help your God?"

"I do." I replied as I placed my hand on the Bible.

"State your full name to the court."

"Jobella Leanne Jordan."

"Ms. Jordan, I would like you to start, by telling the court what your relationship is with the defendant."

"The defendant, Sam Spencer, Uncle Bud, is married to my mother's sister, Ruth.

"What kind of relationship have you had with your aunt and uncle?"

"My mother and father have not had a friendly relationship with either of them since my grandparents died thirteen years ago."

"I understand that they are your only living relatives, is that right?"

"I know of no others. If I have any other relatives, my parents never spoke of them."

"What happened that made you seek them out, and live with them, after your parents' deaths?"

"When my parents died, I lost my home as well. My house burned completely down, and my brother, sister and I didn't have anywhere else to go. When I picked the twins up at the daycare, the sitter found that my aunt was listed as an emergency contact so I called her, and she agreed to let us come to their home until we could make other arrangements."

"Was your aunt receptive to your coming?"

"No, not really, she acted sarcastic towards us, as if we were a bother. Uncle Bud wasn't there when we arrived. He had been late coming home from work that day. Aunt Ruth seemed to be nonchalant about my parents, like she didn't even care that they were killed."

"How did the defendant act when he came home, and saw the three of you there?"

"Aunt Ruth hadn't warned him before he came home, and he seemed to be angry when he saw us."

"Did the relationship improve over the next few days?"

"Before, during, and for a little while after the funeral, they seemed to show a little more compassion for us, especially Aunt

Ruth. I think deep down inside she still cared for Mom and us more than she let on. They pretty much left us alone to grieve over those few days."

"What happened when the lawyers went over your parent's will?"

"They actually said to have my aunt and uncle take care of us if something should happen to them, and they said that they would give them a portion of our inheritance, if they would take care of us until we reached twenty-one. We children wouldn't get our inheritance until we went to college, got married, or reached our twenty-first birthday, and my aunt and uncle would get the ten percent at that time."

"Let the record show that exhibit A is a copy of the will showing the defendant's part of the inheritance." She gave the judge the photocopy of the will, and then turned back to me. "What was your uncle's reaction to that?"

"He thought he should get something right away for agreeing to take us in. The will said he could get a loan against the total amount each year, and if we stayed under their care until we were twenty-one he wouldn't have to pay it back, but it would have to be paid back immediately, if we were to leave for any reason before we turned twenty-one."

"He would not get any money and would have to pay the money back if he were to get a loan, if you didn't stay there, is that what you are saying?"

"Yes."

"You took the children out of the home and brought them to the police station on Sunday, May 30th, of this year. Is that correct?"

"Yes."

"What were the circumstances that led up to the twins removal from their care?"

"The day before, I went to the nursing home, where I volunteer, as usual on Saturdays. When I returned to the house I saw the twins sitting in the corner. They had been crying because they were hungry. My aunt and uncle refused to feed them until they stopped crying. They were missing Mom and Dad. That's what they said their reason was for crying. I became angry when they made the twins go without dinner, so I took both of them out to eat. That night when I was getting them ready for bed, I saw whelps and bruises on both of them. Josh said that uncle Bud had been drinking, and beat him with his belt. Joanie told me that Aunt Ruth had grabbed her by the arms, and shook her. I saw the bruises on her arms as well. The next morning, before my aunt and uncle woke up, I got the children ready and brought them to the police station. I wanted to file a complaint against my aunt and uncle for child abuse. They called in a doctor, and a social worker, and they examined them, and questioned us. It was decided at that time to take the children from my aunt and uncle, and put them in protective custody, and then into foster care. I didn't like it, but I felt it was best for them. Later in the day after my aunt and uncle woke up, and found them missing, they became angry with me. I stayed in my room the rest of the day until my boyfriend, Steve, called me, and reminded my about our youth meeting at the church."

"Did the doctor and police feel like the children were the victims of abuse?"

"Yes."

"It must have made your aunt and uncle very angry to think they wouldn't get their portion of the inheritance because of you taking the children away."

"Yes, he yelled at me through the door of my room, and said that he wasn't through with me, and that they wanted me to be gone by the next day, and not come back."

"Did you feel like you were in any danger from him?"

"Yes, I saw what he did to the children, and I was afraid for myself. I was ready to get out of there, but I didn't know where I would go. I didn't want to face them as I was leaving for church, so that is why I decided to leave out through my bedroom window when Steve got there. We decided to leave using Steve's car that was parked a block away. We went through the back streets to get there."

"Some here would say that wasn't the smartest thing to do in that part of town."

"I was so upset that I didn't use good judgment, I'll agree, but I took my chances rather than face him."

"Did they approve of your going to church?"

"No, they turned away from religion when my grandparents died, and they were opposed to us going to church as well. I felt like I had to sneak around to go to church."

"You've had a very difficult time following the death of your parents. This is hard enough to deal with, but then having to lose your brother and sister two weeks later must have been really hard for you. Did your aunt and uncle show any compassion for your loss at all?"

"No, They might have been okay for a few days, but as soon as the funeral was over they started showing their true colors."

"Can you elaborate on that?"

"My uncle drank a lot. He would come home late from work everyday smelling of alcohol, and he would continue to drink beer at home. My aunt more or less tolerated it but he often became belligerent even with her. Sometimes I think she was afraid of him too. She didn't dare criticize him. She would drink sometimes, as well, but she just became lazy, and depressed when she drank. Uncle Bud was abusive. He would yell at Aunt Ruth when he came home. Sometimes he would slap her, and shove her around."

"Did he ever threaten you physically?"

"No, not in so many words, but I was afraid of him, of what he could do."

"Can you tell me in your own words what happened the night of the attack."

"Around 7:00 pm, Steve came by, and waited outside my bedroom window, and helped me climb out. My bedroom door was locked, but they must have heard me getting ready to leave. Before I left, I heard my uncle yelling at me, and saying that he wasn't finished with me yet and he called me 'Missy' in a derogatory way. Steven and I started running after I got out, and that is when I heard someone coming up behind us. When I turned to look behind me, I tripped over a large tree root. There was a man following us with a ski mask on. He fell on top of me, and started tearing at my clothes. When Steve came back to help me, the attacker started beating him up. Steve fell and he was hit in the head with a rock, and it knocked him out. After he was unconscious, the assailant held me down, and tore off my blouse, and bra, and tied my hands together with my blouse, and started raping me. When he was through, he said, "Missy, I'm not going to kill you, but you're now going to wish you were dead." After it was over, he ran away, took off his ski mask, and threw it over the fence."

"Did you get a good look at his face?"

"No, but I know it was Uncle Bud. I recognized his voice, and he smelled like him, and was the same size and build as my uncle."

"What happened after the attack?"

"I went over to check on Steve. I thought he was dead. He was lying so still. He had blood coming out of his mouth and nose. I held him, willing him to wake up but he never did. Then I remembered that I had my cell phone and called 911. It was a just few minutes before they got there, but it seemed like forever. Steve's parents met us when we got to the entrance of the ER. The police must have called them. After they signed the consents for tests and possible surgery, they rushed Steve through cat scans, and lab work, and then rushed him off to surgery to stop the bleeding in his brain. In the meantime, they took me to a private room to examine me, and run a bunch of tests. They collected the skin under my fingernails and checked for semen on my clothes and me. Then they admitted me, and took me to a room to rest. The police questioned me, and after they left, I tried to sleep. The nurse came in with medicine to help me relax, and also she gave me a pill that they give rape victims to prevent pregnancies."

"Did either of them try to contact you after you were in the hospital?"

"My aunt came a couple of nights after the attack, and tried to apologize, but I didn't want to see her."

"What has your life been like after the attack?"

"I've been on the mental ward in the hospital for depression. I feel like I've lost everything, and I have nothing to live for. My family's gone. My self-esteem is gone. My so-called friends have been criticizing me for things I haven't done. I've lost my faith in God, and I feel like he's even deserted me. I also missed the last two weeks of high school, including my graduation. I feel like he totally destroyed what was left of my life."

I looked over at Uncle Bud, and saw him smiling. His goal was to destroy me, and he succeeded. I was hoping that the judge, and the jury saw his look.

"Mr. Rosen, do you wish to cross examine this witness?" asked the judge.

"I do, your honor." Said the defendant's lawyer while Ms. Freeman went to sit down.

"Ms. Jordan, why did you choose to go to your aunt and uncle's home instead of some friends, or even your boyfriend's home following the death of your parents?"

"I really didn't know anything about them until the sitter gave me their name. Since they were the emergency contact, I figured they would be okay. We hadn't seen them for years, but they were the only relatives that I knew of, and I didn't want to burden my friends."

"How did you feel about calling them?"

"I was apprehensive, and I didn't know how they would respond."

"What was it like when you met them?"

"My aunt seemed somewhat sarcastic, and not very friendly. My uncle wasn't there when we arrived. My aunt made me feel like we were an imposition."

"You walked into their lives after not seeing them for ten years, and you expected them to welcome you with open arms, especially after your loss, is that right? To them, you were an imposition!"

"I'm not sure how they should have reacted. After all my Mom and Aunt Ruth were sisters, but they haven't been on speaking terms for that long. I thought my aunt should have been a little more sympathetic, yes."

"You had to realize that three children would have been quite a change in their lives after living together for fifteen years without children, wouldn't you agree?"

"Yes, but we didn't plan on staying with them forever."

"Oh, I see, you just wanted to stay until you could find a place more suitable. Somewhere, where you wouldn't have to be seen in the slums. Somewhere that was more appropriate to your life style, isn't that the was it was?"

"We didn't have anywhere else to go."

"As soon as you had an excuse to get the children out of that environment, you took advantage of it, isn't that right? You never intended for your aunt and uncle to get any of your money!"

"But the children, they were abused!"

"Ms. Jordan, have you ever received a spanking, or a time out from your parents? Have your parents ever grabbed you by the arms, and shook you when you were disobeying?"

"I don't remember ever getting a spanking so hard that it left bruises."

"Of course, you were the perfect child that your parents doted on, and so were your brother and sister."

"I didn't say that!"

"If you were so good, you would've accepted your aunt's apology, and moved on with your life, instead of wallowing in self pity."

Ms. Freeman shouted, "I object! The counsel is putting words in her mouth, and badgering the witness."

"Thank you, Ms. Freeman. I was wondering when you were going to stop this tirade against the witness." Said the judge. "Objection sustained, Mr. Rosen, Please tone down your questioning. The witness is not on trial here."

"Ms. Jordan, on the night of the attack, you didn't get a good look at your attacker, did you? He was wearing a ski mask, and it was getting dark. It is even possible that it wasn't even your uncle who attacked you, isn't that right? There has to be more than one man in that area that has the same build as your uncle, and has been drinking. Can you say without a shadow of a doubt that it was your uncle?"

"I'm pretty sure it was."

"Pretty sure, maybe you are just trying to get even with him for hurting your brother and sister, or maybe you are accusing him of all of these things so that he, and your aunt won't get any of your inheritance."

Ms. Freeman jumped up again. "Your honor, I have to object again, Mr. Rosen is still badgering the witness."

The judge responded as before. "Objection sustained, once again. Mr. Rosen, please limit your questions to the day and night of the attack. You will have your turn to present evidence when it is your turn to do so."

"Then I have no more questions, your honor."

"Ms. Jordan, you may step down." Stated the judge.

"Ms. Freeman, would you call your next witness please?"

"Yes, your honor, I would like to call Mrs. Hannah James."

Steve's mother approached the witness stand, and took her oath to tell the truth.

"Mrs. James, can you tell me what the relationship is between your son and Ms. Jordan?"

"My son, and Ms. Jordan is engaged to be married. They plan to be married in about two years, after they complete some of their college."

"What do you know about the night of the attack?"

"My husband, and I were in church, and we were waiting for Jobella, and Steven to come join us. He had gone over to her house to pick her up to bring her. When they didn't come, I became nervous when I couldn't reach him, and then I called the police. That's when I learned about the attack. My husband got a call on his cell phone at about the same time, and it was the doctor in the ED telling us that they were bringing them in by ambulance, and to get there right away. We got to the ED about the same time as the ambulance. They already had the paperwork started for us. Steven looked horrible. They had a monitor hooked to him, and IV's going. He was lying on that stretcher, and not moving. We quickly signed all the paperwork, and they rushed him back for tests and surgery."

"How did he look?"

"It was awful. His face was all bruised, and swollen, and he had blood all over him from the bleeding from his mouth and nose. We took one look at him and thought he was dead because he wasn't moving at all.

"Did you see Jobella?"

"Yes she was being treated also. She told us what happened. She was very upset of course. She was crying and saying it was all her fault."

"Why would she say that?"

"She said it was her idea to go the back way, instead of through the front door, and being picked up at the front. She just didn't want to deal with her aunt and uncle on her way out because they were angry with her and she was afraid of them."

"Can you tell us how long your son has been in a coma?"

"He hasn't woken up since that night. It has been almost six months since the attack."

"Have there been any signs of improvement since that time?"

"Well the doctor's are hopeful because he has lived this long, and he is not on any type of life support. He's breathing on his own now. The doctors, however, can't give us any hope on any lasting effects this might have. We won't know if there is any brain, or muscle damage until he wakes up."

"Thank you. Your witness, Mr. Rosen."

"Mrs. James, how long have Jobella and Steven been dating?"

"They've been friends since childhood, and have been formally dating since the beginning of his senior year in high school. They started talking about getting married since last Christmas."

"If they were that close, why didn't you offer to take the Jordan children in?"

"They had already made the decision to go to her aunt's house before I found out what happened. Besides it probably wouldn't look so good if she was living in the same house as her fiancé, and then there were the twins."

"You still could have offered to move them to your home after you found out about their living conditions."

"By the time I realized what they were going through, the will had been read for them to be in the custody of their aunt and uncle."

"You didn't try to fight the will, and offer your home to them? You had to know the state of their living conditions. Did your son not tell you? He had seen their home, and knew from Ms. Jordan what was going on inside that home."

"I guess I just didn't think about that."

"You're future daughter-in-law, and the twins living in squalor in a poor part of town, and you didn't think about it? Maybe you just didn't want to be bothered with the three of them!"

Mrs. Freeman shouted. "I object!"

The judge looked at Mr. Rosen. "Mr. Rosen anymore of this badgering the witnesses, the victims of this crime, and you will be removed from this case. Is that clear? Please remove the previous comments from the record."

"No further questions your honor."

"Thank you, Lord." sighed the judge. With that the audience smiled.

"Mrs. Freeman, do you have any other witnesses?"

"Yes I would like to call in Mrs. Ruth Spencer."

Aunt Ruth came into the courtroom from out in the hall, where she was kept until her time to come in. Sam Spencer stared at her as she walked to the stand. There were several people in stands whispering, as she walked by. After all the media coverage of this trial, she was embarrassed by the whispers. She knew that none of the audience was saying anything good about her.

The bailiff approached her. "Mrs. Ruth Spencer do you solemnly swear to tell the truth, the whole truth and nothing but the truth so help your God?"

"I do."

"You may be seated. Can you state your full name for the court?"

"Mrs. Ruth Applewhite Spencer."

"What is your relationship to the defendant?"

"I am his wife."

"Are you aware that you do not have to testify against your husband?"

"I am aware of that but, this is something I want to do."

"How long have you been married to Mr. Spencer."

"Fifteen very long years."

"What kind of relationship did you have with your husband?"

"It started out okay, but it's been goin' down hill for a very long time. Lately he'd be comin' home drunk everyday after work. Him and his buddies would stop by Papa Joe's Pool and Pub for some beer and ale, and play a game or two before comin' home. Sometimes, iffin' supper wasn't ready and warm, he'd slap me around, but I never knew what time he was comin', so I didn't know what time to have it ready."

"Why did you put up with the abuse for so long?"

"I didn't think that I deserved any better. Heck, I wasn't any better than any other women I knew. Most of my friends in the neighborhood were treated the same way. It's just the way it is. I know different now."

"You didn't have to put up with that. I know you know that now. There are places to go like a woman's shelter, or even to your sister's. Could you not confide in her at least?"

"Nah, we went our separate ways when our parents were killed in a car wreck. Both of us were escaping the tragedy of it all. Gabrielle had her family, and I escaped by going to bars and drinking the pain away. Jobella was three years old at the time. Same age as the twins are now. Of course they lived in the ritzy part of town. I felt like I wasn't good enough for the likes of them. When I was hanging around bars, I met Sam. He was a handsome devil back then. Couldn't tell that now, but he was somethin'. When he asked me to marry him, I jumped at the chance. He was working in construction at the time, and was making well enough to buy us a little house, and I was able to stay at home. He liked it that way. After a while we settled into a routine and I was little miss homemaker, and he was the breadwinner. For a few years it was okay. I had a couple of miscarriages along the way, and then we finally gave up on having children. I think Sam took it harder than me because he started drinking, and staying away more. It finally got so we just tolerated each other. It was in the last couple of years that he has became more violent."

"What went through your mind when your niece called, and said they were coming over because of her parents death, and their house burning down."

"I was really surprised. Regardless of what anyone says, I was unhappy to hear about my sister's death. I wouldn't wish what happened on anyone. I guess I was in a state of shock, and tried to joke around with the kids to lighten the tension, and make them feel at home. I guess they interpreted my remarks as sarcasm. I was willing to make it work with the children."

"What about Sam? What was his reaction when he saw the children?"

"He at first didn't know who they were, and thought I had gotten a baby sitting job, then I explained to him what happened, and that the kids were going to be staying with us. He started wondering how we were going to afford taking care of them when we could barely make ends meet with just us. He wondered if we were going to get anything out of it for taking them in. Like the government would treat us as foster parents, and such. He also knew that the Jordan's were rich, and he thought maybe we could get some money out of their estate."

"And how did that turn out?"

"Well they read the will, and they said we'd get a tenth of the five million dollars that they had in their estate that was to be left to the children, if we raised them until they were twenty-one, or on their own. We could also take an annual loan of ten percent that would be taken out of the end total, if we needed it to raise them."

"Did you receive any of the money yet?"

"No it had to clear through the court system first."

"How did Mr. Spencer feel about that?"

"He was really anxious about getting that money. It takes a lot of money to take care of three children, especially since they lost everything. We weren't use to having kids around, and we don't get much money from his job anyways."

"Well you had enough money it seems for alcohol and cigarettes!"

"I object!" shouted Mr. Rosen. "Look whose badgering the witness now!"

"Objection sustained. Ms. Freeman, don't bring up unnecessary details about the witness's private life. Strike that last comment from the testimony."

"I'll withdraw that comment." Replied Ms. Freeman. Mrs. Spencer can you tell me in your own words what happened on the day of the alleged abuse of the twins?

"My niece went to volunteer at the nursing home like she said she did every Saturday. After she left, the twins started carryin' on somethin' awful. They started crying because she left them, and they wouldn't stop. They wouldn't do anything they were told to do. I haven't had to put up with that type of behavior before, and I had been drinking some beer to calm my nerves. I made some sandwiches for lunch, but I told them wouldn't get anything to eat until they shut up that noise. I didn't realize how bad it affected my nerves. I'm afraid that I became a little out of control when they wouldn't stop. I started shaking Joanna, and I put her in the corner. I made her stay there. About that time, Bud came home, and saw what was going on, and he pulled his belt off, and started hitting Joshua with it. He was in a rage and wouldn't stop. He then grabbed him, and put him in the corner with his sister. Of course that made both of them cry all the more. So I just left them in the corner until they stopped, and I refused to feed them. I was afraid of Bud. If I tried to calm them down, he would come after me for pampering them. I was really fed up with the whole situation. When Jobella got home they were still sobbing in the corner. Bud had gone in our bedroom to take a nap. She took the children out to get something to eat. She was really angry with us."

"What happened when they came home?"

"They were very quiet, and went straight to their room. Later that day when their sister gave them a bath she saw the bruises on them from the shaking, and the whipping. She was very angry, and slept in their room with them that night."

"Do you feel like what you did was wrong?"

"I know now we should've handled it differently. We were use to getting whippings, and being disciplined when we were kids, but I know we shouldn't have been that rough with them. They've been through a lot with losing their mom and dad and all."

"What happened the next day?"

"When we got up the next day, Jobella was gone along with the children. We didn't know where they had gone. I figured they went to a friend's house, or church, or somethin'. When she came back, the twins weren't with her. I had no idea that she'd taken them to the cops."

"What happened later that day?"

"Well I just stayed at home, and tried to straighten the house up in case someone came by asking about the twins. Bud went out to the bar with his friends, like he usually does on Sunday afternoons. I heard Jobella in her room crying, and talking with someone on the phone, or she could've been praying for all I know. I didn't want to bother her so I left her alone."

"What happened when Bud got home?"

"It was close to suppertime when Bud came home drunk as a skunk and started rantin' and ravin' about Jobella, and how she screwed up his life, and how he was gonna' get even with her. He yelled at her through the door to her room, but it was real quiet in there. We knocked on the door, and no one answered. Bud busted open the door just as Jobella was climbing out the window. Bud said he was gonna' go out, and try to find out where she was going."

"What did you think about that?"

"I was assuming he meant to look for her, and bring her back home to ask her why she did what she did. It isn't safe to run around our neighborhood after dark. Everyone knows that and he may have wanted to try and protect her. He was gone for a good thirty minutes. When he came back his clothes were torn, and dirty, and he had some blood on his clothes and hands. He said he was attacked when he was looking for her. He said he didn't see her, and wanted to take the car to go look for her, but he wanted to get cleaned up first."

"What happened then?"

"He wanted me to come with him so we could look real good for her. I hesitated because he was drunk, and I knew he shouldn't be driving because if he were to get another DWI he would lose his license."

"The highway patrol picked you all up driving out of town on the interstate. Can you tell me why they stopped you?"

"Bud was driving like crazy man. He was all over the road, and he was speeding to boot. I asked him why he was driving so fast when we were suppose to be keeping an eye out for her, and he told me just to keep quiet, and continue looking for her. I knew something was wrong then. When I asked him what really happened he just kept quiet and stared straight ahead. Then I heard the sirens. I swear I wanted to kiss that trooper when he pulled us over. I was scared out of my mind being in the car with him. The cop cuffed Bud, and then put us both in the patrol car and brought us to the police station. They locked up Bud, and then they came out to talk with me. That's when I found out they were looking for him for the possibility that he beat up Jobella and her boyfriend."

"Can you tell the court why you weren't arrested along with Mr. Spencer?"

"I didn't have anything to do with the attack, and I didn't know anything about it until the cops arrested Bud. They charged me with participating in the child abuse but later let me go when I agreed to be a witness against Bud."

"No further questions your honor."

"Mr. Rosen, do you wish to question the witness?"

"Yes, your honor." He replied.

He stepped toward her. "Mrs. Spencer, you are saying you made a plea agreement with the prosecution, is that correct?"

"Yes."

"You would turn on your husband after fifteen years of marriage. You must have had a really bad life with him to want to put him away for the rest of his life."

"Yes sir, I did."

"Bad enough to make up a story like this to get back at him for beating you, and making your life miserable?"

"I wouldn't make up some story just to get even. He did do this to them."

"Has Sam ever done anything like this before when he was drunk?"

"Not that I'm aware of. As far as I know, I'm the only one he ever attacked."

"Do you mean that a man who is so drunk that he can barely stand can't be overtaken by a couple of healthy sober young adults?"

"He can be very strong, even when he is drunk. He works in construction, and is very muscular. He could overcome someone if they had fallen, or been caught unawares."

"Is it so hard to believe the story he told you? Maybe he was fighting off that neighbor and that neighbor is really the one who attacked them. Maybe his DNA was found on the mask that was found at the crime scene because he took it off the real assailant with his bare hands. Maybe their blood was found on him because he tried to help them."

"I doubt that very seriously. He wouldn't help anyone, especially if he felt that someone was out to get him."

"Just because he doesn't help you? Maybe you just wanted to raise the kids yourself, and put him behind bars, and you collect the money for raising the kids yourself."

Mrs. Freeman arose. "I object, your honor he's badgering the witness again. She's not on trial here."

"Mr. Rosen, the objection is sustained. I'm warning you that to continue with this line of questioning will put you in contempt of court."

"I'm again sorry, your honor."

Ruth's face paled as she frowned at the defense lawyer.

"No more questions for this witness."

"Ms. Freeman, do you want to cross examine this witness again?"

"No your honor."

"Ms. Spencer you may step down. Court will recess until tomorrow morning at 9:00 am."

After everyone left, I stayed behind to talk with Abby. I had to wait on her until everyone left because she was to take me back to the hospital following the session. Mr. and Mrs. James stayed behind as well.

"What is Mr. Rosen doing?" I cried. "He's making uncle Bud sound like the good guy! Why is he doing that when he knows he's guilty?"

She replied. "The job of the defense lawyer is to give him the benefit of doubt, and to plant seeds of doubt in the jury. I really don't think that the jury is buying it. We have too much physical evidence, as well as your eyewitness report of all these crimes, and that is enough to bury him. Mr. Rosen is pulling at straws right now. The next card he'll play, if this doesn't work, is to make him look like he didn't know what he was doing. Maybe he'll have Sam confess, and then make him look like the victim. They are all strategies that the defense uses. Remember he's trying to win the case as well."

"You don't think he'll win, do you?"

"No this is too serious of a crime for the jury to let him walk away without any jail time."

As I checked back into the psych unit that night, I felt like all the inpatients, and nurses were watching my lawyer, and me as we entered the ward. Most of them that were coherent enough, knew what was going on, and wanted me to tell them everything. Abby warned me not to discuss the trial at all, not even to my psychiatrist. I had been sworn to silence, and Abby quickly reminded me of that.

After supper I went straight to my room, and the nurse brought me a sedative, and my anti-depressant, to calm my nerves. She didn't make me stay in the dayroom that night after supper. She knew I needed some down time after the trial. The next day I would have to get up, and do it all over again in the court. They would be presenting all of the physical evidence that day as well. I would just have to sit and watch. I wasn't looking forward to seeing everything again through the photos and documents. The crime scene investigators would be the ones in the witness stands tomorrow. My part was done.

That night I prayed that God would heal my beloved Steve, and calm my nerves during the rest of the trial. I prayed for victory in the courtroom. I felt a little more at peace, but still wary of what was to come in the following days.

The next few days the trial seemed to drag on. The prosecutors had really done their homework, and called on witnesses from the crime lab, police department, and social services. They showed pictures of the wounds on the twins, Steven, and myself. It was hard to look at the photos that were blown up to poster size so everyone could see them. The pictures that were especially hard for me see were the ones of Steven. His face was swollen, and bruised beyond recognition, and blood was running out of his nose and mouth. They showed the rest of his body with bruises on his torso, and arms where he was kicked unmercifully. Then they showed pictures of him lying in the hospital with the tubes, monitor wires, and ventilator hooked up to him. They showed pictures taken at the crime scene with me cradling Steve's head in my arms, and my clothes torn and bloody. They also took pictures of me in my hospital room with my cuts, and close cropped and jagged edged hair, and wrapped in a bloody sheet. They presented the evidence of my terrible rape. They told about the ski mask with the evidence of DNA from the saliva, and hairs found inside the mask that matched Uncle Bud's. It was all irrefutable evidence that Sam Spencer was indeed the person who committed these terrible crimes.

Finally the day came that Sam Spencer was to testify on his own behalf. What kind of lies would he tell? Would he be able to convince the jury that he was the hero in all this, as his lawyer would have them believe?

The day began the same as the previous days with the courtroom opening up, and the judge coming in. He called the two lawyers to his bench for a briefing, and a stern warning about the personal attacks he had to stop the previous days. The courtroom was more crowded today. Everyone wanted to see what Sam had to say about everything. It was a high profile case because my family, and the James's were highly thought of in the community.

As I was making notes just to pass the time, I heard Mr. Rosen call Uncle Bud. This was the day the defense was to take the stand.

"I would like to call Mr. Sam Spencer to the stand your honor."

On this day Uncle Bud was dressed in a suit, and he was free of his shackles. He was clean-shaven, and looked almost presentable except for his sarcastic grin. He looked at me, and smiled on his way to the podium.

He placed his hand on the Bible. Mr. Rosen said. "Do you swear to tell the truth, the whole truth, and nothing but the truth, so help your God?"

"I do"

"Please state for the court your whole name."

"Samuel Lamont Spencer."

"I understand your nickname is Bud, is that correct?"

"Yes your honor, I've been called that since I was in grade school."

"Sam, how long have you been in prison?"

"For six months."

"There was no one to bail you out until your trial?"

"I have no one that cared enough to do that, besides they wouldn't let me out even if I could afford it."

"How has prison life been for you?"

"It was awful at the beginning because I couldn't get a drink. I started having DTs, and other withdrawal symptoms. They wouldn't do anything for me. They said I had to ride it out but I'm clean now!"

"Sam, would you tell us in your own words what happened that last weekend in May of this year?"

"I was playing pool and drinking with my buddies Saturday afternoon and when I got home, the brats that came to live with us were screaming their heads off because Ruth hadn't fed them. I can't tolerate much foolishness when I've been drinking. So I gave them what for, and made them sit in a corner. I was angry with my wife because she didn't feed them, and then I went in my room, and crashed. Later I heard their sister come in from her volunteering at the nursing home. I could tell she was angry with us, and took the twins out for something to eat. At least it was quiet for a while. She came back a little while later, and thankfully they were all behaving for once. Jobella took them to her room, and played with them or something."

"What happened that night?"

"Evidently they still had marks on them where I had spanked them. They deserved it though. They needed to get over the deaths of their parents by this time. Anyway, like I started to say, Jobella had given them a bath, and put them to bed. We were sleeping in late on Sunday morning. It was very quiet so we were able to get some extra shut-eye. When we got up, the kids weren't anywhere around."

"Did you have any idea that Jobella might have taken them to the police station?"

"I didn't even think about that. I thought she might've taken them to church or to a friends house."

"What happened later when Jobella returned without the twins?"

"I was hoppin' mad. She said she took the children away, and they wouldn't be back. She went straight to her room, slammed the door, and wouldn't come out. After I ate a bite, I went down to the pool hall and pub, and had a few rounds with the guys. I was trying to calm down, but it didn't go any good. I was still too angry. I didn't like the kids much, but with them gone I was out of the money I would've gotten. That was all I could think of."

"What happened that evening when you got home from the bar?"

"I don't remember much. I recollect getting home and trying to talk to Jobella but she stayed hole'd up in her room. The more I talked, the angrier I became. I heard her leave through the window, to go to church with her beau, and then I lost it. The next thing I can remember, I was speeding on the interstate, and being pulled over by the cops. The rest is history as they say."

"You don't remember allegedly raping Ms. Jordan, and beating up Mr. James?"

"No, I was too drunk to remember anything during that time."

"No more questions for this witness your honor."

Ms. Freeman do you wish to cross examine?"

"You'd better believe it, your honor."

"Mr. Spencer, your wife said that you, and her met in a bar over fifteen years ago, is that correct?

"Yes, I believe that's right."

"So you frequented bars, and came home drunk multiple times during your marriage. You stopped there after work almost everyday, is that also correct?"

"Yes, I'm ashamed to say that's right."

"You also said that you blacked out, and don't remember anything that happened that Sunday night. So what you're saying is that when you are drunk, you aren't aware of your actions?"

"That's correct."

"So what you're saying is you've spent the last fifteen or so years in a state of oblivion, and aren't responsible for anything that has happened to you, or others around you for at least fifteen years? You're not responsible for all those DWI's, and the wrecks you caused, you're not responsible for hitting your wife on several occasions, and you're not responsible for losing several jobs due to alcoholism, and you're not responsible for abusing Joshua and Joanna, and last of all you're not responsible for raping and beating Jobella, and nearly killing Mr. James, and destroying their lives. Is that about right, Mr. Spencer?"

I looked at uncle Bud, and saw that he hung his head after the tirade of my lawyer.

"Yes, he said, I didn't know what I was doing."

"You are either the worst liar in history, or the most pathetic person, in this courtroom. I believe you know exactly what you did because the attack on Jobella, and Mr. James, was premeditated in that you searched and found the ski mask that was used in the incident, and you tried to clean up your mess afterwards, and plotted along with your wife to cover it up, and flee from the crime scene."

"Leave her out of it. She had nothing to do with it. I did it all, I knew exactly what I did, and I'm not sorry!"

"No more questions, your honor."

The courtroom all of a sudden became so quiet you could hear a pin drop. Uncle Bud just confessed with his own mouth that he was guilty, and he was without remorse. We all stared at him.

The judge spoke with uncle Bud, and to the rest of us at the same time. "Because of your confession and taking responsibility for the crimes, I'm going to relieve the jury of their responsibility of making a decision. We will return in two days, following the weekend, with my decision on your sentencing." I would like to thank both councils for their participation in this case. Your duties will no longer be required at this time."

He had the guards handcuff Uncle Bud, and took him back to the jail to await sentencing.

He then had Mr. and Mrs. James and me stand up before him. "I wish to make my apologies for the agony you have had to endure during the assault, and the following hospitalizations, and then having to relive it in my courtroom. Mr. Spencer had the right to a trial by jury, even though his confession then eliminated the deliberation by the jury. I will see to it that he will be reprimanded to the fullest extent of the law, and you will not have to worry about him any longer. Please go, recover, put this time behind you, and by God's grace live the life you were meant to live, and have no fear from retaliation by him against yourselves or your families. God speed, and bless you."

The trial was finally over, and the sentencing phase was two days away. I felt like I could relax now, and figure out what the next steps would be for my life. Abby gave me a big hug, as did Mr. and Mrs. James.

Chapter 10

That night after I got to my room, I felt relieved that it was finally over, and I survived, but I still had a nagging feeling that it wasn't over. Maybe it was a feeling of guilt over the way I handled everything with my aunt, and with the twins, or a feeling of isolation from the God that I loved, and worshiped so much. I don't know what it was, but I just knew that I had to do something. I prayed to God to show me the way back to him.

It was two weeks until Christmas. I should have been finishing my first semester at college along with my friends. Steven and I would have been starting to make plans for our wedding next year, and the twins should have been enjoying their last year home with mom and dad before going into pre-kindergarten next year. So many exciting things to look forward to, but right now none of these things were going to happen. It's a sad thing when the only thing you have to look forward to is the sentencing of the person who changed everything about your life.

Saturday came with the promise of more wintry weather. It seemed colder this year than usual. We don't normally have a white Christmas here in the south, but they said that this could be the year.

After breakfast was over, I had the rest of the day to myself. The doctors said that I was showing a rapid improvement over the last two months, and I could have a day "off" here and there, and today was one of those days. I was sort of enjoying the time to myself when the nurse came to me and said I had a visitor. Thinking it was Abby coming to see me, and give me an update on the sentencing, I came out to the dayroom in high spirits. Again, it was a kind of a let down when I found out it was my so-called friend, Zoe.

"Can we go somewhere to visit, Jobella? This place gives me the creeps."

"We can go to my room if it's okay with the nurses."

We got the go ahead to visit in my room. It usually was against the rules to have visitors in the rooms, but they made an exception for me, since I was doing so well. We visited for a little while. I found out that she was home on break from her college for the Christmas season.

"You are looking well, Jobella. I guess I was kind of afraid to see you because Billie and Eliza said how bad you looked. I must say I'm pleasantly surprised."

"This was all the doing of my lawyer friend. She took me out prior to the trial for a make over, and I had my hair done. I really made a mess of it when I cut it off after the attack, and of course most of my scars have healed up, and what's left of them can be covered with makeup."

"Is the trial over? I heard that they had arrested your uncle. That must have been horrible for you to be attacked like that."

"They are going to sentence him on Monday. He confessed in court yesterday."

"I hope they put him away for good for what he did to you, and your family!"

"I don't think I'll ever have to worry about him again. So what about you? I'm anxious to hear about college, and boyfriends, anything."

"Not much to tell really, school is school. I'm doing okay, but no boyfriends at the present."

"What did you want to see me about? You must have wanted to visit for some reason after all this time."

"I just wanted to see you, and let you know that I've been praying for you. I know how rough it has been."

"I've said a lot of prayers as well since I been in this place, but God seems to have forgotten me. I've been lonely, and all of my so-called friends seem to not care anymore. No one from school has been by to see me except one time by Billie, and once from Eliza. This is the first time you've been in to see me in six months as well. No one seems to care about me, that I was once so close to. I not only lost my family, but my boyfriend, who is still in a coma, by the way. His parents haven't even visited me since I've been here. I just now this past week have seen them, and that was only because of the trial, and we were thrown in together. I guess the only reason people liked me was because of my family's money, and my 'so called' popularity. Where is it now? What have I done to make people despise me so?"

"I can only answer for myself. Life has gotten busy, and we've had to go on without you because you were in this place. I still like you as a friend, and I'm sure Billie, and Zoe feels the same way. Maybe when things kind of get back to normal, we can hang out again during our breaks from school."

"So you're saying, you can only like me if I'm go back to being myself, like I was in high school? Well guess what, it isn't ever going to happen! I'll never be the same person. What happened changed me, and changed the view I had on life."

"When you criticize your friends for not coming to see you, should you blame them for not coming back? You hurt their feelings by not making them feel welcome. Like today, I wanted to have a nice visit with you, but you acted like I was bothering you. I heard the way you treated them when they were here as well. You think you are so pure and innocent, and wonder why all of these things happened to you, even though you've always been so pure. What would God say if he revealed everything about you, what your heart, and mind were really like? He punished you more than what you thought you deserved. You said you you've been praying but you can't seem to find him through supplication and prayer. You can't know everything about God. No one can stop him from punishing unbelievers. He knows who the vain people are. You've always believed yourself better than anyone else because of your standing in the community, and all the goody-goody stuff that you've done."

"That's not true. I didn't believe I was better than anyone else!"

"He knows the wickedness in our hearts, and in our thoughts, but if you will prepare your heart, and reach out to him, he will forgive you. Don't dwell on the evil that has happened. Remove all that bitterness and thoughts about God punishing you, and about your uncle's attack, and about your parents' death, and then maybe then you will be able to talk with God again, and stand again without fear and hate. Soon you'll be able to look forward to a life full of hope, love, and happiness. You'll be able to lie down at night, and sleep in safety, and without fear. The wicked people who attacked you, and said bad things about you, won't go unpunished. They will dig a hole for themselves, and not be able to escape unless God has mercy on them."

"I know God as well as you, and my other 'so called' friends. I have been preached to by all three of you now, but you didn't tell me anything that I don't already know. God's hand is in everything. He created the world and everything in it. He is the only one who knows my heart. He created me, and only he knows my every thought, and he knows everything that I've been going through. But tell me, how is it fair that evil people sometimes prosper, and seemingly have no problems at all, while good church going people like my family is punished. I just don't understand it."

"Our life here is temporary. The evil person, even though he may have it good now, he will feel the wrath of God for eternity. He may even be prosperous, but he will lose what he has at the time of his death. He can't take anything with him. Whereas people like your parents will spend eternity in the presence of God, and those that mock God, will spend eternity in hell. Your parents are with God now, and I know he will make everything all right with you again. Wicked people will never see heaven, and what they have done on earth will die with them when they die."

"But the wicked person that is prosperous has a legacy that lives on through his heirs. Mom and Dad were wonderful Christians, and so was I, and we lost everything, and have nothing. The wicked, and the Christians both die, and their bodies deteriorate in the ground. What is left for us? How can I go on with nothing to build on? Your comforting me is lost on me now. Maybe some day I'll look back on all your words, and remember them. Maybe I'll get back to honoring God again. I'm just having a hard time doing it now."

"Well, I'll leave you alone then. I was only trying to help." Zoe sighed.

"I appreciate your coming, and I appreciate your friendship. Maybe next time we see each other things will be better. I do hope you have a Merry Christmas and a great New Year."

"I hope for you the same. Maybe I'll try to get back to see you before I go back to school."

With that she left, and I was all alone with my thoughts.

That night I was restless. I thought about everything that my three friends had said. Were they right? Was I disobedient to God? Did my parents or me sin, and this was God's way of punishing us? Was God so vengeful to do us harm, and let other people who are worse than us go free from disaster, and prosper? I couldn't believe that of God. My friends had to be wrong, but they did make a few good points. I know I have to get my faith back on track, and learn to love, and hope again. But where do I start? Why does God feel so far away? Why won't he help me? I don't want to become an unbeliever, and believe God doesn't exist, and our time on earth is our only life however short it is. It is better to believe that he is there for us during our times of sorrows, and to lift us up when we need it. I don't want to be hopeless like those who don't believe. It must be sad to think that this is all there is. How sad must be the funerals for those who don't believe that we live forever past our death.

As I was getting ready for bed I prayed harder than I have ever prayed before. I prayed for forgiveness, and pleaded with God to show me the way past my grief. In the quiet of that moment I felt a strange presence in the room. I didn't see anything, but I felt it, and it was swallowing me up. I couldn't even speak. I could only listen. It wasn't an audible voice, but I heard it never the less. It had to be from God speaking to my soul in the only way he can.

"Jobella," He began. "Who were those that tried to comfort you, and speak of things about me? They were without knowledge of how things are. You will need to be strong for the job that I have for you. Only listen to my words. Can you tell me this, where were you when I created the earth, and everything in the universe? Who made the morning stars, and laid the cornerstone of the earth, and caused all of the sons of God to rejoice? Who created the skies, and the seas, and caused the rain to fall to water the ground, and allowed the plants to grow? Who keeps the stars in the heavens in their assigned places? Can you lift up your voice, and cause the rain to fall, and cause the thunder and lightning? Everything is under my control, all of nature. The animals even obey my voice. Shall those that contend with me instruct me of what should be done? He that reproves God let them answer it."

"I am a sinner, what can I say? I have no answers." I replied in humility.

"I need for you to get tough. I have a job for you to do. You will answer to me. You cannot condemn me to make yourself look better. Are you better than me? You need to put on the clothes of righteousness, and array yourself with honor and glory. Cast away your anger. Those who would be proud need to be abased, including you. If the devil comes at you with all his wiles you need to be prepared to fight him off with everything you possess. Even then it will be impossible for you to do so. You need my strength, and honor to put him in his place. You need to be on the lookout, for Satan is sneaky, he can make things look like they came from me, but you need to be wiser than him. Always look to me for the answers before proceeding to do things that you think are right. If you don't, the devil will trick you into thinking that you are doing something for me. Satan is the king of pride, and arrogance. Never be prideful of the things you have accomplished. Satan will use that to keep you away from me. Think about it. If you can think that you can do everything by your own self, why would you need me? Always hold up doing what you think is right in your own heart, and seek my guidance before proceeding even if it does seem like a good thing. Wait on me to show you the way. Allow me to do good things through you. Do not be in a hurry. My timetable is not the same as yours. If you seek wisdom from me, you must allow yourself to be used by me."

I responded to God with great humility. "God, I know you are great, and have created the world, and all it's wonders. I know now that I have sinned by being prideful of all those things that I accomplished without giving you the glory. All those works I have done were to make me look better to those around me, for that I am truly sorry. I know you who have created me, know my heart, and my thoughts, and you always will. Forgive me for my pride, and forgive me for my evil thoughts against you, my enemies, and even my friends. Lord I want to be used as a vessel for you, without any thoughts of my own gain. I hate myself for what I have done, and I beg your forgiveness. I made a mockery of Christ's sacrifice for me on the cross because I didn't seek him for forgiveness of my sins. God I see now that I need you, and I need Christ to fully control my life in everything I do."

"My daughter your sins are forgiven. Always seek me, and stay strong against the devil. Go to all those who did you wrong, and forgive them also, and tell them the better way. Let them know that only 'I AM' has the power of forgiveness for them as well, if they will seek my face in prayer, and supplication. Let your friends know how much you love them, but teach them the right way, only I can forgive, and I can't be found by doing good works. Only when they seek guidance from me, can they enter into my family as you have. And Jobella, one more thing, your mother and father are here with me in everlasting peace. They have done well in life, and their home is now in heaven. They didn't die because of anything that they may have done, or didn't do. It wasn't through me they were taken, but through the acts of Satan. You will be restored, and have many years left of your life to do my will. You must be a witness for me, and through your work, many will be saved including those who did you harm, and spoke against you. Go now in peace now, your life has been restored.

That night after communing with God, I fell into a deep restful sleep. I felt peaceful, and forgiven. That night was a turning point for me. God and his Christ were more real to me than ever before. I knew then that even though life could be really hard at times there would never be a time that he wasn't with me to see me through it.

Chapter 11

The next morning I woke up refreshed, and in an upbeat mood. It was a beautiful Sunday morning. The first day of the week, and the first day of the rest of my life. After I ate a hearty breakfast I asked if I could go to the chapel service here in the hospital. I needed to continue to feel even closer to God. Because I've been doing so well recently, and seemed to be so alert and untroubled when they checked me, they did allow me to go. They said that I had to wear hospital clothing, and a hospital ID, and I wasn't allowed to go anywhere else except the chapel. I didn't have any problems with that.

When I got to the chapel, I was surprised to see Steve's parents there. They were kneeling at the altar as I went in. I quietly walked up to kneel and pray at the altar beside them. I didn't want to interrupt their prayers. I saw that they were both sobbing.

My heart seemed to stop in my chest when I saw them like that. I waited until they were getting ready to get up.

"What's happened? Why are you crying? Has something happened to Steven?" I asked fearfully.

"We'll say!" said his dad with a big smile on his face. "Steven finally woke up during the night!"

"That's awesome! Is he talking yet?" I asked cautiously.

"Not yet but the doctor is hopeful that he will be soon. He has a long way to go before the doctor can give us a realistic prognosis. It's just wait and see, at this time," added his mom.

"I wish I could see him, but I'm not allowed anywhere right now, except the chapel."

"How come they let you come without a chaperone?" asked his father.

"I guess they trust me." I laughed. "Besides, where would I go with this muumuu on? It's hideous."

"You don't look so bad. It's not very becoming, but at least your covered," said his mom. "You look especially good today, what happened?"

"It's a long story." I smiled. "I'll be happy to tell you about it sometime, but let's just say that God is wonderful, and I'm happy that I belong to Him."

"Amen to that, Jobella. I totally agree!" answered his father.

"When you see Steven give him my love, and give him a big hug and kiss for me."

We went back to the pews, and waited for the service to begin. There were just a few of us there. They opened the service by singing 'Great is Thy Faithfulness'. There was no stopping my tears as we sang, because I totally believed those words of that song now.

After the sermon, we sang 'Just as I am' for the invitation. My heart melted at that song, and I couldn't help but go to the front, recommitting my life to Christ. I felt lighter than air, and the happiest I've been for a very long time. Mr. and Mrs. James came up to support me, and the preacher prayed for us, and for the continued improvement in Steven.

When the church service was over, Mr. and Mrs. James took me aside to talk with me. His mother spoke up first. "Jobella we would like to ask you something, and I want you to really consider it before you answer. We would like for you to come, and stay with us when you get out of here.

"Are you serious? I would love to. You are the closest people I have to a family right now, but what about when Steven goes home? Aren't you afraid of how it might look with both of us living in the same house before we're married?"

His father replied. "We'll cross that bridge when we come to that. Steven will probably be in the hospital quite a while longer, because of rehab. His recovery will be slow at best. Later on when he does get home, you will probably be away at school somewhere. Besides, I'm not worried what other people think, anyway. We have full confidence in both you, and Steven that you'll always do the right thing, and that's all that matters to us."

"In that case, I would love to!" I cried.

After I left the chapel, I was higher in spirits than ever. Maybe things would get better after all. The doctor would be by later, after he goes to church. I would need to remind him that I need a pass to go to the sentencing tomorrow morning with Mrs. Freeman.

I told Dr. Habersham of all the events from last night. I'm glad he was a Christian otherwise he would really think I was crazy. He would've thought I was hallucinating and on drugs or something. I think he believed me when I told him about my conversation with God. I told him that I rededicated my life this morning to do God's work, and that I felt wonderful. I also told him what Steve's mom and dad said about me staying with them.

"Jobella, I do believe you, I do, but I'm still going to have you stay for at least another week in here and I'll reassess you on Friday to make sure you still feel this way after you are tapered off your medication. If it looks good, I'll let you go at that time. Just in time for Christmas I might add."

"Thanks, Dr. Habersham. I won't disappoint you, I will be well enough to go home by then."

"That will be wonderful, but I will miss you!"

"No you won't. We go to the same church, remember? I will see you there."

"You are right, of course. It will be exciting to see what God has in store for you."

I finally saw the proverbial light at the end of the tunnel. Things were looking up for me. I would try to remember what God had said about not letting Satan getting control of me. I know this week would seem to be very long as I continued on the ward with the other patients. It would be hard going to group therapy, and listening to their problems when mine were all but taken care of. I would have to struggle to not be brought down by the talking, and commiserating with the others. Then there was also that other matter to be faced with this week. The sentencing of my uncle Bud, and facing him one more time in the courtroom.

When I went to bed, I thought of uncle Bud, and the horror he put me through. I would be so glad to see him get what's due him for hurting my loved ones and me. As I tossed and turned, I kept seeing him come at me. The vision turned into a nightmare. "Jobella," I heard a voice say, "See what I done. I've ruined your life. You will never forget what happened. No matter how happy you are now, it won't last. I will always be there, to remind you that you, and your family were violated. You will never see your parents again, and your relationship with your brother and sister will never be the same. They will hate you for sending them away. You believe in God? There will be times when He seems to be so far away you will call on Him, and he won't answer you."

I woke up, suddenly afraid. Did I really hear those words or was it my imagination playing tricks on me because of the sentencing tomorrow. I prayed to God to stay by me until I fell back to sleep.

I opened my Bible and read in 'Psalms 30:5 and 6: For his anger endureth for the moment; in his favour is life; weeping may endure for a night, but joy cometh in the morning. And in my prosperity I said, I shall never be moved. Psalms 30:11-12: Thou hast turned for me my mourning into dancing; thou hast put off my sackcloth, and girded me with gladness: To that end my glory may sing praise to thee, and not be silent. Oh Lord, my God, I will give thanks to thee forever.'

With the reading of those verses the darkness lifted, and I knew that it was Satan that was trying to attack me, and make me doubt my conversion, but that wasn't going to happen ever again.

I woke up early the next morning to read my Bible and pray before breakfast. Abby would be picking me up around nine to take me to the courthouse. I was in the day room waiting on her when she came. When she saw me, she stepped back and stared.

"What happened to you?" She exclaimed. "You look great! You're absolutely glowing!"

"A few things happened. Most important I had a talk with God, and he saved me. Really! The same night I had that experience, I found out the next day that Steven woke up from his coma. I went to chapel yesterday, and his parents were there, and they told me all about it. They also said that I could stay with them after I got out of the hospital, and on top of all that Dr. Habersham said that I could get out by this coming weekend!"

"Wow you are full of good news. That's great! Now let's get through this hurdle this morning, and it will all be over."

"I'm ready."

When we got to the courthouse, I sat at the lawyers table along with Steve's mom and dad. Uncle Bud was sitting at the defendant's table with his lawyer. He was back in his orange jumpsuit and shackles.

We all stood when the judge entered the courtroom as we did before. There was a crowd in the audience including several news services ready to pounce as soon as the verdict was read.

The audience was required to stand along with us. The judge struck his gavel, and we all sat down.

He addressed the lawyers, and wanted to know if either of them had any last minute pleas, or speeches they wanted to verbalize. When they rejected the offer the judge ordered Uncle Bud to stand. We, who were victims, were granted one chance to address the defendant.

Mr. and Mrs. James were first up. "Mr. Spencer, you are in this courtroom facing sentencing for what you did first to Ms. Jordan and her family, and then what you did to our son. We can only speak for our part in this ordeal, and we'll leave Jobella to speak her peace. We have been through many agonizing days and months over the last six months because our son, Steven has lain in a coma. He finally woke up the night before last so you are at least not guilty for his murder, but at this time we don't know what his prognosis is going to be, whether he'll be able to walk, or even talk again. It has been a struggle for us to see what was a young vibrant Christian man, who had dedicated his life to the Lord, to be in service to preach his word, and I'm sure if he recovers, he will still do that. However, as everyday passes, with each new obstacle he faces we will be reminded of how he came to this. It was by your hand, that he is this way now. We will not forget what you did, but by the grace of God we have forgiven you. As you go your way, and work through your sentence, keep in mind that the God who helped us forgive you, wants you to seek forgiveness as well, and to come to a saving knowledge of him. We pray that God will be with you.

I got up after they sat down. I walked over and stood in front of my uncle. "Uncle Bud, what you did was wrong. I know you know that. Joanie and Josh never did anything that deserved what you did to them. I had to take them away to protect them. It tore my heart out to be separated from them, but it was for their own good. Someday I hope to get them back when all of this is over. Then when my emotions were at an all time low, you attacked my boyfriend and me. I'll never forget the look in your eyes as you raped me. It was a look of pure hate. I know that if you hadn't been drinking that day you might not have committed any of these crimes. I also know that if you, and your wife were sober, and your hearts were with God, that none of these things would have happened, and we wouldn't be here today. I feel sorry for my Aunt Ruth. She's had to put up with a lot from you over the last fifteen years. You could've been different, you could have had a better life, but you chose to spend it drinking, and slumming it away. Uncle Bud, I could choose to hate you, and let that hatred tear me up inside, but God has shown me a better way. Although I can't forget what happened, I will use it to make me a better person, a more compassionate person to those less fortunate than myself. I have, as Mr. and Mrs. James have done, forgiven you. I pray that you will get into Bible study, and ask for forgiveness from God. Only God can truly forgive what you have done. You're not beyond redemption. I will pray for you, Uncle Bud, that God will have mercy on you, and that you will be a better man for it."

My Aunt Ruth was in the audience. I turned to smile at her to let her know that I had no bad feelings toward her, as well.

I went back to my seat, and then the judge made his statement to my uncle.

"Sam Spencer, are you ready to receive your sentence?"

"I am your honor."

"Mr. Spencer, Mr. and Mrs. James, and Ms. Jordan have been very compassionate toward you, more so than I would have been if it were an attack on my family or me. Even though they have forgiven you, it doesn't make the crime go away. It doesn't change the fact that you are guilty of the heinous crimes that have been committed. Justice has to be served. So Mr. Spencer I sentence you to serve in the state correctional facilities consecutively ten years on the two counts of child abuse, and fifteen years each for the assault and battery charges against Mr. Steven James, and the assault and rape of Ms. Jobella Jordan for a total of 40 years. You will be eligible for parole at the end of 30 years for good behavior. Do you have anything to say to these in attendance?"

"I want to say to Mr. and Mrs. James, and their son, and to Jobella that I am sorry, the man who committed these crimes wouldn't have done them had I been sober. I know I caused these folks a lot of heartaches, and I know I can't go back, and undo what I did to them. I deserve this sentence, and I'm glad that I am being removed from society to protect them. If I was free to do what I wanted I would probably go back to my drinking, and cause more problems. Thank you, your Honor, and I will heed what they have told me about God, and I thank all of them for their forgiveness, as I don't deserve that from any of them."

As Uncle Bud walked by our table, I walked over to him, and gave him a hug.

I whispered in his ear, and told him I would be praying for him. We smiled at each other, and as we did, I saw the tears in his eyes. He was a broken man, and ready to be used by God, and my healing was complete.

Chapter 12

The day had finally come when I was leaving the psychiatric unit in the hospital. The nurses had brought some party food, and a cake for me, to wish me goodbye. It was great to be leaving, but I was going to miss everyone. I became close to several of the nurses, and the other residents, and of course, Dr. Habersham. Mr. and Mrs. James would be here soon to get me, and I was so excited. I had my bag packed earlier in the day, and now all I could do was wait. Of course all my paperwork had to be finished before I could leave, and the doctor would have to sign off on me.

The nurses got together and bought me a huge gift basket full of toiletries. They knew I didn't have anything, and I would need them in my 'new home'. They also got me a teddy bear to keep me company while Steve was still in the hospital. I was delighted in all this attention, but I told them it wasn't necessary. I had everything I needed now. I had a home to go to, and I had my God, and right now that was enough.

Before we left the hospital I wanted to go by and see Steve in the intermediate care unit. Mr. James took my bags, gift basket, and teddy bear to the car, and Mrs. James, and I walked down to his room. He was sitting up in his wheelchair, and the aide was feeding him his lunch. He smiled at us when we walked through the door, and I knew he recognized me. I walked over, and gave him a big hug, and kissed his forehead. I didn't want to interrupt him getting fed. He still didn't have the strength to raise his arms to feed himself, and that made me sad, but at least he wasn't being fed through a tube in his stomach anymore.

It had been a week since he woke up, and everyday he got a little stronger, and even said a few words, but it would take him a while to get his strength back. Still as we left, I had a smile on my face. I got my fiancé back, and I was thrilled.

As we drove home there was still a little snow left on the ground. Christmas was a week away, and more snow was in the forecast. It would be nice to have a white Christmas this year. We haven't had one in a very long time. The only problem would be, I would want to see Steve but slick roads may be a problem with that. Still it would be nice.

When we got to Steve's house there was a surprise reception for me. All three of my friends were there, along with my aunt, and some of Steve's other family, that lived nearby. I was happy to see them, but all I really wanted now was to get settled, and rest a little bit before supper. I already had one party today, and I really didn't need another, but I stayed, and visited a little while to be supportive of my 'new' family. Aunt Ruth looked like a whole new person. She underwent a lot of changes since she didn't have to answer to Uncle Bud anymore. She said she quit drinking, and had even gone back to school to finish her degree in sociology that she started over fifteen years ago, before she met Sam. I was pleased for her.

I talked with my friends a little while. I told them how much I appreciated them coming by, and visiting with me while I was in the hospital, and how sorry I was that I was rude to them. I told them I wanted to visit with them individually before their semester break was over. I really wanted to talk with each of them alone, but this wasn't the time to go into everything I wanted to say.

After everyone left, I thanked Mr. and Mrs. James for everything that they have done for me, and for taking me in. They showed me to the guest room they had made up for me. It was wonderful. The room was way more than I could have asked for. It was beautifully decorated but my real surprise was when I opened the closet, and there was several new clothes hanging in there! I gasped at what I saw. I told her that she didn't have to do all that, but she said that it wasn't her. It was my three friends that had done it! They still loved me as friends, and that made me very happy.

Later that day when I sat alone in my room in my 'new' home, I reflected on everything that had happened in the last week, and I was amazed at the goodness of God, in bringing me here to this point. He had truly blessed me. I became aware of how easy it was to praise God through the good things, and at the same time to not feel the need to seek him when everything seems to be going our way. I would have to remember that even in the lowest points in my life that God was still there lifting me up, and that is when I should praise him all the more.

After supper, as I settled in, I knelt beside my bed, and prayed. "Lord I praise you for your goodness and for the mercy you have given me by bringing me through my darkness, and into your light. Thank you for your provision for my salvation in dying on the cross for my sins. As I enter into this new stage of my life I pray for strength in what lies ahead. I want to remember my brother and sister at this time, and I pray for their continued health, and love, and I pray for their foster parents that they would treat them well, and will be ready to give them back to me when the time is right. I pray for Steven. I pray that he will be healed, and well again, and I pray for our relationship in the future that it would be honoring to you.

Lord, guide my steps through my future, and let me walk with you, that your will be done in my life. I thank you Lord for the provision of this, my new home, and for the love of Mr. and Mrs. James. Bless them Lord. In Jesus name I pray, amen."

The next day, I woke up still in unbelief of everything that happened. I was riding a high with God by my side but I know there would be more trials down the line because God didn't promise that we would always be on the hilltop. Sometimes when everything seems perfect it's the time to watch out, because that is when Satan attacks us so that we begin to doubt our salvation.

Today was the Sunday before Christmas. We went to church to celebrate the season, and the fact that Christ came down to earth to be born of a virgin, and give himself as a sacrifice for our sins. It was hard to think of a more joyous holiday with the exception of Easter, when he rose from the dead to give us salvation. Christmas met a lot more to me this year because for the first time I concentrated more on the Christ, than on what I was going to get out of it. It was so much more than the shopping, and decorations, and seeing the twin's smiles as they sat in Santa's lap telling him what they wanted him to bring them.

Pastor Stewart read the Christmas story from Luke 2. I've heard it every Christmas my whole life, because my dad would read it to us on Christmas Eve to remind us what the holiday was all about, and then we would light all the Advent candles, and pray. It didn't mean as much then to me, as it would now. I wish I could tell them that, and thank them for being such Godly parents.

After the sermon we sang Christmas songs, and then had the invitation. I wanted everyone to know that I rededicated my life so I went forward. Pastor Stewart welcomed me with open arms, and tears in his eyes. After he prayed with me, I turned to face the congregation. Everyone was on their feet as he told them of my trials, and my conversion. There wasn't a dry eye to be seen. Everyone came to me after the service was over, and hugged me, and said that they had been praying for me.

On the way home my heart was singing. God was so good.

Come Monday morning the first thing I wanted to do was to get all my things from my aunt's house including my parent's car that was left there. I was hoping that it was still there, and in one piece. I would need it when I went back to school, and for trips to and from the hospital to see Steve. Mrs. James drove me to Aunt Ruth's house, but there was no sign of her, and the car was gone. I knocked, but no one answered. I looked in the window, but everything had been cleared out. She had left, and I didn't know where to even begin looking for her.

"Mrs. James, what should I do? She's gone. It looks like she moved out. There's nothing there but some trash lying around. Not even a sign in sight that indicates that she is trying to sell the place. It would help if we could find her realtor."

"We can see your lawyer, or go to the police. If I remember right, Ruth's on probation for a year. She can't leave the area until that time is up, and she was at our party, if you remember. I didn't have an address for her when I invited her, I had seen her at the market, and told her about the party we were going to have for you. I didn't think about getting her address at the time. I figured she still lived here. She is doing mandatory community service at a woman's shelter. So we could start there."

We went to the police station to make inquiries about Aunt Ruth. They sent us to Mr. Rosen, their attorney. His secretary said we would have to make an appointment with him because he was extremely busy. We told the secretary what we wanted, and she said that he wouldn't be able to give us that information without her consent. So we were no closer to finding her than we were before.

The time was getting on, and we wanted to go see Steve, so we decided to give up our search for the day.

When we got to the hospital Steven wasn't in his room. He had gone to therapy. The nurse said that we could catch him there in that department. We took the elevator down to the rehab unit. The speech therapist was working with him.

"He had a setback yesterday evening at suppertime." She said matter-of-factly. "He started choking on his food. We are working with him now to make sure his throat, and esophagus muscles are working properly. Sometimes when someone is tube fed for a while, as he had been, the smooth muscles of the digestive system forget how to work, and we have to stimulate them again to function properly."

We stayed for a little while, and waited but it looked like they weren't going to be done too soon and I wanted to go by my high school to see if there was someone in the office to see what I needed to do to get my diploma so I could register for college.

I forgot that the school was closed for the holidays. So much for getting anything done that day, or any other day in the next two weeks!

I started feeling sorry for myself after we got home. I guess I was hoping everything was still going to be perfect for me, and everything would just fall into place but that just didn't happen. Mrs. James just smiled, and said, "Welcome back down to earth, Jobella. The place that we have to deal with on a day-to-day basis. We can only do so much, and then leave the rest to God. It will get better. It may not be always to our liking, and our timetable but somehow it will happen, and work out according to God's will.

The rest of the day we spent baking, and decorating cookies for the ladies league cookie swap, and give away at the church tonight. I asked her if I could make some extra for the nursing home where I used to volunteer. She thought that was a wonderful idea, and I was excited that I would be able to go, and visit my friends again in the home.

We took the cookies to the nursing home on Christmas Eve day. Mrs. James, and I were welcomed into the visitor's center, and several of the staff greeted us, and it was hugs all around. They asked us to stay, and visit with the residents. I was sad to hear that some of them had passed away while I was gone, but I was excited to see the ones that were still there. We all went into the dayroom, and we brought our cookies, and the kitchen brought in some punch and coffee to go with them. We got around the piano, and Mrs. James played, and led us in several Christmas carols. We closed in prayer, and I announced that as soon as I was able, I would come back, and do some more volunteering if they would have me. Of course there was no objection from the resident's but the administrator said I would have to reapply because it had been over six months since I was there, but she didn't think it would be a problem.

It lifted my spirits to be there. I've always enjoyed visiting with the elderly. They were wonderful supporters. They had lived a long time, and the ones that didn't have dementia were able to give advice from their many experiences, and the stories they had to tell. I always loved listening to those stories.

As we were leaving I heard my name being called, "Jobella, over here." I turned, and couldn't believe my eyes! Aunt Ruth was there, visiting with one of residents!

"Aunt Ruth," I smiled. "What are you doing here?"

"I'm visiting Bud's mother. She had a stroke shortly after Bud's arrest. She is paralyzed on her R side but she is still able to communicate and enjoys company."

"Doe she blame me for Uncle Bud's arrest?"

"No, not at all, and neither do I." she smiled. "Actually, I'm better off without him. I moved out of that old house, and found an apartment I could afford in a better part of town, and I'm in school now to finish my sociology degree. When I was serving my community service with the abused women's shelter I got the urge to make doing things like that a part of my life. The probation officer, and the courts saw what a good job I was doing, and my desire to go back to school, and they suspended my sentence."

"Aunt Ruth, what happened to my car, I went looking for it a few days ago and I didn't see it and saw that you moved. I didn't know where to find you."

"Your car was impounded following our arrests. It was still at the house, and the police went ahead, and impounded it along with our car until someone could claim it. They knew it couldn't belong to us, and they didn't want to leave it there. It was too nice of a car to be trashed by the thugs living in that neighborhood."

"Where did you get the money for your apartment and school?"

"Jobella, that's really my business, but I didn't get it from your car if that is what you are implying. If you must know, I did sell the house. The reason there is not a 'for sale' sign is that I sold it back to the bank. I didn't get as much for it by doing that, but I got rid of it, and that's all I wanted to do. I didn't want to be anywhere that reminded me of that monster. Oh, by the way, I packed up the twins, and your belongings. They were taken to Mrs. Freeman's law firm. You can get them from her."

"I'm sorry, aunt Ruth, I guess I was wondering about that. I'm glad things are working out for you. Maybe sometime I can come, and visit you when I get a car again, if that would be alright with you."

"I think that I would enjoy that very much. I'm really not the person who met you at the door over six months ago. I've really cleaned up my act since that time. I'm sure my mother-in-law would like to see you as well when you come here. She's nothing like Sam"

"I'll be sure to do that. Could you give me your phone number and address? I'm living with Steven's mom and dad now until I can get in school and get my own place on campus. Thank you for letting me know about our things. I'll check with Abby about getting them back."

With that we exchanged addresses, and said our good-byes. As we left I thought about going by the police impound but it was already five O'clock, and it was Christmas Eve, so I knew they would be closed. We made a quick run by the mall to do some last minute Christmas shopping. I didn't have much money to spend, but I did want to get Steve and his parents something for being so nice to me.

Christmas was almost an anticlimax for me. So many good things happened in the weeks leading up to this day that any gifts would pale in comparison. My heart was full already, and spending it with some of the people I loved most made the day that much more special. I did however miss my own parents, and my brother and sister. I missed the excitement that was in the twin's eyes as they came down the stairs, and looked under our Christmas tree, and found their presents. They couldn't read the names on the packages, but Joanie's presents were usually wrapped in Disney Princess, or Hello Kitty paper, and Joshua's was in Toy Story, or Star Wars paper. It was always a struggle to keep them from opening their gifts before mom and dad came down, and we had a chance to take pictures. The thoughts of my family not being together this day was bittersweet. I knew that mom and dad was celebrating with Jesus in heaven, and the twins hopefully were happy with their Christmas at their foster parents home.

After we ate our dinner, we went to the hospital to visit Steve, and bring him the presents we got for him. We found him in his room today. Due to the holiday there was no rehab, or other special activities. The nurses that were there seemed eager for their shift to end so they could go home to be with their families.

Steven looked a little down today. I know he was wishing he were at home, and celebrating with us instead of being trapped in a body that wasn't working so well. He was dressed, and up in his wheelchair when we got there. I wish they would allow us to take him home for a visit but that wasn't allowed until he made more progress in his mobility. He wasn't even able to open his presents without some help. He didn't have enough muscle coordination or fine motor skills yet.

We brought Steven some food from our dinner. The nurses said he was doing much better with his swallowing, and it would be okay to give it to him. We brought him some of our homemade cookies as well. It was hard to know what to give him for presents until he got out of the hospital, but we did get him some new pajamas, a robe and a pair of slippers. His parents got him a new MP3 player loaded with some of his favorite contemporary Christian singers. Any other presents would have to wait until we welcomed him home someday, hopefully sooner than later.

We wrapped his new robe around him, and asked at the nurse's station if we could take him off the unit to go around, and look at the Christmas decorations on the other floors, and in the lobby. They said it would be okay, but not to stay too long. He had to be back for his medication.

He smiled at the décor, and turned to smile at me. He couldn't say too much yet, but what he said warmed my heart, and gave me hope. "Jo, I love you. You too Mom and Dad." We all smiled at each other with tears in our eyes. He knew who we were, and that he was loved in return.

Life wasn't perfect, but we loved the Christ who came to earth on that first Christmas to give us an eternal life that was perfect, and that was good enough for all of us.

Chapter 13

Six months previous, somewhere on the southern end of the island of Java, Kyle Jordan was helping the natives build a new hospital for their small town. He was a missionary doctor, and his wife Sadie, was a nurse. They were working on the building when one of the helpers came running. "Doctor, doctor!" he panted, out of breath from the long run up the mountain. "Telegram for you! It says it's urgent!"

"Thank you Sanji." He replied as he tore the envelope open.

"What is it Kyle!" shouted Sadie, as she came running over.

He was frowning as he read over the letter. "It says my brother and his wife were killed in a house fire, and everything is gone."

"When did it happen?"

"I'm guessing it was about two weeks before this telegram was written. It happened around the middle of May. I can't believe it has taken us six months to get this."

"That's what happens when you live half way around the world, and in the middle of nowhere. We really are isolated, aren't we?"

"What about the girl? Didn't they name her Jo, or Belle or something like that?"

"They didn't mention her, they only mentioned Kevin and Gabrielle."

"It's been nineteen years since you've seen them. You haven't even heard from them."

"Remember, we thought it would be better for everyone if we didn't have contact with them for the girl's sake. We didn't want her to find out that we gave her up for adoption by my brother and his wife. Everyone was to believe that she was their biological daughter."

Kyle and Sadie were dating at the time she got pregnant. They were in college to become missionaries, but one night their passion became more physical, and before they were able to stop themselves they spent the night together. A couple of months later they knew she was pregnant. They didn't want anyone to find out about it, so Sadie took a leave of absence from school, and went to a home for unwed mothers. They didn't believe in abortions, and at the same time his brother Kevin, and his wife were having a hard time having a baby, and they agreed to adopt theirs under the stipulation that no one would ever know that Kyle and Sadie had a baby out of wedlock. The mission board they were going through was very strict, and wouldn't agree to send them if they knew what happened. So everything was done without anyone's knowledge.

When the mission board heard about Kevin and Gabrielle Jordan's death, they contacted Kyle, Kevin's identical twin brother in Java. It took them two weeks to locate them, and when they did it took a month or more to get the telegram to them because they were so remote.

When they found out what happened they wanted to go home on furlough right away. They wanted to see her. They wanted to make sure she was all right. They thought if she was all alone in the world now maybe they could legally adopt her if she was okay with that. She might not have anyone else. They didn't remember any living relatives except her aunt and uncle on her mother's side. Both sets of grandparents were dead as well as far as they remembered. His parents died while he was in college, and he knew that Gabrielle's died fifteen years ago.

They contacted the mission board but they wouldn't give their approval for them to go home right away. They wanted them to finish up on the hospital they were building, and then there was the question of raising the support to get them home. They didn't have the funds they would need for the trip. The mission board didn't understand why it was so necessary for them to see about his dead brother's estate when there was nothing left, and the children were the sole beneficiaries of any money that was left, and that was all tied up until the children became adults.

They would have to wait for a few months or more to finish up here. It would take them that long to get the money to fly back home. They contacted their sending church and told them of the situation, hoping they would be able to help them out, but the church was strapped for cash as well. They could barely send the money for them to live on. So there was nothing else they could do but wait. That, and build a hospital of course.

In Sadie's heart she knew her daughter was still alive. This past six months she had frequent urges to pray for her. Those urges intensified over the last two months. Now after getting the telegram, she knew why she had been feeling the way she did. Once she knew what happened, she prayed even more.

Kyle wrote a letter to the pastor of their church back home, and asked him if he could find out anything about the fire that killed his brother and sister-in-law. He wanted to know if there were any survivors and how they were dealing with it. He also wanted especially to know about his niece. He wanted to know if she survived, and if she did, what happened to her.

His pastor wrote back about a month later, and sent several newspaper articles dealing with the fires, and their deaths, and their obituaries. As expected there was no mention of him having a brother. They didn't know he existed because he had been out of their lives for so long. He left for the mission field about the time Kevin moved to Clairmonte, and became the president of his company. No one was aware that Kyle was on a self-imposed exile from his family. Even though he was doing great things with the natives of Java, he lived with the sadness of never being able to see his family again especially his and Sadie's daughter. He also saw in the obituary that they had three children, eighteen-year-old Jobella, and three year old twins, Joshua and Joanna. *'So they were able to have more children, even though it took them fifteen years after they got their Jobella. Jobella, that was a strange name to give their daughter.* He thought. *'Maybe it was a contraction of Jo and Bella. Yes that had to be it. One of the grandmother's names was Josephine, and the other one was Isabella.'*

He picked through the rest of the clippings. He found another clipping from the same newspaper. Jobella and her boyfriend had been attacked, and her uncle in the attack had raped her. They both were in the hospital in serious condition he continued to read. Her boyfriend was in a coma, and she was in the mental ward. They both were expected to survive the attack but at what cost, he continued to read.

The third article he read concerned the trial of her uncle. He was found guilty, and was sentenced to forty years for the attack, and also for child abuse of the twins. How could all this happen to these innocent children when they had just lost their parents two weeks prior to these attacks? How could her uncle be that cruel? He was glad that he confessed when the trial was coming to a close, and he was glad that they wouldn't have to be afraid of him ever again.

When he shared the articles with Sadie, they both broke down and cried for his brother and sister-in-law, and their children, especially for Jobella. They prayed for Jobella, and those around her. They even prayed for the salvation of her aunt and uncle.

There were no other articles after the trial news. They would have no way of knowing where the children were. They would have to hire someone to track down where they were moved. Maybe Jobella's lawyer would be able to give them that information.

Their hearts yearned to return home, to Clairmonte and to find the children, and make them their own. They would adopt all three of them, and be reunited with their beloved daughter they gave up so long ago.

Chapter 14

After the Christmas and New Years holidays were over, it was time for me to make some things happen. The first thing, the day after New Years, I went to the police impound to try to get my parent's car back. I thought it would be easy. I couldn't have been more wrong. It seems my parent's were still paying on the car. The police checked the title to see who it was registered to, and found that the bank still had the title and if the payments haven't been made since the fire seven months ago, they had no choice but to return the car to the, dealership to be resold.

"That's not fair, you know why the payments weren't made. I should have been told that you were getting ready to send it back so I could've done something about it!" I said to the impounding officer.

"You know you weren't able to get it out of hock. You have no visible means of income to purchase it, or take up the payments of any car, let alone a new BMW." Thousands of dollars of back payments were owed. He replied.

"I know you're right, I'm sorry. I'm disappointed though. I would've thought that my parent's would have paid cash for it. They had enough money for it."

"People often choose to make payment's even though they do have money, to keep up their credit ratings. That's something you will learn as you get out on your own."

"I'll give you the name of the car dealership if you want to go see if they still have the car on the lot. Here are the things we took out of the car before sending it back."

He handed me some change, brochures, and some CD's that were in the car. I thanked him for his help and apologized for being upset.

Out of curiosity, Mrs. James and I went to the dealership to see if the car was still there. We were disappointed to find that it was sold the previous week. I looked around to see if there was something I could afford, but the impound officer was right. I didn't see anything on the lot that would fit in my budget. Especially since I didn't even have a job. The rest of the money in my parent's bank account wouldn't even cover the down payment!

After that I went by my high school, and luckily the office staff had come back to work a few days before school started back. I asked what I needed to do to get my diploma since I wasn't able to take my finals, and graduate. My guidance counselor told me to come in the next day, and take the tests I needed, and she would see to it that it was graded by the end of the week, and then she would get with the principal about giving me my diploma.

I was anxious to get started to college. Before the fire, and everything else that happened I was offered a scholarship to Duke for all four years. I wasn't sure if that still applied. I would write to them, and explain the situation, and beg them to let me still have it. I wasn't able to start last semester, but I would like to see if I could start as soon as possible.

Because of everything that has happened to me this year, I was surer than ever that I wanted to go into law. Ms. Freeman was so inspirational in the way she treated me that I wanted to emulate her. I would go into family law and protect victims like myself, to combat injustices against individuals, and families, and to serve others with an attitude of prayer and godliness.

I hoped that Steve would support me in this endeavor when he gets well, and we get married. That would be important to me to have his blessing. I didn't know what his plans would be in going back to school or if he would even be able to go back now.

We went to the hospital to visit him after I left the high school office. His mother and I looked in on Steve almost everyday. He had some good days when he made some improvement, but other days he relapsed a little. Today happened to be a good day for him. We took him to the therapy department in his wheelchair, and watched him as he worked with his therapist. I think he tried a little harder when we were there. He wanted to show us he was making progress. They were working on arm exercises today. He could catch the exercise ball now, and he could lift some lightweights slowly above his head.

The therapist said that he was ready to start feeding himself, and his diet was advanced to regular foods. He could speak in short sentences now, and make eye contact with those he was speaking to. After getting his upper body strength back, they would begin with his leg exercises. They needed his muscles in his arms strong so he could support his weight on the parallel bars to walk. They wanted him out of the wheelchair ninety percent of the time, before they would consider him ready to go home.

After we left Steve, we ran the rest of our errands. We swung by the grocery store to pick up some fresh vegetables for a salad for supper. When we saw aunt Ruth in the deli area, I turned to go the other direction. I still had a hard time seeing her even though she was trying to do all the right things, and we reconciled our feelings with each other, and with God. I had forgiven her, but I still couldn't forget the way she was with the twins. I guess only time would help with that.

Seeing her made me think about the twins again. They were four years old now, and would soon be starting pre-school. I wondered where they were, and if they had a good Christmas, and if their foster parents were giving them the love they deserved. I hoped that they weren't being abused. I didn't like not knowing what was going on with them. I thought about contacting social services, but I knew they couldn't tell me anything. They didn't want me to contact the foster parents or try to see the children. It would be counterproductive to their welfare, they said. They wouldn't be able to give them back to me until I was in my own home, and was able to support them. Right now I didn't know when that would happen. I still had college, and it would be a while before Steve, and I would get married, and have jobs. It looked pretty bleak for me seeing them again for a long time. By the time I see them again they will probably not even know me.

Mrs. James let me borrow her car to take to the school to take my finals. These were the tests that I was supposed to take the week after my parents died. I pretty much aced most of my classes so my guidance counselor said I only needed to take part of the tests. That made it a lot easier on me. I just hoped I remembered what I had learned because I wasn't able to study for them. All my textbooks were destroyed in the fire. There were a few tricky questions, but I managed to muddle through them with a passing grade. The principal and my guidance counselor went ahead and graded them, and then gave me my diploma while I was there. I was able to also get my transcripts at the same time so I could to go ahead and apply to Duke.

I needed to get a car so I wouldn't have to depend on Mrs. James to take me everywhere I needed to go, especially when I left for college. To do that I would have to see if I could get a job. I didn't want to keep on imposing on them without giving them something in return towards my cost of living.

So with the paperwork sent to Duke, I got to work looking for a job. Because I found out that I wouldn't be able to start at the university until the fall semester due to turning in my paperwork late, I wanted to find something to do until then. I couldn't sit around for eight months doing nothing.

There weren't a whole lot of jobs in our little town. I checked in with the nursing home, the hospital, and the manufacturing plant where my father was the CEO until his death. I checked the want ads daily, and checked the Internet job sites as well. I also asked my lawyer if she knew of any kind of job with her firm.

I asked Abby about getting some of the money from my inheritance for a car, but there was so much red tape to getting it. The hold up was that I wasn't in college yet, and I was only nineteen, and not living on my own. I told them I needed enough of the money so I could get a car, and get a job. They said they would check into it.

The following Sunday we went to church again. As usual Pastor Stewart's sermon hit the mark. It was on the subject of asking God for something. If we asked for anything in his will, he would answer it. God knows I have praying quite a lot lately; for Steve's healing, for the twins, and now for school, a job, and a car. I found out I needed a lot of patience to get things I desired. The answers didn't always come overnight. It wasn't so easy waiting on the Lord when you want everything, when you want it. Life wasn't always handed to us on a silver platter. We also must accept it when God says no. So it was with me over the next few weeks.

We went to visit Steve again Sunday, after church, and brought him some lunch. It was a pleasant day for January, almost like spring. We rolled him out to the deck off his unit to let him get some fresh air, and we ate with him outside. He seemed to enjoy that. The sunshine, and the garden area on the deck felt very relaxing. He told us about his week, and how they finally started doing his leg strengthening exercises. They were going to start him on the parallel bars this coming week. It was encouraging seeing him so upbeat about his improvement. He was able to talk in complete sentences now, and was looking forward to walking again.

On Monday, the law firm that employed Mrs. Freeman called me in. They received my application, and wanted to interview me for a paralegal position. They wanted to know if I could come in on that very day! Talk about excited! That would be so perfect. They said their paralegal had given her two-week notice, and they had to find someone right away.

Mrs. Freeman along with the rest of the staff sat in on the interview, and asked me several questions about why I wanted the job, and about any past experiences that would qualify me for the job. Of course the only experience I had with the legal system was the trials that I was involved in. They said they would get back with me in a day or two.

I sat on pins and needles waiting to hear back from them. They didn't give a clue about how I did on my interview. Mrs. Freeman gave me a sympathetic look but no indication whether I had a chance or not. I'm sure there were a lot of applicants, some with a lot more experience, so I was surprised when they called me the next day. They wanted me to start immediately so I could be trained before the current paralegal left!

Mrs. Freeman, or Abby, as she wanted me to call her, came to pick me up the next morning. She insisted on getting me so I wouldn't have to depend on Mrs. James to get me to and from work. We parked in the parking deck across from the law offices in the courthouse. Imagine my surprise when I saw a BMW next to where Abby parked that looked a lot like my parents old car. I was even more surprised when Abby took a key off her key ring, and handed it to me along with a thick envelope of paperwork. At first I thought that it was a key to the office, and my new hire paperwork. Then she took me over to the car. I asked her what was going on, and why was my mom and dad's car was there.

I didn't know it at the time she handed me the paperwork that Mr. and Mrs. James followed us into the parking deck, and got out after we did. Then saw a couple of flashes go off.

"Jobella, welcome to your new job, and your new car!" Abby laughed.

"When did you do all of this?" I was astounded. "I can't afford to buy this car. I know I'm not going to make the kind of money I need to make payments on this!"

"If you're going to work for a law firm of our caliber you need to have the wheels to go along with the job. Just one of the few perks of your new employer." She teased. "Don't worry, we all got together, and paid for it. It's yours. You just have to pay the taxes, and license on it every year, and the gas, and maintenance that goes into it, of course. Your paperwork that I gave you includes the title free and clear."

"How, when, what happened? When we went by the auto dealership a couple of weeks ago it was gone!"

'That's because we had bought it! It was just in the shop being checked out."

"What if I hadn't gotten the job here, or I accepted another position somewhere else?"

"We thought about that. We would have figured out another way of getting it to you, but we were banking on you coming here for a job because we knew that you were interested in becoming a lawyer."

I was so excited! The other lawyers in the firm were getting out of their cars, and came and gathered around us and cheered. "Who would've thought that lawyers could be so nice?" I laughed.

After everyone left the parking area, Abby and I made our way to our offices. I was to do general secretarial duties, like filing and sending letters, and scheduling appointments. Not too difficult of a task for me. '*This is something I can handle.*' I thought to myself.

Everyone I worked with was very patient with me. It would take a few days to learn their routines, and get use to each one, and what they expected of me. It wasn't hard at all. Abby even let me go into court with her a few times. Not that I needed to see what they did, but she was glad to have me for company, and to take notes for her while we were there.

After a while I settled into my routine of working nine to five. I would go out with my co-workers at lunch, and they would teach me some tips on how to make it as a lawyer. I learned a lot from them, and was anxious to get into law school now so I could take all this information, and incorporate it into my studies. They let me borrow books from their libraries, and look at old cases to learn the ins and outs of what happened in those cases, and see what worked, and what didn't in them. It was an education that was invaluable to my future courses.

About a month after I started working there I was sorting through the mail, as I did every morning, when I came across a letter from Java. It was directed to Mrs. Abby Freeman. The fact that it came all the way from Java was strange enough, but when I saw the return address it floored me. It was from a Dr. Kyle Jordan. What on earth could it mean? Was it from a relative or was it a mere coincidence that we had the same last name? It had been marked 'personal' and those letters the lawyers didn't want me to open. I took it into Abby, and she looked as puzzled as I did. She sent me from the room, so she could read it privately. She didn't say anything else about the letter and when I asked her about it, she changed the subject. She obviously didn't want to talk about it.

Chapter 15

I didn't have much time since I started working to visit Steve. It was pretty much limited to the weekends now. It was springtime, and when we visited we went out on the deck to enjoy the fresh air. The flowers and trees were coming into full-bloom. It was beautiful, and my life was becoming beautiful again. Everything continued to be going my way. I always felt that the other shoe was going to drop at any time, because everything was almost too good to be true!

Since I was given my car, I had more freedom to come and go as I pleased. I didn't have to wait until Steve's parents came to visit him, I could visit him at anytime. It was nice to have this time 'alone' with him. We shared secrets, and our hearts. I told him about how my work was going. I could sense a longing, and a jealousy in his heart to be where I was at this point in my life. Here I was living with his parents, enjoying their company and support, and working at a job, where I was making a decent amount of money, and everything was going my way. He was stuck here in his 'prison' of immobility unable to walk or even stand without nearly falling over. He also was afraid something would happen before he got out of the hospital. He was worried I would find someone new that wouldn't be a 'burden' to me. I told him he was my 'soul mate' and the one God had given to me. There would never be another I could love as much as I loved him. I reassured him even if he was never going to walk again, I would still love him, and we would find a way to live with that. But I knew God would heal him. He told me so.

After our visit he was taken to therapy again. It was an everyday event for him now. He'd been out of his coma for over four months now. He felt tired at times, and discouraged even though he had made great strides in overcoming the brain damage that he had suffered. Walking was really the last thing that he had to get back. He just felt that it was taking too long.

I prayed with him, and told him I would bring Pastor Stewart next time I came, and maybe we could have a prayer time together. With that, I gave him a hug, and held him the best I could while he was sitting in the wheel chair. As he raised his arms to hold me I felt his body trembling, and I knew he was crying. When I let go, and looked at him I saw the tears in his eyes. I knew then that whatever it took to get him walking was the most important thing in both of our lives. I would be his number one cheerleader!

I told the therapist when they came to get him that I wanted to go with them to encourage him. They told me I could observe only, and not do anything to distract them or Steve. I told them I would, but I wanted him to see me, and know that I was there for him.

They tried to stand him up with a gait belt. His legs were weak, and his knees didn't want to support him. He had almost no muscle mass in his legs left, after being in bed, and in a wheel chair for so long. I prayed to God to give him strength to at least stand, and take the first step. Steve looked at me with tears in his eyes. He was determined to do his best, but under his own strength he couldn't do it. He would need to be lifted up by God.

The therapist finally gave up on trying to get him up. They decided they would have to do some more leg strengthening exercises on the weight machines before trying it again. After I prayed, I begged them to try to get him up one more time. They said it was impossible right now. I told them with God nothing is impossible. So they tried one more time. They wrapped the gait belt around him once more. This time when they stood him up. He was able to stand for ten seconds before having to sit back down. He smiled at me, and gave me two thumbs up. It wasn't much, but it was a start.

The next Saturday I visited him again, and as I promised, I brought Pastor Stewart with me. When he saw both of us together, he smiled.

"It's good to see you again, Steven. Jobella has been keeping me up on your progress. Its good to see you looking so well. She also told me that you've been discouraged about how long it's taking you to recover."

"It has been discouraging. I'm tired of living here in the hospital. I need to get out of here, and get on with my life. I've missed a whole year of school. I'm ready to get back into it, even if it's in a wheelchair.

"God has his own timetable. He's teaching you patience. He's already worked miracles in your life. He will continue to do so. When I saw you eight months ago after your attack I thought that you would never get over it. I really thought that you were going to die that night. Then after being in a coma for six months, I didn't think that you would ever wake up. The doctor's had all but given up on you, and was ready to put you in a nursing home for the rest of your life. When you woke up, and knew everyone around you, it was a real miracle. Now look at you. You're talking and interacting with those around you, and you have the strength back in your arms, and you have function with your hands and can feed and dress yourself."

"Yes, I have all the attributes of a toddler, only I can't pull myself up and walk." He frowned.

"It will come. I have faith in the God that has brought you this far. Your church family, and I will continue to pray for you. You will walk again. I'm looking forward to the day that your family, and Jobella bring you into the church to worship, and then later for your pre-marriage counseling, and then your wedding. It's all going to happen, Steve. You have to believe."

"Steve gave a short laugh. I'm afraid that will be a long time coming. I hope that Jobella will still want me, after all of this." He winked at me.

"I brought his hand that I was holding up to my lips, and kissed it. You don't ever have to worry about that, Steven."

As we left, I promised him that his family, and I would be by the next day. It would be Easter Sunday. We planned on bringing Easter dinner, along with an Easter basket filled with all kinds of goodies, and Easter eggs made especially for him. His mom made some hot cross buns for breakfast, and we would throw in a few of those as well.

The next day was beautiful. It seemed that it was always beautiful on Easter Sunday. It was like the universe was celebrating the resurrection of Christ. After church we packed up the food we would take to the hospital. We would make a picnic out of it to share with Steven.

He was thrilled when we came through the door with all our goodies. We called ahead to the nurses' station, and told them we were coming with food for him, so they wouldn't give him a food tray from the kitchen. We were all starving by the time we got there.

We went out to the garden area, and laid out our spread on one of the picnic tables. We rolled Steve to the end of the table in his wheelchair. And we sat close to him. It was a wonderful meal. Mrs. James had out-done her self with the meal. We had ham, deviled eggs, potato salad, and green bean casserole. My offering was the coconut cake for dessert. We also brought a gallon of sweet tea.

After we ate, and packed the left overs back into the picnic basket we went back to his room to visit a little while. Steve had a big smile on his face. He had a present for us as well. He called the nurse into the room, and he whispered something in her ear. We saw her smiling at us as she walked out door.

In a few minutes she returned with a walker in her hands.

"Now I have a surprise for you all as well!" he smiled. With that he put the locks on his wheel chair, and stood up gradually. He then grabbed the walker by each side handle, and walked to each one of us, and gave each of us a hug. We all sobbed with joy. He was walking. We couldn't get over it! It was the best Easter present ever!

"The doctor told me that if I continued to do this well, that as soon as I can walk a hundred yards or more even with a walker I'll be able to go home. He said I would still have to continue to build up my leg muscles, but between eating the right foods, especially protein, and continuing my exercises I should get all my strength back and be totally back to normal!"

It was truly a day for celebrating God's goodness for us, and for the world.

I couldn't wait to get home, and call the pastor, and let him know what happened. I knew he would be thrilled with our news, and for the answered prayers of all of our friends that knew Steve.

All the next week Steven walked as much as possible with his walker. He was bound and determined to get out by the following weekend. The doctor's were amazed at his progress. They never seen anyone with as much motivation as he had, to get well. There was no stopping him! He was up in the halls on his unit, and walked constantly. First with the walker, and towards the end of the week he could walk on his own. He liked to go to the nurses' station, and harass them about anything and everything. They got a kick out of him, and his teasing. He begged them to contact the doctor to let him know how well he was doing.

Finally on the Friday after Easter, we got the call. Steve was coming home. We were thrilled, but it did cause a concern for me. I was still living with his parents, and I was concerned about staying in the same house with him while we were still dating. I knew Steve and I were waiting for marriage before being intimate, but what would people like those at church, and our friends think of us being under the same roof. His parents and I didn't think that he would have gotten well so soon. I still had four months until school started, and was able to move to the dorms on campus. That would mean that we would be under the same roof all that time. When we were alone at home there would be too many temptations.

I made up my mind to look for an apartment. I wanted to continue to work at the law firm while I was in college anyway, so I started looking for a place that would be somewhere between where I worked, and my school. Duke was about forty-five minutes away from the James's home in Clairmonte and my job. So I would have to commute twenty to thirty minutes either way. 'That was doable' I thought. So I started looking for an apartment the next day in that general area.

I told Abby about my search for an apartment, and that I was going to move out on my own, and also I would be in college soon, so she started the procedure about getting me some money from my trust fund. I was only planning on taking a small portion of it, something that would cover my expenses in school, and pay for the down payment on the apartment, rent, and some furniture. It was going to be exciting having my own place, and not having to depend on someone else, but it was also going to be extremely lonely. I was glad for my job in Clairmonte, my church, my job and the nursing home, where I could socialize with others. Also, Steve was there in Clairmonte as well. My apartment was just going to be a place I came home to eat supper, and fall into bed.

❧ Chapter 16 ❧

Abby finally had time to settle down, and read the letters she received before Easter. She had taken her a spring vacation from her practice, and this was her first day back. When she got down to the bottom of her pile she found the letter she had received from Kyle Jordan two weeks ago.

She racked her brain wondering where she had heard that name before, especially someone that lived in Java. She reread the letter, and then it all came back to her.

Kyle wrote:

Dear Mrs. Freeman,

I don't know if you remember me or not. But you helped me, and my girlfriend at that time, Sadie, make arrangements concerning our baby that was born out of wedlock. We did a private adoption through your law firm, where my brother, Kevin and his wife Gabrielle, would get our child, and we would go away, and not try to see her, or claim her. We did that because we were studying to be missionaries at the time, and didn't want anything to prevent the mission board from approving us, and having a child out of wedlock would disqualify us from going. Sadie and I have since married and we haven't been in touch with either my brother or his wife as per our contract.

It has come to our attention a few months ago that my brother and his wife were killed in a fire, and then the subsequent problems, and trials of Jobella and the twins. We learned about it when the mission board notified us of their death, and the pastor of our home church sent us articles about all the other things that happened.

I'm afraid that the mail in and out of here takes a while so I don't know when you will receive this. I know it took as a while to get notification of everything that happened.

Mrs. Freeman, I would like to see if there is any way that we could be considered in legally adopting all three of Kevin's and Gabrielle's children. We are the children's next of kin. I understand that Jobella is getting ready to start college, and that Joshua and Joanna are in foster care homes now. I don't foresee Jobella being able to handle the twins while she is trying to go to school, and we would be most interested in caring for all of them.

We are currently here in Java doing mission work, but if we were able to get the kids we would ask the mission board to allow us to spend some time there in your area, and possibly be reassigned to a local church, and physician practice.

*We could get the funds needed on short notice if
we need to fly home to meet with you.*

*Please contact us as soon as possible to work out
any details if we are able to do this.*

*God Bless you for helping Jobella and the twins
with all their problems.*

*Yours in Christ,
Kyle and Sadie Jordan*

"Oh my, who could have seen this coming?" She said to her partner when she showed him the letter. "I don't want Jobella to see this in case things don't work out. Just imagine, this is Jobella's biological parents, and it would give the twins a permanent home with real family members, that would actually care for them.

"We can't say anything to Jobella, I agree, until we find out everything we need to know about them. We need to make sure they are someone truly interested in getting the kids and not just interested in getting their inheritance money. I would like to help you do background checks on everything before we proceed."

Abby went through her files from nineteen years ago, and found what she needed. She found the court papers on Mr. Kyle Jordan, and Sadie, his wife. He was right in saying that they were Jobella's parents. She found the contract that they had signed giving up any claim on their daughter, and promising that they would not visit or have anything to do with her, or Mr. and Mrs. Kevin Jordan. A copy of Jobella's birth certificate was also in the file. Kyle and Sadie kept their end of the bargain evidently because she would have heard something from the Jordan's if they had try to come back to claim their daughter.

They would also have to go through, and do a criminal background check, and other paperwork to make sure they were fit to raise a family. They would also check with the mission board, and check any activities that they were involved in during their mission trips. After the preliminary background investigation, they would write, and let them know if they were qualified to make an application for adoption.

Social services would also have to be involved in the background checks, and home life of them to make sure they would be fit parents.

Because the twins were now wards of the state, the Jordans would have to establish residency in the state. They would have to qualify to be foster parents before they could care for the twins, and then they could consider adoption after that.

"So we are agreed." Said Abby, to her partner. "We will write to them, and let them know what the plan is so they can start getting their affairs in order in Java. We'll proceed with the preliminary investigation while we are waiting to hear further word from them. This is one letter that we will definitely need to keep from Jobella. We won't want to get her hopes up that she has a family that she didn't know anything about. Especially since it is her biological parents that want to adopt them. Also I know that Jobella was talking about getting the children back, after her and Steve gets married, and raise them as their own children, so this may be a problem for Jobella as well."

Her partner replied. "On the other hand this may prove to be a blessing for her. Her and Steve wouldn't be saddled with two young children when they are both in school, and starting their own household. They will have enough to keep up with school, and work, and it could be hard on their new marriage with all the stressors that having kids would bring. I'm sure they both will try to work while they are in school as well. At least I hope Jobella will continue to work here part time. She's been a good worker. I'd like to keep her until she gets a degree, and then work her into the firm when she graduates and passes her bar exam."

Abby replied, "I want that as well. I'm going to write Kyle and Sadie and let them know that we'll consider their request after the background checks have been processed. I think that this would be a wonderful solution for everyone. If it all works out Jobella and the twins will have a new family with Godly parents who will love them, and treat them as the family they already are.

"I'm glad that Jobella is off for a few days apartment, and furniture hunting, and getting ready to settle in on her own. It gives us time to look into a few things without her asking questions, and wondering why we are being so secretive."

Abby looked through all of her folders she had on the Jordan's. She crossed referenced them with all of the files she had on Kevin and Gabrielle Jordan. She even looked into their ancestry on the web. She put all of Jobella's, and the twin's records with them. Between everything that had happened over the years with all things regarding this family she could have filed the Jordan family in their own file cabinet.

She wrote letters to the mission board that Kyle and Sadie belonged to. They wanted to get any updated information from them on their recent history, and what they were doing now, and how long they were committed at their current mission site, and if they would be able to get out of that commitment if they wanted to settle back here in their home state of North Carolina. She explained what happened to his brother's family and their desire to take care of the children. She didn't give them any more information than that. Of course they already knew about the fire because they are the ones who told the Jordans what happened. The mission board was able to supply the address from their sending church as well so she was able to get with the pastor to get any information he could supply.

They went into the police records on the Internet and put in their names, and current address. They didn't find anything against them, but they didn't think that they would.

In the next few days they learned all about the history of Kyle and Sadie Jordan. They were indeed the brother and sister-in-law of Kevin and Gabrielle Jordan, but of course she already knew that.

There was nothing against them in any of their information. They were, as close to being perfect of anyone she knew. They didn't have any more children after she gave birth to Jobella. It seems she had complications in that delivery, and had to have a hysterectomy. They made their missionary work, their life. They would have loved to keep their little baby girl, but they didn't want anyone to know she was theirs.

In the investigation they were even able to find out where they went to school. Kevin and Sadie met in college. Kevin graduated near the top of his class in med school, and was now a doctor working at a medical center in Java. Sadie went to the same college, and was also in pre-med but she dropped out the year she was hiding her pregnancy, and when she went back, she decided to take up nursing instead, and is now a registered nurse working in the same medical center as her husband. They were working on building a field hospital about fifty miles out of Jakarta. They were close to finishing that, and were eager to complete it before coming back to the states. When he came back to North Carolina he would have no problem either setting up a practice as a physician, or working for a church. He was qualified in either job. His wife too, as an RN, could also find work if she wanted to. Nurses were always in short supply, and it would be easy for her to find a job.

The mission board wrote back, and told them that they had no issue with them returning to the states once the hospital was up and running. They would prefer that they finish what they started, however. The Jordan's had no problem with that stipulation.

In the next two weeks they gathered the information back from all their sources. Everyone had stated that the Jordan's were above reproach. Everyone thought that they would be great parents for the children. Now they just had to wait on the Jordan's to get things done in Java and they would have to keep all this information away from Jobella.

Chapter 17

Steven was bored staying around the house all day while he was waiting to get reinstated in the seminary. He had completed his first year when he was attacked, and almost killed, and spent almost the whole second year recovering when he should have been in school. It was late April now, and he went to the campus office, and filled in the paperwork to sign up for his sophomore year courses. They told him that he could get a few credits over the summer to make up for the ones he missed if he wanted to.

The seminary was close enough for him to commute to classes. He was thrilled that he could go ahead, and get back into the routine, and get the attack behind him. He had no residual brain damage, and his walking was getting stronger everyday. The doctor's were amazed at his recovery. They said that it had to be God because there was no other explanation for his complete recovery. He should have been in a permanent vegetative state after what he had been through.

I finally received the letter from Duke letting me know that I was accepted for the fall semester, and I did get at least a partial scholarship because of my activities I had done in high school. I also got information stating that I needed to complete, and pass the LSAT prior to taking any law courses on campus. All my first year classes were prerequisites anyway, so I had plenty of time to take it, but I wanted to do it right away in case I had to take it again.

My friends at the law firm gave me a party when they found out I was accepted. They said they would do it again when I passed my LSAT, and was accepted into the law school at Duke. They were always up for a party! At least there would be no drinking at their parties. They knew that I was a Christian, and didn't believe in drinking, and some of them that worked there felt the same way, including Abby, so they abstained from alcohol to honor us. They said that they would do what they could to help me pass the law school entrance exam.

Things were really pulling together now. Steve was living with his parents, and would continue to do so until we were married, and while he was still in school. I, with the help of Steven, and his family, helped me move into my apartment. I didn't have a lot of furniture yet, but it was comfortable enough just for me. Luckily the apartment was close to Steve's school as well so he would be able to commute from our apartment once we were married.

I was enjoying my independence for the first time in my life. I had a job that I loved. I was getting ready to go to college. I had the love of my fiancé and his family, and I now had my own apartment. Most of all I had the love of God. I should have been very happy but there was something missing. With everything I had, I continued to miss my family. My mom was always my best friend and I shared everything with her. My dad was a constant source of inspiration to me. My goal was to live up to my parent's standards. I missed them both terribly, and I cried every time I thought about them, and how I would never see them again this side of heaven. I longed to go to my parents, and let them know that everything was working out in my life. I wondered if there was a window in heaven, and that they could see everything that was happening with me.

Most of all I missed my brother and sister. I wanted to feel their small hands in mine. I wanted to feel their arms around my legs when they clung to me. I wanted to help them learn to cope in this world. I know that between school, and work I would have little time to spend with them, but at least I'd be able to see them part of each and every day and to tuck them into bed at night, and read them stories, and pray with them, and tell them about God's love. I wondered if they got that kind of love, and support in the family they staying with.

As I was pondering all of this, the phone rang. Steve called to let me know that his family was having a cookout at the lake tomorrow, and wanted me to come. It would be nice to see them again. It had been two weeks since I moved into my apartment, and I was missing them.

I woke up excited about the day ahead. The sun was bright and the temperature mild. It was a beautiful day for a picnic. It was Saturday, and I called the nursing home to let them know I wouldn't be there that day. It was the middle of May and I didn't think about it at the time but it had been almost one year to the day that my parent's home was burned to the ground and they were killed. I couldn't think about that now. I was going to see Steve, and have a very nice time, and I would try to put my gloomy past behind me.

I drove to the James's home, and listened to Christian music on my CD player in my car. I loved this type of music, and it always put me in a worshipful frame of mine. God was so glorious. He made this gorgeous day. When I looked around at the spring flowers and the trees coming to leaf, I thought how could anyone deny that God existed. All of the living things in the world cried out His name. In Him all things were possible, and beautiful.

As I pulled into their driveway, they were already packing their van with picnic baskets and blankets. Steve came walking up to meet me. I was continually amazed at his ability to walk on his own after his ordeal. He looked so handsome. I was the luckiest girl alive to be courted by him. He gave me a big hug to greet me, and we walked hand in hand to his parent's car.

On the ride to the lake everyone was unusually quiet, totally uncharacteristic for their talkative family. I wondered if they were thinking about what happened a year ago as well. Steve and I were in the back seat. He had his arm around me and I rested my head against his chest. I would've been content to stay like that forever, but I still wondered what was going on with them, and that made me a little uncomfortable.

The signs for the picnic ground at the lake lay just ahead. The lake had public areas for picnics, and other areas where you could spread a blanket. Those areas were more private, and that is what we chose.

When we got to the lake, Steve and I decided to go for a walk to be alone. It was still a little cool to go for a swim, but we just wanted to be by ourselves for a bit. Steve's father was grilling some hamburgers and hot dogs, and his mother was preparing the picnic spread while we were gone. When we were finally alone he turned to me and, held me in his arms. I savored the feel of his strong arms around me, and the tender touch of his lips as we kissed. I loved the way he made me feel cherished.

"Jobella, I know we've talked about it over the last couple of years, but nothing has ever been made official. You know I love you more than anything in this world and I would never want anything to come between the love that we share. Mom and Dad told me about what happened after I was knocked out. I know what your uncle did to you, but none of that matters to me. I love you, and I always have. I admire you, and what you have done to put all of this behind you. You're the most amazing person I've ever met. So I'm officially, and forever your biggest fan." and then he got down on one knee, and continued. "So Jobella, officially, will you marry me?"

Then my tears came. "Of course I'll marry you. I have never doubted my love for you, and the way you loved me. Nothing will ever separate the love we have for each other."

With that he pulled out the proverbial black velvet box and as I teared up, I saw what was the most beautiful diamond ring I had ever seen. He put the ring on my left ring finger, and then we hugged, and kissed. It was the most romantic kiss we ever shared. My heart was full, and our love complete.

"Jobella, I know we said we'd wait a couple of years down the road after we were in college a while, but we've been through so much this year. I want us to get married sooner than that. What do you think about getting married this August, a couple of weeks before the fall semester starts?"

"I think that would be wonderful, but what about your parents? Are they okay with that?"

"I spoke with them, and told them what I was going to do today. Why do you think we were so quiet coming here? They said that they thought, after everything we went through this year that we needed something in our lives we all could look forward to. They know how we feel about each other, and they love you almost as much as I do." He smiled.

"Then I say, okay! Let's do it!" I jumped in his arms and he whirled me around. "You've made me so very happy."

"And you, me. After we get settled we'll see about your getting Josh and Joanie back. Let's see what we can do once we get our classes, and work schedules figured out. Okay?"

"That would be wonderful. Thanks, Steve for being so understanding. Now, let's go see your parents. I'm starved!"

When we got back to the picnic site we were walking, holding hands, and smiling. Mr. and Mrs. James ran up to us, and gave us both big hugs. They knew what Steve's plan was, and our smiles could only mean one thing. I accepted.

As we ate our lunch we talked about setting our wedding date in August, and everyone was okay with that. Since it was only three months away we would need to start making plans soon. "Maybe after we eat. Will that be soon enough?" I laughed.

"We can do that." Mrs. James smiled. "We're going to be family now. You can call me Hannah, and my husband, Nate. We don't have to be so formal. You can even call us mom and dad if you want to."

I was thrilled. After I marry Steve, I'll have a whole new family, and they were way more than I could ask for.

I was thinking about my wedding, and who I would have stand with me. I thought how great it would be if the twins could be there. They would be a great flower girl, and ring bearer, but I know that the social worker that was handling the case wouldn't let me see them until they were out of foster care. So we had to rule them out.

As for my bride's maids, I would ask my three friends from high school. As I thought of them, the Lord laid it on my heart again, that I promised Him that I would talk with them about needing to have faith in Christ rather than good works. I would ask Abby Freeman to be my matron of honor because of everything she had done for me. She really was my best friend in the entire world right now. She was in her forties but she had been my lawyer, and my mentor for over a year now. She was a strong Christian, and someone I really looked up to.

Steve, of course, would choose his own attendants, and he did have a niece and nephew that would be perfect to be our ring bearer and flower girl. I wasn't aware that he even had an older brother until now. He was several years older than Steve, and had moved out before we met. He lived on the other side of the country, and wasn't able to come home when Steve was in the hospital. I looked forward to meeting them, and their children. Steve said that his brother would be his best man, and he had some friends from his Bible college that would be his ushers.

Now that our wedding party had been chosen we would decide on a date for the wedding after talking with Pastor Stewart to make sure he could do it on our chosen date. Pastor Stewart had been our pastor for the past ten years, and had been our spiritual leader through all of our ordeals.

We accomplished much during that afternoon picnic. We got engaged officially and started planning our wedding. The rest would be the fun part of planning everything else. I was so excited! Now if everything we planned already, would work out.

Chapter 18

Kyle and Sadie were putting some finishing touches on the hospital clinic that they were helping to build along with the natives and other missionaries outside of Jakarta. It soon would become a reality, and then if God willed it, they would head back to North Carolina, and be reunited with their biological daughter, and her brother, and sister.

Kyle's secretary called him to tell him he had a very important personal letter waiting for him back at his office. He hurried to his office in the clinic next door because he hoped that this was what he was waiting for. Sadie came running following him up the steps to his office.

When he read the letter, a smile came over his face. He hugged Sadie, and gave her the letter to read. It was from the attorney's office. Mrs. Freeman wrote it personally to them.

Dear Dr. and Mrs. Jordan,

After going over all of your files, and the files of Mr. and Mrs. Kevin Jordan, and their children, and also after doing background checks on everyone, and checking with the mission board, we decided to grant your petition to adopt the three children of Kevin, and Gabrielle Jordan.

There is one problem that will have to be resolved however, but I'm sure under the circumstances it will be in your favor. Jobella Jordan has asked the court to grant her custody of the twins. She's getting married in August, and she plans to petition the court shorty after that for her requests.

We are planning for a December court date for her because she will be in school at the time, and wants us to examine this during her winter break. Prior to this hearing, we will contact the social worker for the children, and set you up with her to see if you can take over the foster care of the children until that time.

Hopefully you can wrap up your work in Java expeditiously so we can begin the process. Let us know where you are in the progress of your completing your work, and when you plan to get back to North Carolina.

Sincerely yours,
Abby Freeman

P.S. Ms. Jordan and her fiancé know nothing about our arrangements. I would like to keep it from them until the hearing. I think that they will be excited about our plans. I hope so, anyways.

"I didn't think about how this would affect Jobella. I hope she'll be all right with this adoption. She and her husband-to-be will be greatly affected by this no matter which way it goes. I would think that being newlyweds, and students, the addition of two young children would be hard on them right now. I can't imagine them having a problem with this." Sadie said.

"It will be hard to keep this from her. I want to see her, and get to know our daughter, and the twins! Now we have extra incentive to get this hospital finished, and quickly."

They felt like singing and glorifying God. The part of them that was missing for so long would be theirs again.

They hurried back to the hospital where they were finishing the cabinets, and touching up the paint at the nurses' stations. Boxes were lined up in the hallways. They contained the furniture for the rooms, and offices, and the cabinets, and locks for the medication areas. There was so much to do but they would need to have it done before they could leave. Even if it meant working day and night, seven days a week!

They wrote to the mission board to let them know that they were going to be finished with the facility in two weeks, and then they would be heading back home. The board said it would be okay as long as they were through with the hospital.

Then they contacted their home church to let them know about their plans, and the need for a little extra money for their plane tickets. Their church had a special love offering for two weeks prior to getting the letter from the Jordans in anticipation of their return. They sent the money special delivery, and they got it within a few days.

They would be all set to arrive sometime in the middle of July. It would be hard for them to stay away from Jobella, especially for her wedding in August, but they would try to refrain, honoring their contract with her lawyer.

Many of the locals in their Java congregation learned about their plans to leave after the hospital was built. Some of them were doctors and nurses as well. Before the Jordans came to Java to their small village the locals had to sometimes go fifty miles or more over rough terrain to get to a clinic. Through Dr. and Mrs. Jordan, they were able to complete their medical training under them, and knew enough to give basic medical care to the people in the village. They felt the hospital, and clinic was a gift from God, and many became Christians through Dr. Jordan's preaching, and example. When they heard that they were leaving, many of them banded together, and helped in the construction, and finishing of the hospital. They offered free labor in thankfulness for what God was able to accomplish through Dr. Jordan.

The day before they left, the newly minted staff of the hospital, and clinic came together, and gave them a going away and grand opening party combined. It was a bittersweet moment for them. The natives were happy to have the new clinic, and hospital ready to open, but were sad to see this couple who gave the last fifteen years of their lives to them, leave.

After several days of packing, and shipping their household goods back to North Carolina, it was time for them to leave as well. They found a storage unit in their hometown on the Internet, and arranged to have everything shipped there. They would retrieve their meager household items when they found a permanent home. They planned on looking for a rental home as soon as they got there so they would be able begin the procedure to foster the twins right away.

They notified Mrs. Freeman, and the social service agency of their planned arrival time. Mrs. Freeman was going to meet them at the airport, and help them get settled in their hotel. After they rested a day or two they would get together with Abby, and the social worker, and plan for the transition, and get all the paper work filled out. They thought that it would be better to do it there in the hotel room rather than the law office because they didn't want Jobella to know anything about it.

All these things passed through their minds as Kyle and Sadie boarded the plane in Jakarta for the long trip home. It would take them twenty-four hours from Jakarta to Raleigh including layovers. The trip was very tiring with the jet lag, and sitting for so long. They would lose a whole day through the time changes as well.

"Are you excited to be going back home?" asked Kyle.

"I am but I can't wait to see the kids more." Sadie responded.

"Me too." Smiled Kyle. "I hope they like us and want to make a home with us."

"We'll, we're two very likable people, how can they not?" she laughed.

As they circled the Raleigh airport they became excited and nervous all at the same time. They hoped that Mrs. Freeman would be waiting for them. It had been almost twenty years since they had seen her. They hoped that they would recognize her, and she them. They have changed so much since that time. They were college students at the time, them going to Chapel Hill, and Abby, was just one year out of law school from Duke. That seemed like a whole lifetime ago.

As they got off the plane and walked through the airport they saw a woman with a sign with their name and knew they found her.

"Wow you guys look great." Abby said. "You haven't changed hardly at all!"

"You either!" replied Sadie. With that they threw their arms around each other in a friendly welcome.

"It's so good to see you and, good to be home!" added Kyle. "We'll be ready to go as soon as we get our luggage. We sent all our household possessions to the storage unit to be stored, so we don't have much with us."

As they drove around town looking for their hotel they were amazed how much everything had changed in the fifteen years they were away. The area had really built up, especially with many new apartments, and new businesses.

"How are the prices around here for apartments?" Kyle asked, as they passed several apartment complexes. "We would probably be more interested in renting a house for at least a little while, while settling in to work. We thought that we would look around while we are staying at the hotel. We are anxious to get settled, and to set up in a practice somewhere close by. We want the children to live in a great neighborhood, though. That's very important to us."

"The twins are living with a wonderful older couple in Clairmonte. That's where your brother, and his wife lived. I can show you their property if you like. It has gone on the market because it had been foreclosed on due to no one paying on it for the last twelve months. It would be great if you could buy that, and rebuild there. It is a lovely neighborhood, and it covers almost two acres of land. I know Jobella was thinking of getting it eventually, and building a home similar to their parents. But it will be several years before she'd be able to get it, and it won't stay on the market that long."

"Yes, I'd like to see it! Maybe we can go by there in the next day or two. It would be good to keep it in the family. If there were any records of the blueprints, and pictures for us to look at, that would be great too. My brother, and his wife had great taste from what I can remember. Maybe we can make a house that is similar to what they had."

"The kids would love that! I can set you up with the architect that worked on it if you'd like."

"That would be great. Could you take us to the property tomorrow?"

"Sure. After the meeting with the social worker we'll take a little road trip to Clairmonte."

After Abby left them, they went for a bite to eat in the hotel restaurant. The first thing they would need to do would be to rent a car for a week or two until his funds came through. He did have an inheritance from when his parent's died that was put into a special savings account for them. It was around a hundred thousand dollars.

It would be enough for them to get set up, but they would have to get to work soon to maintain a suitable life style. Sadie started looking for a job that she could begin soon as well. It should be easy for her. Nurses didn't have a problem getting jobs. There were usually tons of them in the want ads. She could almost work wherever she wanted. They would get the daily newspaper that was left at their door this morning to look over. The paper felt strange in their hands, and they 'devoured it' from cover to cover. They wanted to catch up on what was happening in the area as well as look in the classified section for a car, a home, and jobs.

The next morning around ten, Abby showed up at their door. They visited for a while as they waited for the social worker.

They were sitting at the table in the room when they heard the knock on the door. Sadie let the social worker in, and Abby arose from her chair. She couldn't quite believe what she was seeing.

"Ruth, Jobella's aunt Ruth? What are you doing here? Where is the social worker? I was looking for a Ruth Applewhite. She's suppose to meet us here."

Ruth laughed. "I'm her. After Bud went to prison for those unspeakable crimes against the kids, I filed for a divorce. Applewhite is my maiden name. I reverted back to that following the divorce. I didn't want anything else to do with him including his name!"

"You look amazing! You look nothing like the woman I saw in the trial, and I forgot about Applewhite being part of your name. What have you done over the last year to yourself to look so good?"

She came over to the table to join everyone. She smiled "Well, the first thing I did was to rededicate my life to Christ. Then I cleaned up my act both literally and spiritually. I sold that shack of a house in "shanty town" and moved into an apartment close to the college I was going to. I had almost completed my education in social work when I took up with that bum, Bud. I just had three more semesters to go, so I hurried through, and finished them up quickly. My probation allowed me to go back to school, and believe me, I got a real education working at the women's shelter as part of my community service sentence. The school actually let me use that as my clinical experience as well so I was able to complete the rest of my classes in two semesters. So, to make a long story short, I am a fully certified social worker now, and I've been assigned the case of the twins. My boss didn't realize they were my niece, and nephew at the time, and I know I should have said something about that but I wanted to see the twins, and see how they were making out. Because of the changes I made in my appearance, etc. the twins didn't recognize me either."

"Because God has forgiven you, and you have been shown to be a vessel that God could use through your work, we have no problem with you representing us with getting the children under our care." Kyle smiled at Ruth and shook her hand.

"I see that the twins, and Jobella have joined us together as family. You are their aunt on their mother's side, and we are their aunt and uncle on their father's side." Added Sadie. "I know you will have their best interest in heart."

"Ruth, I'm going to tell you something that you might not be aware of, and you are not to let it go out of this room, now or at any time in the next few months. Can we trust you with some very delicate information?" Abby asked.

"Yes. I'm bound by confidentiality rules the same as doctors and lawyers. I can keep a secret no matter what it is."

"As you can probably tell, Dr. Jordan is the identical twin of Kevin Jordan."

"Yes, I'm becoming aware of that. He looks just like him." She smiled at Kyle.

"What you may not be aware of, is that Jobella was adopted by Kevin and Gabrielle when she was an infant. They went away for a few weeks nineteen years ago, if you remember, and came back with a new born infant."

"I seem to remember something like that. I was still a teenager at home. I thought it was strange because she didn't look like she was pregnant, and boom all of a sudden she was a mom."

"Well, what happened was that Sadie was pregnant with Kyle's baby, but they weren't married. They wanted to be missionaries, but wouldn't be accepted by the mission board if they knew she was pregnant so she went away and had the baby in secret and Kevin and Gabrielle adopted her. Jobella is Kyle's and Sadie's biological daughter."

"Wow, I didn't know that, I thought that she was all theirs but come to mention it, I thought it was strange that Jobella had red hair when no one else it the family did. Now that I see Sadie, I see why!" she laughed. "Don't worry, I'll be totally discreet about everything you're telling me today. Won't Jobella be surprised when she tries to file for her own adoption of the kids, and finds she has a family she didn't know had!"

"That's why I don't want her to know about anything about this yet. I'm sure she'll be really excited when she finds out, but she just doesn't need to have too much on her mind as she prepares for her wedding, and starting school. That's all the stressors she needs right now."

Ruth added. "Well, let's get all this paperwork signed and then we can proceed to the next steps. As soon as you have a permanent or semi-permanent place to live we can start letting the twins ease into the transition from their foster parents to your home. You will initially take them on as foster children until the adoption is complete. By the time we have the final hearing in December, they should already be in your care. In the meantime I will try to set up a time when you can meet the children and their foster parents in their home. We'll give you a week or two to get settled and then we'll get back with you to set up that visit."

Ruth left, and Abby remained behind. They were going to drive to the vacant lot to look around, and see if it would be an option for them and if they wanted to put an offer on it.

They rode around for about a half an hour. On the way they were on the lookout for someplace they could rent, until they either built a house, or bought one. They saw a couple of ads in the paper earlier, and they asked Abby if she minded stopping by those.

Abby called the realtor while she was driving to the lot to see if he could meet them there. He said that he would be glad to show them around, and he would also bring some listings for some homes in the area that he was renting out.

They entered the neighborhood where his brother and his wife lived. They were amazed at all the beautiful homes. Quite a change from their little wooden and sod shack in Java. The yard was beautiful. Shade trees and fruit trees were in abundance. There were a few remains of what must have been beautiful gardens. The house of course was no longer there. You would've not even thought that there ever was a house on the property. They had done a great job of clearing out the rubble from the fire. The bank, along with the realtor, had their landscapers keep the law cut, and hedges trimmed so it would look presentable to sell.

They got out of the car, and looked around the grounds. After they were there about five minutes, the realtor came to meet them. He introduced himself as Ted.

"You must be the Jordan's." He said. "You look just like your brother!"

"Yeah, I get that a lot." He laughed. "I guess it's because we were identical twins."

"I never knew Kevin had a brother. You didn't visit much did you?"

"We've been half way around the world in missions." Answered Sadie. "It was too expensive to be jetting back and forth all the time. We've been in Java for fifteen years, right out of college."

"What kind of missions did you do?" Ted liked to get a background on people to make sure he wasn't spending his time on people who couldn't afford to buy real estate.

"I'm a doctor and my wife, Sadie, is an RN. We plan on settling in this area, and I would love to buy back this lot that belonged to my brother. I plan to rebuild something like he had here."

"That would be great. The lot is pretty expensive though. The bank is selling it for a hundred grand. We've had some interest in it, but no one has given us a firm offer so if your interested we can get some paperwork moving on it."

Kyle and Sadie spoke quietly to one another, and agreed that they'd like to get the property. "Yes, we would like to do that. Can we get with you tomorrow? We need to go the bank, and make sure we can get at our inheritance money. We will have to live on that until our jobs start paying, but I believe that we can handle it."

"Here's my business card. Let me know as soon as possible." Replied Ted.

"Well that's a start. I think that what we need to do is go to the bank, the first thing, and try to get that money. Then we can make whatever other plans we need to next." Said Kyle.

Ted added. "I almost forgot, would you like to look at some houses for rent? I actually have a couple close to here. Your children, if you have them, will be in the same school district as this property. The schools in this district are great, the best in the city!"

"Sounds good. Would you mind if we look at those, Abby?" Added Sadie.

"I've actually scheduled the whole day with you, today. We can even go by your bank if you want to, and then maybe go by a car rental place so you'll have a way to get around until you can get a car."

"You are a God send Abby. Thank you."

"Well, when you have God, He makes everything great in His own time. I believe you possess that kind of faith in God, and I believe he is going to work out everything for you."

They stopped by the two properties that Ted told them about. One of them was just a block away. It was a nice medium sized

Victorian. The realtor went to get the owner. She lived next door, and was happy to show them around. It was kept up very well, and you could tell that she had a lot of pride in it. The owner's name was Mrs. Bradshaw.

"How much is the rent on this?" asked Sadie.

"About fifteen hundred a month, plus utilities." He said. "The phone and electricity are already hooked up so you won't have to worry about the connection fees. It's ready to move into anytime."

"Do you think you can hold it a few days until we get our money from the bank? It shouldn't take over a week."

"Sure. I can do that." She said. "I don't have any other offers on it yet. Say, you look very familiar to me. Do you have any relatives that live around here?"

"My brother and his wife lived one block over. Mr. and Mrs. Jordan, the couple whose house burned down about a year ago, killing them. We are actually going to try to buy the property, and build another house on it. That's why we're looking to rent in this neighborhood until we can get a house built."

"Oh yes, I remember them. You look a lot like him. This house of mine would be perfect for you!"

"That's what we are thinking. Thank you for your help, Mrs. Bradshaw. We'll get back with you, hopefully before the week's over."

"Looking forward to it! You can call me Fannie. Mrs. Bradshaw is way too formal for the likes of me. We're going to be neighbors after all."

"We'll be seeing you soon!"

After they made their future living arrangements, Abby asked what bank they used. Kyle told her and she drove them straight there for their next stop.

They entered the bank, and spoke with the receptionist at the entrance. "We would like to speak with your manager about withdrawing some of our inheritance money. We need some cash to get a few necessities to begin a life here. We'd also like to set up a checking and savings account."

"No problem, sir. Someone will be with you shortly." Smiled the receptionist.

The bank manager was very supportive when they told him about their situation. They told him that they would need at least enough money for the down payment on a car, the land, at least six months rent, and cost of living expenses. That should be more than enough until to get them set up their jobs.

He looked up their account that their inheritance was put into, and found that it had accumulated quite a bit of interest over the last fifteen years while they were away. Instead of a hundred thousand they had another ten thousand in the account. They decided that sixty thousand should be enough for the time being to get them going.

They went ahead, and set up their checking and savings accounts. Kyle had brought a few hundred dollars with him to set up their accounts. Everything went through without a hitch, and the bank manager told them that they should be able to access their money within the next twenty-four hours.

Things were moving along so smoothly they were starting to worry that everything was too good to be true, but sometimes the Lord does allow things to work out especially if they are in his will.

After leaving the bank they went to the DMV to get their driver's licenses for North Carolina. Since it had been so long, they had to be retested, but they both passed with flying colors. It had been fifteen years since they last filed, and they were worried that something had changed or they forgot some of traffic rules in the United States, but they guessed things hadn't changed all that much while they were gone. After all they've done that day they still wanted to go to a rent-a-car company to get a car so Abby wouldn't be saddled with them, as they looked for jobs the rest of the week.

It was around five in the afternoon when they finally finished, and arrived back at the hotel. Things were happening so fast that when they finally touched down from their whirlwind activities of the day they became aware of just how exhausted they were. Abby left them for the day, but she said she would touch base with them the next morning to see how everything was going.

After taking a short nap, and showering, they felt refreshed and happy. The day had been very productive, and they had accomplished many things. They ended the day with a season of praise to God for what He had given them that day.

The next day they were still glowing in all of the happenings of yesterday, but they still had a lot to do before moving on to the next steps of getting set up here in town. They picked up the morning paper outside the hotel room door and scanned the want ads for jobs. They were excited to learn that there happened to be a clinic nearby just outside of Clairmonte looking for a physician. They would start there.

Chapter 19

After we left the picnic we decided we'd drive by the land that my house use to sit on. I wanted to eventually rebuild a house on it for us. I made a promise to Josh and Joanie that once Steve and I got married, maybe we could build a house just like the one we had, and they could have their own rooms, and decorate them just the way they wanted.

As we passed by we saw the 'for sale' sign in the yard, and on closer examination we saw the words 'under contract'. "What's this?" I cried. "I didn't even know it was up for sale! I thought it belonged to us, and was part of our inheritance!"

"I guess not. I thought it was also. I guess we'd better contact Ms. Freeman, and find out what's going on." Suggested Steve.

I dialed Abby's number while Steve was driving. She picked up after a few rings.

"Mrs. Freeman speaking."

"Abby, this is Jobella. Steven and I just drove by my parent's property, and saw that it was for sale and under contract. What's going on, I thought it was our property now?"

"Jobella, I guess you didn't know. Your parent's were making payments on their house and land. They had a mortgage with the bank. The payments hadn't been made in over a year since their death, and the property was foreclosed on. It became the banks to sell. Even with your inheritance money you probably wouldn't be able to afford it. I'm sorry I didn't tell you about it sooner. I know the couple that is buying it though. They are very nice, and you are going to love them."

"I couldn't love anyone who is living on the land that was supposed to mine."

"It would have been a long time before you were able to afford it, Jobella. You are young and there are a lot of things that you don't know about yet in earning a living, and being able to pay your way. The inheritance money won't last all that long after you get through paying for school, and have to use it to pay for room and board, and cost of living essentials while you are in school. The only way you can get your inheritance at this point is for school, and for your wedding, and enough money to get by on until you are twenty-one, and then you can get the rest of your part of the money. It would be too late at that time because someone would get the land for sure before that time was up. The bank wouldn't wait until then to sell it."

"I suppose you're right, but I'm extremely upset about this. I was counting on getting it, and building a house like my parent's for the twins."

"You would've been way over your head with that. They had a million dollar property including the kind of house that they had built on it! You won't even be through with school for six years. It will take a few years after that to get what your parents had. The twins would be grown, and out on their own, before you could afford that kind of house!"

"I'm disappointed but I guess I didn't really think about all of that. Thanks for bringing me back to reality, Abby." I replied. "Abby, while I have you on the phone. Steve and I have set our wedding date. We are officially engaged now. I would like for you to be my matron of honor, if you want to, that is!"

"I would be honored! When is the date? I want to make sure I'm in town, and don't have any plans that I can't get out of."

"It's going to be August twenty-six, on a Saturday. Steve and I both start classes the day after Labor Day, and we want a short honeymoon before school starts."

"I thought you were going to wait a couple of years before getting married, after you've been in school a while."

"We decided with everything we've been through that life is too precious. We both, and his parents were thrilled that we decided to go ahead with it."

"Well, congratulations. I can't think of a reason why you both shouldn't do this. I know you'll be very happy! Will you be in the office on Monday? We can look at my calendar then. That's a little over two months away. I shouldn't have anything planned that far in advance. If you want, I can help you pick out colors, dresses, and plan a party. Do you have your brides maids figured out yet?"

"I'm going to check with Eliza, Zoe, and Billie. Hopefully they won't be in school at that time or have other plans. I'm going to call them this week. Wow, there really is a lot to do. I hope I can get it all together. Maybe you, and I can spend our lunch breaks together and go shopping."

"That would be a lot of fun. It's a date."

I felt a lot better after I talked with Abby. It was disappointing about the land, but I could see what she was talking about. Maybe whoever bought the property would do it justice by building a nice big house and let us come, and visit with them sometime.

Steve took me back to my apartment, and we looked through the sample books I brought from the stationers. The first thing we had to do would be to choose our invitations. They would have to go out right away.

It seemed kind of strange when I went back to work on Monday. Everyone seemed quieter than usual. Maybe they were just busy. Abby must have told them about my engagement because everyone was smiling, and congratulating me. News travels fast in lawyer circles, I smiled thinking of all my friends I had here in the office.

Abby and I decided we'd start our search for wedding dresses during the lunch hour today, and look at some brides maids dresses to get an idea of what colors, and styles we would want. We went out to eat, and then spent a little time at David's Bridals. We saw the prettiest lilac colored dresses for her and the bridesmaids. My search would take a little longer for my dress. I decided the best thing to do would be to take a catalogue home along with a couple of brides' magazines. It was so exciting! I only had a little more than a month and a half. I'm glad it wasn't much longer, but the time would fly by, and the wedding would be here before I knew it.

That evening after I got home, I made phone calls to my three friends. I asked them if they wanted to be in my wedding party, and if so, could they come to my house for tea this coming Saturday.

They all said yes, and they were available on August twenty-sixth, and they were free this Saturday! Everything was going according to plan, even with this. Other than losing out on my family's property everything else in my life was going great, almost too great. I kept waiting for the other shoe to drop. Nothing in life is great all the time. I knew in this season of my life that something was bound to happen but maybe God was giving me an extra measure of happiness in my life after all of the horrendous things that happened this past year.

That evening after work I stopped by the stationers, and ordered the invitations Steve and I chose. He told me they should be ready to be picked up late Friday afternoon. What timing! Maybe I could get my friends to help me out with those while they were there on Saturday. After all, I reasoned, what are bridesmaids for?

I looked over the catalogues and magazines back at my apartment. I decided I would love to have a simple strapless a-line dress with lace across the top and a lacey train. I chose a pair of over the elbow gloves that would co-ordinate with it because the dress had no sleeves. It would look more elegant than bare hands and arms. My veil would be attached to a tiara. The whole ensemble would be understated, but gorgeous!

The next day at work I showed Abby what I decided on. She thought everything was beautiful, and she said that I had exquisite taste.

I had to get with her about helping me get some of my money out of my inheritance account. After all, I was able to use part of it for my wedding, and school. I had to watch my expenditures. I couldn't get carried away with too much, because by being in school I would have to live on that to supplement my income for the next six to eight years. Steven and I would both need at least a master's degree for our job field and if I get the twins it would take up even more money to live. Abby and I agreed if I got a hundred thousand, it should take me through next summer. We agreed that amount should cover what I needed each year. If Steven and I watched our spending it should more than cover us per year, and by the time we finished school we would still have over five hundred thousand left in the account. We both still planned on working part time as well, so we should have enough to be comfortable.

After we filled out all the paperwork, Abby said everything looked okay, and we should get the money by the end of the week. I would have to re-file each fall to get the next installment of the hundred thousand per year.

I would go to the bridal shop after work that afternoon, and try on the dress I had chosen so any alterations could be made in time for the wedding. They didn't have that particular dress in stock, and she said they would have to get it from another store. Ugh, my first road block to the perfect wedding. I hoped they could get it. I had my heart set on that one. She showed me a few other dresses similar to it but I couldn't get excited about them so she promised she would call me when she located one.

Things were a little quiet the rest of the week. The time seemed to drag on. I wanted to go shopping for school, and my wedding but until my money came through I was kind of stuck. I wouldn't even get my paycheck from the firm until Friday. I spent my evenings looking up information about the law school at Duke, and studying for my LSAT, and when I got really bored I went on line and did some virtual "shopping" at my favorite stores, and dreaming about what I could get when I had some money.

When I did my Bible study that night I was reading in Matthew. I've been studying the Sermon on the Mount. It was one of my very favorite passages in the Bible. Jesus was teaching the apostles, and a multitude of others. He had a lot to say to us in our day as well. In Matthew 6:31-34, Jesus said:

'Therefore take no thought, saying what shall we eat? Or what shall we drink? Or wherewithal shall we be clothed? (For after these things do the Gentiles seek) for your Heavenly Father knoweth that ye have need of all those things. But seek ye first the Kingdom of God, and His righteousness; and all these things will be added on to you. Take therefore no thought for the morrow; for the morrow shall take thought for the things of itself. Sufficient unto the day is the evil thereof.'

With those words touching my heart and soul, I closed the computer for the night, and got down on my knees, and prayed that the Lord would work everything out according to His will. I prayed He would forgive me for my worrying, and I decided I would let God have his way in even things so mundane as what kind of clothes I would wear. I also stopped to thank Him for the way things have worked out in the last few weeks. I've been so caught up with everything that happened, I didn't remember if I even thanked him, and gave him the praise for everything he's done for me.

God gave me another little nudge on my heart. He reminded me as I prayed for my friends that I hadn't honored his request to speak with them about what he told me on the night he had redeemed me from my sinful past. About how he was almighty, and how we could never be good enough to enter his kingdom through good works, as my friends had suggested. He reminded me to tell them only through Christ's love, and sacrifice on the cross, could we be saved by believing in him. I prayed God would forgive me for not obeying him, and not putting him first in my life. He urged me more strongly to pray for my friends.

I couldn't wait until Saturday to get here. I longed to see my friends again. I spoke with each of them on the phone during the week to firm up our time, and what we had planned to accomplish during their visit with me. I gave them directions to my apartment. They decided they were going to come together, and save some gas money.

I was able to get my money on Friday, and it was directly deposited in my account along with my paycheck from the law firm. I went by the printers and picked up my wedding invitations. Tonight I would start working on them. I wasn't too close to a lot of people except for some of the church members, and I guess I would invite my aunt Ruth since she was my only relative. I would invite the people I worked with, and of course Steve's family, and friends. I still didn't have anyone to "give me away". That made me kind of sad because my mom and dad wouldn't be there. The twins couldn't come either. I was forbidden to see them until the hearing in December.

I decided I would ask one of the partners at my law firm to do the honors of giving me away. When I called him he told me he'd be thrilled to do that.

As I wrote out my list of invitees, I prayed for each of them. I thanked God for them, and asked his blessing on each of them.

Saturday started out bright and sunny, and my three friends would be over around noon. When they got here, we had a light lunch, and then discussed our plans for the wedding. I showed them the catalogue with the bridesmaid dresses, and told them I wanted my colors of my wedding lilac and pink. Their dresses were to be lilac but they could choose the style of dress they wanted to wear. We needed to get them ordered so we decided to meet at David's Bridal after we got off work on Monday. We also looked on line at the type of corsages, bouquets and flower arrangements we wanted on my wedding planners web site. Then we looked up local bakeries, and decided on the cake, and snacks we wanted. I would discuss those things with the wedding planner when Steve and I met with her.

It was so much fun planning all these things I almost forgot what God told me to do. The feeling came over me that I needed to do this and I couldn't wait another day.

After going through everything I gathered everyone together. I brought out a platter with tea, and petit fours and sandwiches.

"Girls" I began: "God has been very good to me over this last year."

"That is an understatement." Laughed Billie.

"We are very happy for you, and the way everything has worked out for you." Added Eliza.

"I've never seen anyone's fortune turn around like it has with you, Jobella. It make's me envious, but it couldn't have happened to a better person. I'm almost jealous!' smiled Zoe. "Of course I wouldn't have wanted to be in your shoes a year ago.

"God wanted me to speak to all of you. He wanted me to respond to the things you had spoken to me when you visited me in the hospital."

"Oh no, here it comes." Zoe said rolling her eyes.

"I knew there was a reason you wanted us to come today to plan your wedding. You could have made most of these decisions without us." Billie said crossing her arms over her chest.

"We didn't know we were coming to hear a sermon." Added Eliza. "You really haven't changed much have you?"

"Oh, I've changed a lot actually. The Lord spoke to me just before I got out of the hospital. It's actually one of the reasons I recovered so quickly last November. The Lord told me at that time the things that happened to me wasn't because of anything my family, or I had done wrong, as you all had suggested. He wasn't punishing my family or me. He said Satan was in the world, and because he was there, we would always have sadness and trials. Life couldn't always be perfect like it is in heaven because there is sin in this world. He said I was to tell you Christ died for our sins, and even though we aren't perfect, we can be saved by believing on him."

"I thought you always believed that." Zoe stated.

"I did, but I also thought I would have to earn his love by doing good works."

"That's why you were always into everything, and were good at everything you did!" added Billie. "You were the most perfect person I ever met. I was shocked when all those things happened to you."

"With God all we do are as filthy rags to him. We can never do enough to be perfect enough to get into heaven. As soon as we believe that, we are already sinning, because we call God a liar!"

"I never thought about that." Eliza hung her head.

"When God finished speaking with me on that cold November night, I prayed like I never prayed before. I asked God to forgive me, and then for Jesus to come into my heart as my Lord and Savior. I acknowledged I wasn't able to do anything to earn my salvation. Only after God spoke to me, and I took Jesus into my heart, and not just into my mind could I be healed."

"And she lived happily ever after." Smiled Zoe.

"God wanted me to talk with you all because he, and I want all three of you to be the Christians, he wants you to be. He wants you to trust fully in him. You never know what life's going to hand you, and you never know when he's going to come again, or if you die before he does come, you would be saved, and live forever with him in heaven."

"But we're already Christians." Said Eliza, speaking for the three of them. "How can you think we're not? All three of us went to church with you when we were growing up. We know about Christ."

"It's not enough to know about Christ. You have to have faith that you can only be saved by trusting in him. Like you, I thought I was saved but God showed me I wasn't. I had head knowledge of him, but even Satan knows Christ, and that didn't save him, did it? God wanted me to talk to each of you for a reason. Evidently He thought it was important for you to make sure of your salvation. He impressed it on me to talk with you today."

"And here we thought you called us here for wedding planning." Said Zoe.

All of a sudden we were interrupted by a loud crash of thunder. One of our famous storms that come up out of nowhere, moved into the area.

"Well, that was well planned, God is speaking to us through his thunder and lightening!" laughed Billie.

I was upset my friends took what I had to say so lightly. I really wanted them to heed what I told them about God and salvation, but it seems like they were just mocking me. I didn't feel like I got through to them at all. I prayed that God would intervene. I did what he wanted me to do, but I didn't think any of it sunk in with them.

I heard God talk with me then. "You have planted the seeds my child. That is all you are able to do. Your friends did hear you, and they will be saved, but only through Christ will they understand just as you did."

They seemed eager to get going after I spoke with them. The rain started to be a downpour at the time my friends were leaving. I told them to hold up until after the storm was over, but they were insisting that they had to go.

"I'm meeting another friend of mine in an hour, so I really need to get going." Said Zoe as she was getting her purse to leave.

"And I have a hot date to get ready for." Added Eliza.

As they were all riding together, they all left at the same time. I decided to straighten the house a little bit, and clean up the kitchen, and then I layed down because suddenly I felt very sleepy. Rainy weather was comforting, and I fell asleep right away. A little while later I became very restless, and decided to get up. I turned on the television while I worked on my invitations.

From the television, there came a news flash. There had been a terrible accident on I40, and the police and ambulances were everywhere. They panned their cameras to the sight of the wreck. It was a silver colored late model SUV and it was completely crushed. Identities were withheld until the next of kin could be notified. They only said that there were three women in the car. The investigation showed the car was probably going too fast on the slick roads and tried to pass another vehicle at close range and hydroplaned across the median and hit an eighteen wheeler coming in the opposite direction. Ambulances were on the scene, and the EMTs were assisting the victims, but their conditions were unknown at this time. From what I could make out from the images, the car looked similar to the one that my friends were riding in.

As I sat there, my eyes were glued to the television I couldn't quit staring at the devastating wreck. Could this accident involve my three friends? There couldn't have been any survivors as bad as it looked, could there?

"Lord I don't know if this wreck involved Zoe, Billie and Eliza, but I pray, whoever it is that you would be with them. I pray for their salvation and if they are still alive, I pray that you would be with them, and protect them. and that you would heal them."

I heard a voice from deep within my soul in answer: "Trust me, my daughter. All things work together for those who trust in me."

I sat stunned in front of my television of the things happening at the wreck. I couldn't turn my eyes away as I saw the scene unfold. Were those my friends I saw being pulled from the car? They had to use the 'Jaws of Life' to get the doors off the mangled mess. Surely no one could have survived something like this, but still I prayed. Even if it wasn't them, someone in that wreck needed my prayers.

Then I saw them. I gasped as they were being pulled out of the car, and put on stretchers, and put in the ambulances. It was my friends! They were the ones in the accident! Thankfully, none of them had their heads covered as they were carried to the ambulance. They all had neck braces, and oxygen masks on. At least one of them was having CPR done to them. "Oh my God, is she going to live? God help her please!" I cried.

My heart was heavy for my friends. I spent the rest of the day in intense prayer. God had to make them all right. He wasn't through with them yet. I know He wasn't. It was important to him that they all knew him, and I had to be assured they were saved both physically, and spiritually.

After the news report I frantically dialed Steve's cell phone number. I was shaking so much I had to dial it twice before I got through. "Steve did you see the news on television? My three friends have been in a horrible car wreck! It looked awful. I'm not sure if they are still alive, it was that bad!"

"I was in my car at the time. I thought about coming to see you but I saw the wreck, and they had all the lanes closed off so I pulled off the exit and turned around, and came home. I had no idea that it involved your friends, I'm so sorry! I wouldn't try to get out to see them the rest of the day, however, they need to get situated at the hospital, and treated, and they need to clear the rest of wreck away, and the weather is still way to bad to get out in it." Replied Steve. "I'll call you later. I'll be sure to pray for them, and for you. I know how upset you must be."

I called Pastor Stewart next. The girls and their families were members of our church in the past, and I thought he would want to know. He said he would start a prayer chain, and contact the girl's parents to see how they were doing, and offer his prayers for them.

In all of the prayers, and concerns for my friends, and their families, the last thing I could think of now was how it was going to affect my wedding plans. That just didn't seem important at a time like this.

❧ Chapter 20 ❧

Kyle and Sadie were excited, but nervous about meeting their niece and nephew for the first time. Ruth would be at their home in fifteen minutes to take them to the foster parents home to meet the twins. They decided they would have a short outing and picnic with them in the park. Ruth thought getting to know them away from their current family would work out best. The next visit they could have them in their home for a few hours with supervision from the social worker. She would have to be with them at all times watching their interaction with them until the adoption or at least the foster parent application goes through, and they can take them in as foster kids.

They were living in their rental house now, and had been there for about two weeks. They pretty much had everything unpacked, and in place now with what little they had. They had purchased a few things for the twin's rooms so it would be inviting for them when they finally moved in, but before they actually came to stay they would go shopping with the children, and let them choose what décor they wanted in their bedrooms, and of course pick out their bed linens.

The children still had no idea that Ruth, the social worker, was the same person as their aunt who abused them. She had changed so much with the clothes she wore, and her make up, and changes in hairstyle, and color they didn't recognize her. This Ruth wore a smile on her face, and was always gentle with them.

Kyle's and Sadie's nerves were heightened when the doorbell rang.

"She's here!" called Sadie from the doorway as she opened the door.

"Hello, are you all ready for this?" smiled Ruth.

"We might as well be, we'll soon become parents to these children." Kyle said.

It wasn't too long of a drive to their current foster home. It was maybe two miles, at the most. The Dicksons lived in a lovely older subdivision just outside of Clairmonte. The neighborhood was nice, and there were a lot of children playing outside, as they passed by. They wondered if any of them were the twins.

"Here we are." Said Ruth as she unbuckled her seat belt, and got her briefcase in the seat next to her. She had an SUV, so that she could transport her clients, and children comfortably. "Ready to meet them?"

They both smiled at her, but they were still as nervous as first time parents, ready to meet their new baby!

"I hope they like us!" worried Sadie out loud.

"What's not to like?" smiled Ruth. "Kyle you look so much like their Dad, and Sadie you look a lot like Jobella. They're going to think I brought their family back to them!"

"And their foster parents, are they nice?"

"They are an elderly couple, kind of like your favorite grandparents. They are very nice!"

As they opened the door, the couple hugged Ruth, and stared at us. Then they broke out in a big smile, and gave us a hug as well.

"Come on in, this is my wife Sophie, and I'm Peter. We're so happy to meet you at last. Ruth told us all about you. We didn't say too much to the twins, other than there was someone who wanted to adopt them, and give them a permanent home. They will be down in just a few minutes. They wanted to look their best for you."

"They are such sweet children, but they missed their parents, and their big sister so much, it was hard for them to accept us. They hadn't been around anyone our age before, since their grandparents all died before they were born. We finally won them over, but it took a while. They will probably take to you all really well. We will miss them terribly when they move out. They are like the grandchildren we never had." added Sophie.

"After we adopt them, and they become ours, we will be sure to bring them by once in a while. Like them, we don't have grandparents, and we would be honored to have them think of you as their 'grandparents' if you wish." Kyle said.

"That would be wonderful." Smiled Sophie.

"Joshua, Joanna, our visitors are here." Peter called up the stairs.

The twins came running down the stairs holding hands. They had on new shorts, and t-shirts because they knew they would be going to the park today with Ruth, and some people she was bringing by, and they wanted to look their best.

They suddenly stopped in their tracks, when they saw us. They ran to Peter and Sophie, and hid behind them.

"Come on you two." Sophie laughed. "I want you to meet Mr. Kyle, and Ms. Sadie. These nice people are here to take you to the park. I want you to get to know them. I think you all are going to get along real well."

The twins were four years old now, and had been sheltered for the last year since their parents were killed, and Jobella took them to the police station. It took them a while to get comfortable living with Peter and Sophie. They didn't know what to think about this new couple. They suddenly became aware that maybe someone was going to take them away again, especially since the social worker was with them. They clung to the Dickson's, and hid their faces. They didn't want to go with them. They already had too many changes in their lives.

Sophie took them to the sofa, and spoke with them softly. "These nice people want to get to know you a little better. They are a very lovely couple, and I know you are going to like them, when you get to know them. They've wanted to meet you for a long time. You all are going to have a lot of fun with them, I promise. Now I want you to skedaddle over there, and be on your best behavior, okay?"

Josh and Joanie walked slowly toward them, and the Jordans squatted down to their eye level, and gave them a hug. Josh's eyes lit up when he stared at them a little longer. "You look just like my daddy!" he exclaimed.

And then Joanie added "and you look kind of like my big sister!"

"Ruth, is it alright if we tell them who we are?" asked Kyle.

"Looks like they're going to guess if you don't! She laughed.

"Joshua and Joanna," Kyle smiled. "I look like your Daddy, because I'm his twin brother, just like you two are twins. You are our niece and nephew, and we want to take care of you because we are part of your family."

"How come we've never seen you?" asked Joanie.

"Because we were living a long way from here. We lived on an island called Java. We were missionaries there. We took care of people. I'm a doctor, and Sadie here, is a nurse. She helped me take care of sick people too." Explained Kyle.

"Do you have kids like us?" added Josh.

"No God never blessed us with children, but we would love to have some children just like you, and your sister." Sadie said.

"Maybe we can come visit you sometime." Smiled Joanie.

Ruth whispered to Sophie. "This is too way too easy. I don't think we'll have too many problems with this."

"Don't it look like it!" laughed Sophie quietly so they couldn't hear. "I'm sure going to miss them though!"

After all the introductions were made, and everyone including the children was comfortable, and excited about the visit, they left. On the way to the park they picked up some hamburgers, fries, and happy meals for the twins from McDonalds. They wanted to have a picnic, but they made it easy for themselves by picking up something along the way. They heard that the kids liked McDonalds and they wanted to make sure the twins got something they liked.

The park had some lovely walking areas, and shade trees surrounding the picnic tables, and there was also a playground for the kids including a fountain large enough for the twins to wade and splash in. There was a large sandy area as well for them to build sand castles. They would have to remember this area after they came to live with them.

After they ate, and while the children were playing Ruth, wanted to go over some paperwork with the Jordan's, and scheduled the next appointment when they would be able to bring the children into their home, possibly within the next month. Everything was moving right along, and it wouldn't too long before they could complete the foster parent stage prior to the official adoption in December. If they continued to grow in their relationship with them it would be so much easier in the transition.

The twins came running up to Sadie. "Can we take our shoes off and play in the fountain?"

"Sure, be careful though, we don't want you to slip and fall. Remember, you have on your new clothes, so try not to get too wet!" called Sadie after them when they were running toward the fountain.

"They look like they are having a lot of fun. Wouldn't it be nice to be that young again and have that freedom and no worries?" asked Ruth.

"That will come to us again in the next life. We'll be that carefree in heaven!" Replied Kyle, always the preacher, smiling.

"Well, I guess it's time we get back. We've been gone for almost two hours. That is all the time allotted for the first visit. I would say that we made a great beginning. I feel the twins are warming up to you nicely! We won't want Sophie and Peter getting too worried that you have taken the twins from them too soon. I get the feeling they are not quite ready to part with them just yet!" Ruth laughed.

"And we are ready for them to come live with us right now!" Smiled Sadie. "But I know what you mean about Sophie and Peter. We will keep that in mind."

They called the twins from the playground and dried them off with the napkins we had left over from lunch. They didn't think about needing towels when they left home. They didn't know there was a water feature at the park.

Before they got in the van, the twins came to them hugging them. "We had a good time uncle Kyle and aunt Sadie. Can we do this again?"

"Of course, but the next time we visit with you we are going to take you to our house for a few hours. Then maybe we can come to the park after that, okay?" asked Sadie.

When the kids arrived back at their foster parent's house, they were all excited. They told Sophie and Peter they wanted to visit their aunt and uncle again. They showed them the toys they got in their happy meals and told them all about the park.

"Maybe you can take us to the park, Mama Sophie. We liked it there. Next time we want to take a swimming suit so that we can splash in the fountain and swim in it too. Would that be all right Ms. Ruth?" Asked Joanie.

"Sure, if it's all right with Mama Sophie and Daddy Peter." Ruth smiled. "You can do anything you like with them."

"Yeah, we'd like that." Added Josh.

"Well we'd better be off. We don't want to wear out our welcome on the first visit. I'm sure the kids will be ready for a nap soon." Sadie nodded to the twins. "We'll be back in about a week to see you again. It won't be too long. Next time we see you we are going to show you where we live."

The twins hugged them, as they were getting ready to leave. They were all smiling now, and they knew what ever came up next in their relationship it would be a blessing for all of them. They were already feeling like family, and were looking forward to taking the twins into their hearts and lives. They continued to feel like God was in the center of everything that was happening. It was all going to work out just fine. Hopefully Jobella would feel the same come December.

When they arrived back at their rental house it suddenly felt like a home. They walked through each room, and looked at it through the children's eyes. They wanted to make sure it would be a happy place for them. They'd only be in it for one or two more years until they built their own home on their property, but this place would be their home until then.

Any furnishings they would buy would be with the children in mind. They were anxious to get the children's rooms decorated but they would wait until they were with them before shopping for accessories. They didn't want to make it too obvious yet that they were coming to live with them. That would come later when they felt that they were ready to move in with them.

Chapter 21

The hospital was crowded as usual when I walked into the elevators to go to the ICU to visit my friends. I didn't want to come too soon. I waited a few days after things settled down a bit. I'd been in touch with each of their parents to get any updates on their progress and to pray with them. I got their permission to visit today.

They all were still alive but all of them were in critical condition. Zoe's heart did stop beating at the scene and they didn't think they were going to be able to bring her back, but God was merciful, and allowed her to live. Things however were still touch and go with her. She coded again after they brought her to the ICU, and she has been in a coma since that time. She had to have emergency surgery to repair some internal injuries that were causing her to "bleed out". She was stable at this time, but still in a coma.

I walked over to her and saw all of the IV's and wires she was connected to. It brought me back to the way that Steve looked a year ago. She was not breathing on her own, and was hooked up to a ventilator. She had IV's going in through her chest, and she was fed through a tube going into her stomach. She looked so pitiful with bruises that were turning yellow, and purple now after three days. Her injuries were many. Her head was wrapped in gauze. And she had lacerations everywhere from the windshield shattering all over her. She had several broken ribs from hitting the steering wheel. One of her ribs punctured her heart, and it had stopped beating from the injury. Another rib had torn a hole in her lung. I honestly didn't see how she could have survived with everything that happened to her. When they brought her in she had to go directly to surgery to repair her heart and lungs, and she would have to have a chest tube in place until her lungs healed.

I bowed my head over Zoe, and prayed. "Lord, I know you can hear me, even in this place. Thank you Lord that Zoe is still alive and still has a chance to come to you and believe in you. I pray you would heal her body if it is your will and she will be made whole. Lord I know you are able to do this. Be with us who are her friends, and her family. I pray for strength for her, and hope for us, and remind us that you are the great physician, and know that you're able to take care of even these things. In Jesus name I pray amen."

Her mom said to me. "Jobella, I'm sorry this happened right before your wedding, I know you were counting on these girls to be in your wedding party. Please don't let what happened change anything with your plans."

"I'm not even concerned about that. I just want them to get well. I'm still going to have my wedding. I know things happen, but it won't be the same without them of course, but I still have my maid of honor and, if that's all I have, than so be it. Maybe later when my friends are all well we can have a post wedding party. By then maybe I'll have the twins back as well, and we can have a huge celebration!"

Zoe's mom gave me a big hug. "Thank you for being such a good friend. You are a real blessing to us. Please continue to pray for Zoe, and us and we will pray for you that everything works out the way you want it too. I know we haven't always been the best of friends with you or your family, but sometimes it takes something like this to happen to realize who our friends really are, and how great God really is. It's a miracle that Zoe is still alive, and we thank God for that."

After I left Zoe, I went into the next room where I saw Billie. She was lying in traction, and her left leg and arm were in casts. She too, was covered in bruises but she was awake. She was groggy from all the pain medications she was on, but she recognized me as I entered.

I was teary-eyed as I came up to her bedside to visit her. "I'm so sorry this happened to you! I'd take your place in a minute, if you would be all well and pain free."

"No you wouldn't, and I wouldn't let you. You are my friend, and you've been through so much yourself. Now it's my turn. Everyone has his or her trials. Like you said life isn't always going to be perfect. I needed to be brought to a place that God would force me to stop and look at what's important. I've been doing a lot of thinking the last few days. All of us should have been killed in that accident but God spared us. Maybe He isn't done with us yet. Thank you for talking to us about God before we left your house the other day. I know God meant for us to be there, and for you to speak to us about His love, and what is important. I believe thinking on those things you said, has helped me during this time."

"God did impress on me to speak with you that day. I didn't want to come across as a preacher or as someone who was lording it over you but, I did need to talk with you all, and now I know why."

"Well I, for one, am very glad you did. I'm sorry for messing up your wedding plans. It sounds wonderful. I probably won't be out of here by then, but I'll be thinking of you!"

"Like I told Zoe's mom, I'll plan on having a post wedding party when you all get out."

"That would be great. I may not be up for it for at least two months though! I'm a little tied up at the moment." She smiled at her own joke.

"I'll keep that in mind!" I laughed. "Do you mind if I pray with you?"

"I'd love that. You can pray for me anytime you want to!"

"Dear Lord, keep Billie safe, and heal her broken bones. Thank you that she wasn't hurt worse, and she can still laugh even through her pain. Lord, be with her family during this time of her healing. Watch over her, and protect her from harm. Let her know you are able to heal the body, and the spirit. Guard her from attacks from Satan that would have her feel sorry for herself when the pain comes in the middle of the night, and she isn't able to do everything she wants to do. Let her know that there are a lot of us praying for her. Our whole church family cares about her, and wants her to get well. In Jesus name I pray, amen."

"When I do get well, I want to get back into church. The Lord is impressing on me that I should do that."

"That would be great!" I gave her a hug, and promised that I would be back to visit her again soon.

"Tell Zoe and Eliza hi for me, okay? By the way, how are they doing? Nobody is telling me anything."

"Well I haven't see Eliza yet, and Zoe is in a coma. She's still in critical condition, but they think that she will recover. I understand that they had to resuscitate her at the crash site, and once again in the ICU."

"That's so sad. I hope she'll be okay. I was in the ICU when she coded. I thought my heart would stop when I heard it."

"Do you remember anything about the crash?"

"It was raining really hard, we couldn't see ten feet in front of us. All of a sudden the cars were slowing down in front of us. Zoe was driving, and had been going pretty fast because we were all so anxious to get home. Well when the cars slowed down we didn't.

Zoe slammed on the brakes, and when she did, we hydroplaned across the median, and into the largest eighteen-wheeler I ever saw! After that everything kind of went dark. You're going to think this is strange, but I could have sworn that I saw something that looked like angels. They appeared between the crushing metal and us, like they were protecting us from being crushed to death. Jobella, we should have all died! When I see the pictures of the car, I don't understand how we made it out in one piece. God must have had his hand in it. He must have sent his angels to protect us! The next thing I knew, I heard the sirens. It didn't take them long to get there. They pulled us all from the wreck, and I saw them working on Zoe on the stretcher next to me. They were saying that they were losing her, and they started doing CPR on her. I thought she was dead, and wouldn't be back. I'm glad they brought her back, even if she is in a coma now. It means there is still hope. When I saw Eliza, I saw she had a neck brace placed on her. They were moving her very carefully to the stretcher. As we were leaving the scene, I saw news crews from the TV and radio stations there. I was afraid our parents, and you would learn of the accident that way."

"I did, but I waited a few hours, before I talked with your parents. I didn't want them to learn it from me. When I called, they were already at the hospital waiting on the doctors to tell them the outcome of the accident."

"I'm sorry you had to go through this. I will continue to pray for you. I'm going to go visit with Eliza now. God bless you."

As I walked into Eliza's room the mood suddenly changed. She too was covered with bruises. She had an IV, a feeding tube, and a catheter just like Zoe, but she wasn't on a ventilator, and was awake. She was in the strangest looking bed I ever saw, and her head had a clamp on it that was attached to some kind of weight.

"Good afternoon," I said to a frowning Eliza.

"What's so good about it? I'm lying here, and I can't move anything. Did they tell you that I'm paralyzed from the neck down?

I can't even scratch my nose when it itches! The only good thing is that I don't have any feelings below my neck either, so I can't feel all the pain that I should be in!"

"I'm so sorry, I didn't know. Can I pray for you?"

"No, I don't want your prayers! If we hadn't stayed so long at your house to hear 'your sermon' we wouldn't have been in such a rush to get home, and we wouldn't have gotten in the wreck!"

"Please, I'm sorry this happened to you all. I wouldn't have wanted this for you. All right, I won't pray for you now, but you can't stop me from praying for you, and asking God to help you recover, even if it's on my own time. You are still my friend, and I care, so let's move on from that. Is there anything I can do for you right now?"

"Can you sponge off my face, and wet my lips? They are awfully dry."

"Sure, no problem there." I said as I did it. "What has the doctor said about your condition?"

"He said I broke my neck. There is a lot of swelling around my spinal cord. They are not sure until the swelling goes down if there is going to be any permanent damage, and if the spinal cord was severed."

"I'll pray after the swelling goes down, you'll be able to move, and feel things again, and there isn't any permanent damage."

"I'll let you do that, I guess. I'm sorry that I'm being mean. I'm just scared. You can understand that right?"

"I can, with everything that I've gone through both with me, and Steve, I can definitely understand."

"Is your parents anywhere around? I'd like to say hi to them."

"They went to the cafeteria for some coffee, and lunch. Maybe you can catch them there."

"By the way, I visited Zoe and Billie before I came to your room. Zoe is still in a coma, but she is stable. The doctor seems to think that she'll be okay. Billie has a lot of broken bones, but appears to be in good spirits."

"That's good they are still alive. The next time you see them, give them my love."

"No problem, I'll be sure to tell them. I will be praying for you. I'll see you again soon, I promise.

"Thanks, I do appreciate that. I guess I need all the prayers I can get!"

I went to the cafeteria, and found Eliza's parents. They stood when they saw me coming, and gave me a big hug. I told them I visited Eliza, and I was sorry for what she was going through. Her mom had been crying, and was inconsolable. I told her about the other girls as well. I told her I would keep all of them in my prayers.

"Would you like to join us for lunch?" asked her father.

"Maybe just some tea, I'm not very hungry. It's been a very upsetting day for me to see my friends like that."

I went to get the tea and rejoined them.

"How are your wedding plans coming?" asked her mom, trying to change the subject. "Are you still going on with them as scheduled at the end of August?"

"Yes, everything has been scheduled and the invitations have been mailed. I hate that my bridesmaids won't be there, though. We're going to miss them. It won't be quite the same without my girls there. I guess I'll just have to make do with only my matron of honor."

"I know the girls will miss being there as well, they were really looking forward to it. They think you and Steven are perfect for each other."

"I plan on getting lots of pictures, and I told them that maybe we could get together after they get out of the hospital, and have a post wedding party. We can have cake, and everything just like the reception they didn't get to come to."

"That would be great! I know the girls will appreciate it. Please stay in touch with all of us, and keep praying for all our girls!

"I plan to do exactly that and I'll come around a couple times a week to visit, if you all don't mind."

"We would love that! You are such a good friend. If we don't happen to see one another again before the wedding I pray that everything from here on out will work out for you. Be sure to give Steven our love!"

I left the hospital to go back home. I really needed Steve now. I needed a shoulder to cry on. It was horrible to see all my friends in their conditions. I prayed to God then, and would continue to do so every time I thought of them.

Chapter 22

The day finally came when the twins were scheduled to spend the day with the Jordans in their home. They were so excited to have them come. They hoped they were excited to visit as well.

A lot had happened since the last time that they saw them. They both got jobs and luckily it was in the same clinic so they could share their ride. The office was closed on the weekends so they both would be off on Saturdays and Sundays, and Sadie could work part-time so she could have more time with the kids. The clinic was actually pretty close to their home.

The decision would have to be made about what to do with the children while they were at work. The best option of course would be to get them enrolled in pre-kindergarten. They would be there while Sadie was working, and she would be able to pick them up after school. The school was to start just after Labor Day. They hoped to have custody of them by that time. Ruth thought that was doable.

At last the doorbell rang. "Welcome!" Sadie said as the twins ran up to them, and gave them each a big hug.

"We missed you, aunt Sadie and uncle Kyle!" smiled Joshua.

"Can we go to the park again?" added Joanie.

"No we have something else planned for you today!

First we're going to have a tour of our house, and then we are going shopping. Won't that be fun?" asked Kyle.

"Yes sir." They said together. "Ms. Ruth will it be alright?"

"Of course, dears. I think you two, and your aunt and uncle can handle that all on your own. I trust you with them completely. I'm going to go, and find me something to do while you are gone. If that's alright.

"You don't mind?" asked Sadie.

"I said so, didn't I?" She replied. "I'll come back in about four hours, will it give you enough time?"

"That would be great. Thank you, Ruth." Said Kyle.

After she left, they turned to the twins. "Lets show you around the house, and we have a surprise for you." Sadie said.

We went from room to room, and finally showed them their soon to be rooms and bathrooms, up the stairs. There were enough rooms in the house that they could each have their own rooms.

"I don't understand. I thought we were just visiting. Why do we have our own rooms?" asked Josh.

"You are just visiting today, but we are going to have you come over more often, and you will be spending the night with us soon. We would like to eventually have you come, and stay with us, okay?" asked Kyle

"Okay, but what about Momma Sophie and Daddy Peter?" frowned Joanie.

"They can come and visit you anytime you like. We want them to be part of our family too!" added Sadie.

"What about 'Bella? How will 'Bella find us if we aren't at Momma Sophie and Daddy Peter's house? Ms. Ruth said that 'Bella would be coming for us soon."

"Ms. Ruth will know you are here, she'll tell Jobella. We will have a room for Jobella, and Steve to stay in when then they visit, okay?"

"Okay, I guess that will be good." Answered Joanie.

"Are we going to each have a room, aunt Sadie?" asked Josh.

"Yes, here is your room, Josh, and next door is yours, Joanie." she said as she opened the doors.

"Look Joshie, we each have a bed and dresser. And we have our own bathrooms! Yippee!" yelled Joanie.

They immediately ran into their rooms, and started jumping on the beds.

"Okay, okay, let's not tear them up already!" Kyle laughed. He winked at Sadie. "You know what? That's exactly what I would've done."

They went back to kitchen, and made sandwiches for lunch while the kids were getting comfortable in their rooms. They made peanut butter and jelly for the twins, and chicken salad for them.

"Did I hear someone say peanut butter and jelly?" said Josh running into the kitchen. "How did you know that was our favorite?"

"Oh, a little bird told me." Sadie laughed. "Hurry up and eat now. We have some shopping to do this afternoon."

"Where are we going?" asked Joanie.

"We thought you might like to help us find some things for your bedrooms. Like sheets, and pillowcases, and bedspreads. We wanted you to pick out your favorite ones so you could decorate your rooms just like you want." Smiled Sadie.

"Could I have a princess room?" asked Joanie. "I like princesses. Daddy use to call me his little princess before he died in the fire." She added with a frown.

"Princess sounds perfect!" laughed Kyle. "I think you will be my little princess as well!" Then he grabbed her and tickled her.

"I like Star Wars, uncle Kyle. You think we can find some Star Wars decorations?"

"We most certainly will do the best we can, to get you what you want." He replied.

After lunch they went to the mall to get everything they needed. The basic furniture was in their rooms but they bought the bed linens, and table lamps, to match what the children wanted their décor to be. They also bought the bathroom accessories, like shower curtains, and matching soap, and toothbrush holders to coordinate with their bedroom themes. The twins were so excited. They couldn't wait to get back, and get their rooms set up so that the next time they came they would be ready to spend the night.

"What about 'Bella's room?" asked Joanie.

"We can get things for their room next time. We still have a little time left before they come, okay?" said Sadie.

They left the mall and started to head home, but they had one last stop to make.

"We have another surprise for you two!"

"Really? This day is great already!" laughed Josh. "How can it get better!"

When they pulled into the animal shelter, Joanie cried with delight. "Are you going to get us an pet?"

"We'll see, do you think that you two can take care of one?"

They cried in unison. "Yes, yes, a million times yes!"

They came to the animal shelter a few days before, and chose a beautiful white angora kitten for Joanie, and a mixed terrier pup for Josh. They wanted them to be checked out, and have gotten their shots, before they brought them home today. They called ahead this morning before the twins got to their house, so they would have them ready when they got there.

They talked with the landlady to make sure that it would be okay and she said she had no problem with pets if they were small, and under control.

The twins squealed with delight when they saw their new pets. They begged Sadie to let them hold them on the way home. They said they could hold them while they were in the animal shelter, but they insisted that they keep them in their boxes while they were in the car.

When they got them to the house they immediately took them out to play with them. They were so cute together. Kyle got out the camera he just bought. He said they had to take a lot of pictures for the first scrapbook of them, all the "new" children together.

While the twins were playing with their new best friends, Kyle and Sadie set up their bedrooms with all their new decorations. Besides the bed linens, and lamps, and bathroom accessories, they bought them new curtains, and rugs to match. They spent the better part of the afternoon decorating. They didn't have much time with the children, but they were content to be in their respective rooms while they were working. Kyle was setting up Josh's room, and Sadie was decorating Joanie's. They were so involved with their new pets that they didn't even pay any attention Kyle and Sadie.

Then the inevitable happened. The doorbell rang. Ruth had come back to retrieve the kids. When she opened the door the twins were clutching their pets, and the Jordans.

"Well isn't this a pretty picture." She laughed. "You're not going to make this easy for me to take the twins home are you!"

"We just wanted to make sure they want to come back!" Kyle said.

"Ms. Ruth, come see our new rooms!" squealed Joanie.

"Yes, come and see mine too!" added Josh.

They dragged Ruth by one hand while clutching their pets with the other, and took her up to their rooms.

"Oh my, these rooms are great! Did you help pick out the decorations your self?"

The twins nodded, "Yes and these are our new pets."

"Do you have names for them yet?"

Joanie answered first. "My kitten's name is Snowball, because she so soft, and pretty, and white like snow!"

Josh piped up when she was through. "My puppy's name is Charlie. Don't you think he looks like a Charlie?"

Ruth had to laugh. "Yes he most certainly does look just like a Charlie."

Ruth stayed to set up the next visit with them, which would be the next weekend. She said they would no longer need supervision, and they could spend the night next time if they wanted to. She wouldn't be able to keep them away! They would be anxious to spend all night with their new pets in their new rooms.

As Ruth got up to leave she called for the children. "We've got to go now. It's time to go see Momma Sophie and Daddy Peter!"

Josh and Joanie walked slowly down the stairs. "We want to stay here Ms. Ruth, can't we stay here now?"

"No, but it will only be a couple more weeks before you can stay. I don't think Sophie and Peter are quite ready to give you up yet!"

"But Aunt Sadie said they could come visit us anytime they wanted to!" said Joanie.

"I'm sure that's true, but we have some more paperwork to do before your aunt and uncle can adopt you."

"Please hurry with that, we want to stay now!" said Josh.

After a little more cajoling, the twins were finally ready to go. They said goodbye to Snowball and Charlie, and they each kissed both of them goodbye, and then they went to Sadie, and Kyle, and hugged them like they never wanted to let go.

"When we come to live with you, will you be our mommy and daddy?" asked Josh.

"We would love it if you thought of us that way. We want to be your forever mom and dad." Said Kyle.

"We will be back next week. Can we take Charlie and Snowball with us to Momma Sophie and Daddy Peter's house?" asked Joanie.

"No they need to stay here, you can visit them here. You'll be with them for a long time after you come to live here. Their food, and litter boxes are here, we can't take all that with us, okay?" Ruth said.

"Alright, Aunt Sadie, will you take care of them for us?" asked Josh.

"I will be more than happy too! I love them as much as you do!"

After they hugged, and kissed them one more time, they turned, and walked out the door, one on either side of Ruth, holding her hands. They were telling her about everything they did today, and how excited they were about their new rooms, and their kitten and puppy.

Kyle and Sadie hugged each other, and smiled. Having them with them was going to be wonderful. Within a month they would be theirs, and they would be a family at last. The only thing that would be more perfect is if they could share everything with Jobella. They were still forbidden to say anything to her until December because she wasn't to know about the arrangements until the hearing.

It was the middle of August now. Only a little over a week until Jobella's wedding, and two weeks until they were to get custody of the twins as foster parents. A month after that they would be hearing back about the adoption status.

Their hearts yearned after Jobella. Now that they were here, and settled they longed to see their daughter. Would she look anything like them? Those that know her said she did bare a resemblance to Sadie. Especially since she had her red hair. They were dying to see her get married, and they tried to figure out a way they to do it without her seeing them. They would've loved to help her prepare for her wedding as well if they could, but they resigned themselves to knowing that wouldn't be possible.

Kyle and Sadie decided that they would go by the church next week, and talk with Jobella's pastor. Jobella's church was quite large, and they talked with Pastor Stewart to see if there was a place they could view the wedding where she wouldn't see them.

He knew many of the members of the congregation would be there, and he thought if they just blended into the crowd she might not notice them. Jobella had never seen her *'aunt and uncle'* before and wouldn't be expecting them to be there so they might just be able to pull it off.

"Besides," he laughed. "She'll only have her eyes on Steven."

Could they pull it off? They might just do it. It would be hard for them not to go to her, and hug her and tell her everything that day but they knew that wasn't possible.

Through their lawyer, and Jobella's best friend, Abby, they learned of her grief over her three best friends getting in a car wreck, and nearly killed, the three friends that were to be her bride's maids. Their hearts went out to her as they wondered why this had to happen at this time. Hadn't she been through enough this past year? Of course her pain wasn't anything compared to the pain that the girls' families were going through right now. They wanted to go to them, and share with them God's love, and to let them know they were praying for them. However, they didn't want to take the chance they would be recognized, and go back and tell Jobella that her aunt and uncle came by to see them when Jobella didn't know she had an aunt and uncle in the area, and would start asking questions.

As a doctor Kyle did have privileges at the hospital where they were patients. He thought he might at least check on them. Maybe they wouldn't recognize him. From what Abby said they were in pretty bad shape, and one of them was still in a coma. Maybe he could take a chance. He just wouldn't tell them his last name.

Chapter 23

One week, and counting I thought excitedly as I got out of bed on the Saturday before my wedding. It was a beautiful day, and Steve would be by around about nine for a full day of getting some last minute wedding preparations done.

Most of the people we invited have sent their responses, and most have said they would come. Even my friend's parents said they would be there as well. They wanted to get a lot of pictures so they could share them with their daughters when they were well enough to see them.

I looked at the picture of my family. It was the picture I found in my Bible that was laying next to my bed, in the rubble, after the fire. I had it restored and slightly enlarged and put it in matted antique frame, and hung it above the mantle of my fireplace. It looked new, like it had been taken days ago instead of a year and half ago. and then been through a fire. Tears came to my eyes when I thought about them not being there, and how my father wouldn't be there to walk me down the aisle, and my mom wouldn't be there to help me with my wedding dress, and the twins wouldn't be there to be our ring bearer, and flower girl. I missed all of them so much!

I went to take a shower, and tried to wash the tears away, and put on some fresh makeup before Steve came. I always wanted to look my best for him, and he didn't need to see me crying. I didn't want him to get depressed because I was missing my family.

While I was putting on my makeup, the doorbell rang. I was expecting to see Steven, but standing at the door was a deliveryman from the florist. He had a bouquet of the most beautiful lilacs and peace lilies I had ever seen.

"These are gorgeous! Thank you!" I cried, as I signed for them. "Who are they from?"

"I'm not allowed to say." Said the deliveryman. "The card is signed *your guardian angels'* and the buyer said not to divulge who bought them."

I was sure it had been Steve, or his family. As I went to the kitchen to set them on the table Steve came to the door. I brought him into the apartment, and gave him a big hug, and kiss. As he looked over my shoulder he gasped! "Where did the beautiful flowers come from? They look just like the flowers we are going to have at our wedding!"

"You mean you or your family didn't send them?"

"No we didn't even think about it. We've been saving all our money for the wedding."

"The card said *'from my guardian angel'*. Oh, you know what? I bet they're from Abby!" I laughed. "It's something she would do."

"That must be it!" smiled Steve.

"How are you holding up? Are you excited about getting married, and moving in with me?" I laughed.

"I'm great, I can't wait! I'm glad we decided to go ahead, and get married before starting back to school. I don't know if I could've waited another year to have you in my arms, and love you the way you deserve to be loved, the way that God intended for us to love each other. How about you?"

"Me too! I'm ready to get the wedding over with though. This is way too much work. I don't know what I would have done without Abby's and your parent's support. It's kind of hard to be excited without my parents being here to help me, and be excited for me, though."

"I'm sorry for that too."

I fell into his arms again and the tears came for the second time today. I didn't want to cry in front of him but I couldn't help it this time.

We stayed together holding one another until the tears dried on my face and he loved me into being able to smile again.

"Well, we'd better get going. We are meeting with our wedding planner for the final arrangements in less than an hour and we have to drive to Raleigh to meet her."

A million thoughts went through my mind as we drove to Libby's office. Libby was our wedding planner, and I honestly don't know what I would've have done without her.

Libby was able to help me a lot when it came to arranging my purchases, and coordinating everything, and helping with the cake and flowers especially after I lost the help of my bridesmaids. She had the connections with the caterer's and florists and bakeries I didn't have, and I didn't want to bother my future in-laws with so many of the details of the wedding. Libby was truly a Godsend to me and worth every penny I was paying her.

On the way to Libby's I called Abby. I wanted to thank her for the flowers. I didn't know where she would be so I called her cell. She picked up after the third ring.

"Hello, this is Abby." I heard her say.

"Thank you for the flowers you sent! I know it was you because you are my guardian angel!" I laughed. "I was down in the dumps today, and they made my day!"

"What are you talking about? I didn't send you any flowers. I wish I would have though, but I really didn't think about it!"

I laughed again. "It had to be you! No one else besides you, Steve, his family, and Libby knew that I was going to use lilacs and calla lilies in my wedding!"

"I swear it wasn't me or, anyone in the office that sent them."

"Steve or his family didn't send them either."

"Have you checked with Libby or even your friends parents?"

"I'm on my way to see Libby now, but I doubt my friend's parents would have thought about it. They have enough to think about with their own girls right now. I doubt if they are even thinking about me, and my wedding right now."

"Well anyway good luck with your wedding planner. You and Steven have fun today. I'll see you in the office on Monday."

We drove around the block a couple of times before we found Libby's shop and office. Before coming today, I spoke with her about everything on the phone, and on Facebook. I had gone online on her web site, and chose everything that I had wanted, and she promised to have the items I had chosen in her shop today for me to look at, and finalize everything. Who would've thought that planning a wedding was such an undertaking, certainly not me! I guess that's why its so handy having parents helping. They've been through it all before.

Steven and I entered the shop and looked around a bit. There were so many choices! Libby came out from her office to greet us when she heard the door chimes. She came up to us, and hugged us like we were long lost friends. She was friendly, but at the same time professional. She took us back to her office where she had a sample of each of our choices laid out including assorted small cakes for us to sample so she could order the cake on Monday.

Everything was even prettier in reality than it was on the website. She showed us a sample of the centerpieces for our tables at our reception, and we sampled the cakes. We decided on an Italian cream cake with cream cheese icing. There would be lilac looking decorations starting at the top of the cake, and winding down around the sides. There would be dark purple violets to give the lilacs a little contrast. It was stunning, and it would be too beautiful to eat, but it would be too delicious not to. The centerpieces for the reception would be bouquets of lilacs and violets, to coordinate with the cake. The caterers would provide finger sandwiches, and fruit and veggie trays. She showed us samples of stemware, and silver accessories, and we picked our favorites. The candelabras would be rented of course, and she quoted us prices for those. The last thing we decided on was the flowers for the church, and our corsages, and bouquets. We had already decided on lilacs and calla lilies. After looking and tasting and ordering all our food, and decorations we paid her for everything. She promised she would be at the church the first thing next Saturday morning. We didn't have to worry about anything else. She said it would all be ready by the time we got married next Saturday afternoon at 3:00. All we had left to do would be to make sure we got our tuxes and gowns, and get to the church on time. After we paid her, we left smiling. It was finally going to happen and regardless of all the set backs we would be married in one week.

"Oh," I remembered, on our to Steve's house. "I forgot to ask her about the flowers I got today."

I pulled out my cell and dialed her number.

"Libby, I forgot to ask you something. I got a beautiful bouquet of flowers this morning. Did you send them? There was no name on them."

"No, I don't know anything about that. Trust me, if I sent them, it would have had a business card attached, but I already had your business." She laughed.

Steve's mom wasn't expecting us for a couple more hours for supper, so Steve and I went to the travel agency. His parent's had booked us on a cruise that was leaving out of Charleston on the Monday morning after our wedding, and we needed to go pick up our boarding passes. Steve also wanted to go by the men's shop to check on his tux. He had a black suit with a light purple vest and shirt. He didn't want me to see him in it although, I don't know if it is superstitious for me to see him in his wedding clothes, or not. I knew he was going to look great in it though.

Finally when we were finished with all our running around, we got to Steve's house. I was really tired, but exhilarated as well, from everything we were able to accomplish today. I really felt like everything was under control now. Monday after work, I would pick up my dress, and then I'd be set!

When we arrived at Steve's house there were several cars parked up and down the road. 'Someone must be having a party or barbeque' I thought. When I stepped into the doorway Steve called out to his mom. "Where is everyone, we're here."

"Surprise!" Everybody jumped up and shouted.

There in the living room they had a card table set up covered in presents, and the dining room table had a beautiful cake, sandwiches and treats for everyone.

I hugged Steven, and then I hugged my future in-laws. All of my friend's mothers, and some of the ladies from my church, and of course Abby, was there. She was one of the ones that set it up. She was able to keep the secret well, because I didn't know a thing about it. She didn't even hint at it when we spoke this morning.

"Steve, did you know anything about this? Is this why you didn't want to bring me back here too early?"

He just smiled.

It was a very pleasant surprise. Tears came to my eyes when I saw the caring of the ladies around me.

"I think that we men will go out on the back deck, and get the barbeque cranked up." Steve's dad nodded to Steve, and his brother.

Steve's brother had arrived in town just yesterday. I met his wife, and their two children for the first time today. Their children were about the twin's age. Seeing them running around reminded me of how much I missed Joanie and Josh. His kids would be our ring bearer, and flower girl.

His nephew had gone outside to be with the men, and his niece wanted to stay inside with the ladies. She oohed and aahed over the table of presents. I hoped she wasn't too disappointed that they weren't for her. She must have thought it was Christmas with everything going on.

Everyone gathered around the food table, and we all got our drinks and snacks. We mingled for a bit while we ate. I enjoyed getting to know Steve's sister-in-law Kari. She was a few years older than me, but we hit it right off. Her daughter, Laurie came up to me and introduced herself.

"I'm Laurie. What is your name? I'm going to throw rose pedals when you, and uncle Steve get married. I'm so-o-o-o excited!"

"I'm Jobella, and I'm excited to meet you too!" I smiled. "Just think, next week, when your uncle Steve and I get married, I'm going to be your new aunt!"

"Will I be able to call you Aunt Jobella, then?"

"Of course you can, I would be happy for you to."

"Thank you Aunt Jobella, I love you!" with that she ran into my arms and hugged me.

I would never be able to get enough of this love of my new family. It was the next best thing to having my own back.

I visited with my friend's moms then, asking them about how Zoe, Billie, and Eliza were. There hadn't been much of a change they said. Billie, the most alert and positive of the three was getting anxious to get home, although she was still in a lot of pain. She would have to be in traction a little while longer, so she would have to stay a little longer in the hospital. Zoe had shown little change, but there was an increase in brain activity, so the doctors were hopeful that she would regain consciousness soon, and Eliza was still paralyzed from the neck down. She had to have someone do everything for her. She continued to be in the special bed and would continue to be so until she was re-evaluated. I told their mothers that I would try to get by and see them again, tomorrow after church. They each hugged me, and told me how grateful they were for my friendship.

Opening presents was so exciting. I got everything from pots, and cooking gear to fine china dishes, and silverware. A few people even got me clothes for my honeymoon. Laurie looked a little sad because she didn't get anything, but her grandma went to her room and pulled a few presents out of her closet for her, that she had hiding. Laurie squealed with delight when she saw them.

"Nana, you got me something too? I'm not getting married!"

"You're not, but you have to be ready to be in the wedding with Aunt Jobella and Uncle Steve."

Laurie tore into her presents. Her Nana got her a beautiful purple flowered dress to wear, along with a tiara. She also bought her a little basket to carry, and a pair of white patent leather shoes and lacy socks.

"Can I put them on, Nana?"

"Of course." She laughed. "I want to see how they look on you."

Laurie took all her presents, and ran into the bedroom. When she came out she was glowing. "Nana, I look like a princess! Can I wear them the rest of the day for the party?"

"Only for a little bit. I don't want you to get them dirty before the wedding."

"I won't, I promise! Thank you Nana! You're the best Nana in the whole world."

She ran to her, hugging her, and then ran to me and hugged me, and then immediately ran outside to see her brother, grandpa, Uncle Steve, and her father. They were throwing a football around in the yard while they were waiting for their grill to get hot enough for the hamburgers, and hotdogs they were going to fix for supper.

"Daddy, Grandpa, look at me I look like a little princess!" As soon as she said that, she tripped over a small hole in the ground and fell skinning her knees and tearing her dress. As she sat there holding her knees, she started crying.

"Daddy, Mommy is going to be so mad that I ruined my dress for the wedding." She sobbed.

"She will be upset with you, but she'll forgive you. Let me take you inside, and get you cleaned up, and then we will have you change into your play clothes. We will see if Nana and Mommy can fix your dress, okay?"

Kari was upset when she saw Laurie being carried in by her daddy, and even more upset when she saw her skinned knees, and torn dress.

"I told you not to ruin your dress! Why did you go outside with it on?"

"I wanted to show Daddy and Grandpa!" she sobbed.

"Well let's go ahead, and get your new things off, and we'll treat your sores on your knees. Maybe we can mend your dress so it looks almost as good as new." Said Kari comforting her. "Just remember, next time when I say to be careful, I mean it, okay?"

"I will, Mommy. I'm sorry." She sobbed.

After the party, and all the ladies left, the guys joined us again, and we prepared our dinner, and had a time of fellowship with Steve's family. Steve's brother was just a few years older than Steve. His name was Jacob, and his wife's name was Kari. Jacob was a salesman for a computer company, based in Washington State. Kari was an elementary school teacher. Jacob had a two-week vacation, and Kari wasn't going back to school until the day after Labor Day. Laurie, her five-year-old daughter, would be starting kindergarten this year at the school where she was teaching. Her son, Aiden, was four-years old, and would be starting pre-kindergarten this year. I couldn't wait to be their aunt. I wanted to spoil them already.

After supper I talked with Kari. I told her about my dilemma of not having any bridesmaids because they were in a serious accident. I asked her if she would be willing to be one, so I could at least have one. She agreed. Her husband had already been chosen by Steve to be his best man, and the children were both in the wedding also.

"Why not, I would love to be your bridesmaid, Jobella. It will be fun. I don't have a gown to wear though. Could we go to choose one?"

"Sure, I need to go by David's bridal to get my gown on Monday, anyway. Do you want to meet me there? I found some lilac colored gowns that we were going to look at for my friends. Maybe one of those would work for you. Maybe you can get grandma and grandpa to babysit the kids and we can shop, and maybe grab some dinner while we are out! It'll be fun!"

"It's a date! I'll enjoy that a lot. It will be great getting to know my new sis-in-law, and getting away from the kids for a while!" She smiled.

At the end of the day, Steve and I loaded up his SUV with all our gifts, and we took them back to the apartment. I invited Steve to stay a while, and have a cup of coffee. It had been a wonderful day, but we both were very sleepy. We curled up on the sofa to watch an old movie, and the next thing we knew the sun was rising. We had fallen asleep.

"Oh no, what are people going to think!" Steve exclaimed. "We spent the whole night together!"

I laughed. "Don't worry about it, we'll just explain what happened. I'm sure people won't think a thing about it. They all know how tired we were. I'm actually glad you didn't try to drive home as sleepy as you were."

Chapter 24

Steven and I went to church the next day, and met up with Steve's family. We explained what happened, and they had no problem with him spending the night under the circumstances. They said they had total confidence in us, and they were glad he didn't try to drive when he was so sleepy.

Pastor Stewart announced our wedding, and the following reception in the activity building for the following Saturday. All of the church members were invited. He had us both stand, and then Steve's family along with us so everyone would know who we were. He told a little bit about some of our trials over the last year. He didn't have to do that. Most of the congregation was aware of everything that happened. We smiled as everyone stood and applauded us.

After church his parents invited us to dinner to eat the leftovers from the day before. Jacob and Kari stayed home with Laurie and Aiden. They decided to sleep in. They were just getting out of bed when we got there. I wished they would have gone to church with us, but they said they 'had gotten out of the habit' after they moved to Washington.

Steve and I would have to work on that, along with his parents. I didn't understand how his brother could be so different. Steven was always religious and his 'call' to be a preacher wasn't anything he ever doubted. Jacob had grown up in the church along with his brother, but he never took to it, the way Steve had. When he moved away he met Kari while he was a student going to Washington State. He was working on his MBA at the time and Kari was in elementary ed. Both of them had liberal ideals, and going to church wasn't part of their agenda. They had actually turned from God, and he was not a part of their plans.

I would make a mental note to talk with Kari, and tell her about my experiences, and then to pray earnestly for her, and her family. I just prayed that nothing would happen to them before they had a chance to get to know God.

Before Steve took me home, we stopped by the hospital to visit my friends. Zoe was getting bathed when we got to her room. She was semi-comatose now. She would drift in and out of consciousness. We promised to come back, and then went on to visit with Billie. The doctors had removed her traction from her leg, but of course, she still had her cast on. She seemed to be in good spirits. They decided to release her later this week, after she was able to get around a little better. She would be in a wheelchair for most of her recovery, since she had a broken arm she could not use a walker or crutches. She was just excited to get out of the hospital. Her mom told us that she would be staying at her house until she could get back on her own. Her mom promised that she would bring her to the wedding, if she felt up to it.

Next I went to Eliza's room. After the last encounter I was a little cautious about going in. I dreaded finding her still straight as a stick in bed like last time. I was pleasantly surprised to see her up in a wheel chair. She still had the collar on her neck though.

"Hi, how are you doing?" I asked

"A little better, now that I can sit up in a chair."

"So have you gotten anymore results, yet? Are you able to move or feel anything?"

"I had an MRI on Friday. They won't tell me the results until tomorrow. I'm getting a little tingling sensation in my fingers and toes. They say it's a good sign that I'm getting my feeling back, even if it is annoying. I still can't move anything though."

"How are things emotionally and spiritually for you?"

"I guess I'm doing okay, emotionally. I'm starting to get use to the idea that I may never get to use my body again, but the slight feelings in my hands are giving me some hope. I'm going to therapy now, and they do range of motion exercises with me, and are teaching me to do things with my mouth and nose that I never thought I'd use them for. They are teaching me to type on the computer with a stick in my mouth. Who would of thought?" she smiled. "Spiritually, I've had a lot to think about laying here in bed. I've listened to what you told me, and I remember what I told you when you were down. I guess I have a head knowledge of God and Jesus, but I just don't feel it in my heart yet. I've done a lot of praying, really I have, but they seem to stop at the ceiling. I don't get a response to my prayers, at least not the way you did, Jobella. I'm still angry with God for what's happened to us in the wreck. Billie came to visit me yesterday. She's pretty upbeat about everything. She told me about her seeing angels at the crash site. I have a hard time believing that. If angels were there how come I'm in the shape I'm in, and Zoe is still in a coma?"

"I can only answer this. By looking at the videos, and pictures of the car, and what awful shape it was in, all three of you should have been killed. I believe God spared all of you for a reason. I believe he did send his angels to protect you from death. He wanted you to be a believer, Eliza. He wanted you to live so that your life would be redeemed from hell, and you would live for him. I can't say whether or not God's purpose is to use you by allowing you to fully recover, or by witnessing from a wheel chair, but I know he wants to be used by you."

"Thank you, Jobella. I'll be thinking on these things. I'll pull up the Bible on my I Pad that mom brought me along with my 'stick' she got me for my mouth." She smiled. "I can actually read the Bible that way with the Bible app I downloaded."

"I'm going back to visit Zoe now. I'm sure she must be through with her bath by this time. I'm going to continue to pray for you that God will continue to heal your body, spirit, and soul."

I went back to Zoe's room in the ICU. She was groggy, but more awake than when I seen her last. "Good afternoon! It's so good to finally see you awake! I missed you so much."

Her mind was still slow to respond. "Who are you?"

"I'm Jobella, your friend. You were driving home from my house on the day of the wreck. We had been talking about my wedding plans and you being a bridesmaid, remember?"

"Oh, I think I remember that. I was with Billie and Eliza right?"

"That's right." I smiled and hugged her. "I'm so glad you remember. That is a good sign."

"That's not all I remember, Jobella. I remember that I think I must have died. At the moment of the crash I started seeing angels. They were cushioning us from the total impact but I starting floating above the wreck. I saw the workers taking us from the wreck and the angels were helping them. I was worried about Billie and Eliza. They looked like they were in a lot of pain. Eliza wasn't moving at all and Billie was screaming out in pain. Her whole L side was mangled. I tried to cry out to them that I was sorry that I had gotten them in a wreck but I don't think they heard me. They didn't look toward me. The next thing I saw was that they were doing CPR on me! It frightened me to see that, but I was calm at the same time. I didn't even feel the shocks or the compressions. I didn't know what was going on. The next thing I knew I was being comforted by what looked like angels. They wanted to take me somewhere. I looked to where they were pointing. It was beautiful, Jobella. It was brighter than anything I had ever seen and there were bright beautiful colors and golden hues. It was a beautiful garden full of the most gorgeous flowers I had ever seen. I think I saw Jesus there, Jobella. He was glowing. He looked like he was tending the garden when the angels and I approached Him. I saw a multitude of people strolling around. I saw my grandparents and my little sister that died when she was a baby and I saw your parents too! They told me that when I returned to tell you that they loved heaven. They missed you, and the twins but they would always be with you in spirit. They wanted me to tell you to be happy in your new marriage and they would be looking in on the wedding this coming weekend. They also said there was going to be a surprise at the end of this year, one that would warm your heart. They didn't say what it was though. They said to continue trusting in Jesus because he is very real and I can tell you for a fact that heaven is a real place as well. After I finished visiting with them the angels said they needed to bring me back. Jesus wasn't through with me yet here on earth. I didn't want to come back. I can tell you that! But I need to talk with anyone who will listen about Jesus, and his heaven. Jobella, I just want to thank you for you telling us about what it means to be saved. Now I know, and it will always be in my heart and I'll always remember what my eyes have seen when I was temporarily away from my body.

After Zoe told me her story about what she saw I had to hug her! "Zoe, you just made my day! Not only because you are no longer in a coma but what you told me was wonderful! It just confirmed for me even more so that heaven is for real! Bless you Zoe! I would like you to do me a favor though. I was visiting Eliza and she is still feeling down. She is paralyzed from the neck down, and she really doubts God, and his existence. I don't think she is a Christian at this point. When you get well enough to move around some and are allowed off the unit to visit her, I would love for you to go to her and tell her what you have just told me. I really think it would help put her over the edge into accepting Christ. Billie could use a visit as well but she is supposed to be leaving the hospital to go stay with her mom and dad by the end of the week. So I don't know if you'll have a chance to see her before she leaves."

"I'll go talk with Eliza when I get a chance. Sounds like she needs some healing. Jobella, you were right all along. I didn't know everything when I talked with you when you were in the hospital, but I know now about salvation and I praise God for a second chance to do something to change the world, at least my world!" She smiled.

I gave her a final hug goodbye and told her to call me and let me know how it went with Eliza. I was grateful for all my friends. I would continue to pray for them in their newfound salvation and for ways for them to share the word, especially with Eliza.

Chapter 25

Monday afternoon, after work I met Kari at the bridal shop to buy a dress for the wedding and to try on my gown to make sure all the alterations were right. I was going to enjoy getting to know my new 'sister'. Today would be our time together, just the two of us, without the distractions of the rest of the family.

We got to the bridal shop and looked around. We found a pretty, simple, but elegant lilac colored dress similar to the ones that my friends, and I were looking at. We decided on the one that she tried it on. She looked stunning in it, and we both liked it right away.

Then the sales lady brought my gown out. I tried it on with Kari's help. It was beautiful. "You are gorgeous in this." She said. "I can imagine how great you'll look with it all put together along with your hair and makeup done. Not that you need much to look great, you're already so pretty!"

"Thank you, you're too kind. You look really pretty in your dress also. I think lilac is your color!" I smiled.

"You chose well, in deciding your colors for your wedding. By the way, whatever made you chose that color and lilacs for your flowers anyway?'

"We had lilac bushes on our land outside our house that burned down. I always loved the fragrance of them and their color. Mom would sometimes pick a bouquet of them for our dining table. They always looked so elegant. I guess part of the reason I chose them for my flowers was in honor of my parents."

"That is such a neat story, and a neat thing to do. You chose well because the color is gorgeous. I can't wait to see what the decorations and bouquets look like!"

"Me too, I hope my wedding planner comes through for me with good choices!"

"I'm sure she will, that's why they are paid the big bucks!" She laughed. "They usually have very good taste."

"I'm not worried. I liked what she showed us."

After we left the bridal shop we went out to eat. This was going to be our girl's night out, so we were going to splurge, and go to a good restaurant. I wanted to find a place where it would be somewhat private because I wanted to talk with her about Steve's, and my faith, and find out how things were with her, and the Lord. I had to find a way to talk about it without actually putting her on guard, or worse, not wanting to be with me anymore for fear I wouldn't accept her if she wasn't a Christian.

After we were seated at the table at the restaurant, the waiter brought out our menus, and some ice water. We made our selections and while we were waiting for our orders, we started to talk. I thought that the best way to lead into my witnessing was to tell her all about my experiences. That usually works the best when trying to tell someone about what it means to be a Christian.

"So, are you and Steve ready for this wedding to get over with?" She asked.

"It's definitely something to look forward to. I'm excited about it, but a little nervous. I just want everything to go alright, and I know with God's help it will."

"It looks like you planned it well. I'm glad that I could step in for at least one of your bridesmaids. I'm excited about it, actually!"

"Yes, I'm glad you could do it too. It does make me sad to see what my three friends are going through though. I wouldn't wish it on anyone. They seem to be holding up well. Thank goodness they know the Lord and are depending on him to work out everything in their lives."

"How is that?"

"Well, they all thanked me for talking with them about my faith, and what I went through and how God helped me. All of them are actually getting stronger everyday, and Billie and Zoe both claimed that there were actually angels that helped them survive the crash. That had to be true because if you saw the condition of the car they were driving you would know they had to have some kind of divine intervention because they all should have been killed. Zoe had a near death experience, and said she had actually gone to heaven briefly. She said she saw my parents, and some of her relatives along with Jesus. They gave her a message to send to me. My parent's were happy about my wedding, and they told her I would be happily surprised at something that was going to happen to me in December. That will be something I'll have to see to believe when the time comes."

"Wow, that is really interesting! I've never known anyone who had an experience like that. It really does make one think. What about the third girl, Eliza, I think her name was?"

"She is having a little harder time. Right now she is paralyzed from her neck down. I've been praying for her to recover, and she is getting a little sensation back in her hands. She knows in her mind that Jesus is real, but she's having a hard time believing it in her heart, but she is slowly coming around. Everything happens for a reason you know. We just have to trust what that reason is, and that God will be able to pull us through our difficulties."

"There was a time when I thought I had that kind of faith, but things happened that made me doubt all of it." Kari said.

"Oh, really? I didn't know. Do you want to share with me what happened?"

"Sure, my parents and I went to church when I was young, but something happened in our church with our youth pastor, and there was a big scandal. It was blown way out of proportion, and they just got fed up with the whole thing. Dad said they were just a bunch of hypocrites in the churches, and he didn't want anything else to do with any of them. Dad became so bitter that it was difficult to live with him after it happened. He started drinking, and being abusive. My parents divorced soon after it happened. I blamed the church for destroying my family. Jacob, and Steve grew up in a Christian home and Jacob started out trying to get me to go to church with him when we first dated, but when he saw I had no interest whatsoever, he gave up. He loved me, and decided he'd rather have me with no God, than to have God without me."

"I'm so sorry that you went through that with your church, and family. It looks like Satan had a foothold in your church, and caused the division, and then used it to destroy your family. Yes there are hypocrites in the church, just like there are in any areas of life. The only difference is that the hypocrites in church if they are saved are going to heaven. If you don't mind I would love to talk to you more about my church and my relationship with Christ. It's really important to me to help you understand it more. Not all churches are like the one your family went to. As a matter of fact, if your mom and dad had visited other churches, and found one that they were comfortable in, and one that taught the real love of God, your family might've still been together, and they'd all been saved."

"I would have liked that, and I would like to talk with you some more about your experiences. Maybe we can get together later this week if you have time."

We left off talking at that time. Our dinners were being served, and we were both hungry. It made me feel glad that we at least had an open line of discussion on religion now, and she didn't completely turn me away. I would look forward to talking with her again.

During the rest of our meal we talked about the wedding, and how all the plans were going, and what the next steps were. The rehearsal, and rehearsal supper were scheduled for five o'clock on Friday evening. I didn't know if I would be able to get back with her before then.

Steve and I would be busy with our jobs, and the evenings would be spent packing, and getting ready for our honeymoon cruise, and getting our apartment ready for the two of us to live together. He had to pack up all of his clothes, and the few pieces of furniture he had to move in. He kept just enough clothes at his home to get by until Saturday. After we got back from our honeymoon we would have just a couple of days before our classes started for the fall semester.

I was able to get off early everyday that week. My boss knew I had a lot to do. Abby offered to come home with me to help me clean, but I told her that it would do me good to work on my apartment. It was a kind of therapy for me. I relished getting our home ready for my new husband, and it also kept my mind off the fact that my parents wouldn't be at my wedding, and neither would my brother and sister.

I didn't have a chance to visit my friends at the hospital that week either. I would need to get back with them after the honeymoon, and things were getting settled down. Billie would be out of the hospital by then, and her mom said she might try to get her to the wedding. Eliza still had a long way to go to her limited recovery. She would probably still need to be in rehab working with her new limitations unless God cured her, but even then she had a long way to go. Zoe was still pretty weak as well. She had several internal injuries, and still needed some recovery time from being in a coma. She was awake but she had a lot of muscle strengthening to do before she could get around better.

Steve and I had everything pretty much the way we wanted it in the apartment by the time Friday night came. We felt that we were ready to move in together at last, after the wedding, and honeymoon of course!

Steve came by the apartment around four o'clock on Friday. We were both excited, and nervous at the same time. We would be meeting our wedding party, and his parents at the church around five. Steve's brother was his best man, and he had a couple of his friends from school as his ushers. Abby was my matron of honor, and Kari, my future sister-in-law was my bridesmaid. Aiden, my future nephew, was our ring bearer, and Laurie, my future niece was our flower girl. Libby, my wedding planner, and Steve's parents were also there.

Pastor Stewart hugged Steve, and I before the rehearsal started. He knew everything Steve and I went through this past year and he was so thrilled that the day had finally come that we were preparing for our wedding. I thought about Kari and our conversation at the restaurant the other night as the pastor prayed for us and for our families. I wondered how this outreach of love from our pastor had affected her. If she could see love in action from a church congregation that loved the Lord maybe it would affect her and Jacob. I would pray for that at any rate. Maybe the next couple of days will be a turning point for her.

Chapter 26

It was finally here, the day of my wedding! I was so excited I hardly slept a wink. It was a gorgeous day, and it was like God was smiling down at me from heaven. I thanked him for this day, and I prayed he would open up a window in heaven so that my Mom and Dad could see me as well, at least be with me in spirit!

Abby would be coming to get me around eleven. We were going out for a light lunch, and then to the beauty shop to get our hair styled, and have a professional makeup session. Then it would be on to the church to meet up with my new mom, Kari, and Laurie to get into our dresses. The wedding planner would already be at the church assembling the decorations and catered items including the cakes.

Abby was right on time. "We'll are you ready for this, Jobella?"

I flashed her a big smile. "You have no idea! I've been ready ever since I met Steve!"

"He's a good one that's for sure! Good looking and God fearing, you don't get that combination everyday!" Abby laughed. "No one deserves this happiness more than you! I've been with you from the beginning of your trials and I must say that this day is something that we all hoped would be yours, and Steve's to have and look forward to."

"A little over a year ago, I didn't think I would ever be happy again. God is so good!"

"Your apartment is really adorable. I love what you, and Steve did to fix it up. I know you'll be anxious to get back from your honeymoon, and start your life together as a married couple!"

"After we get settled, we want to have everyone over for a little get together. There's a clubhouse with a barbeque that we can rent out for an afternoon as long as we give the landlords a couple weeks notice. I'll be seeing you at work so I can give you a heads up when we have it."

"Sounds like fun! I'll be looking forward to that! Well, I guess we'd better get going! It's almost time for our 'beauty' appointment, and we still have to get a quick bite. I don't want you passing out on me when you're walking down the aisle!" She laughed.

I felt like I was moving out of the apartment with my overnight case of makeup, and my wedding dress in tow. I also brought a change of clothes to wear back to the apartment after the wedding. I didn't want to ride back in my wedding gown.

We were going to spend our wedding night here at the apartment since we were leaving Monday to go on our cruise. We would just have a romantic night alone here in our apartment, just the two of us for our first night as husband and wife.

After leaving the beauty shop I felt like a model. My makeup, and hair were beautiful. Abby had hers done as well, and she looked beautiful, but she was an attractive, distinguished looking lady to start with.

"Jobella, you are gorgeous! You're pretty even without make-up, but what they have done with you, wow!!! You look like you could walk anyone's red carpet. I can't wait to see you in your wedding dress as well!"

"You too! We are both going to be turning heads today!" I laughed.

When we got to the church we tried to avoid the areas that we knew the men would be in. I didn't want Steve to see me until the final 'unveiling'.

We came to the Sunday school room that was set-aside for my party and me. Laurie was already in her purple flowered dress. It had been torn at her Nana's house but it was repaired beautifully. It looked as good as new.

"Laurie, you look so pretty in your new clothes and your tiara. You look just like a little princess! Do you have your basket all ready with the rose petals?"

"Aunt Jobella, you look pretty too. Yep, I'm already!" with that she twirled around to show me the full effect. When she did, she dropped a few of the petals out of the basket.

"Laurie, what did I tell you about being careless? Make sure you pick every last one of the flowers up." Commanded her mom.

"She's just excited, Kari, no harm done!" I winked at Laurie.

"I know, but if I don't rein her in, she'll get even more carried away." Laughed Kari. "You do look beautiful, though. Steve is a very lucky man!"

"I'm the lucky one!" I replied as I slipped into my gown.

Kari and Abby put their dresses on after I had mine on. The colors of their gowns blended perfectly with the flowers we were going to carry. The dresses were simple A-line dresses with an empire waist and they wore a lacey drape around their shoulders. My dress was an off-white color satin, with a lace bodice. It was a strapless gown with a bolero lacy jacket to match. It was an A-line dress as well, and it had a long train. My veil was attached to a tiara similar in style to what Laurie wore.

Laurie squealed with delight when we were finally finished getting ready. "We all look so beautiful. We're all princesses and Aunt Jobella is the queen!"

We all had to agree as we looked in the mirror. We all did look beautiful. The photographer came in to photograph us after we were all in our dresses, and before we headed down the aisle.

My boss stuck his head in the door and motioned that they were just about ready for us. I had decided to let my boss give me away since I didn't have my Dad to do that. He had been great with taking me under his wing at work, and encouraging me to get my law degree. He was also the one that helped me to get my family's car back.

Abby and Kari and then Laurie lined up at the door of the sanctuary waiting for their cue to enter from the organist. I had to stay behind with my 'surrogate dad' until they were in position at the front of the church. Laurie and Aidan looked adorable as they walked side by side. Aidan proudly held the ring pillow high as Laurie began to sprinkle the flower pedals.

At last it was my turn. The strains of the wedding march came through the door. My boss opened the door for me to enter the sanctuary. Everyone stood up to watch me walk down the aisle. I just prayed that I wouldn't stumble or have a missed step. I looked ahead at Steve. I thought to myself 'wow does he look handsome, and how lucky I am to be getting him for a husband'. He was smiling at me, and hopefully thinking the same thing.

When my boss gave my hand over to Steve he stepped back. He winked at Abby before sitting down. Steve, and I were lost in each other's eyes when we said our vows, and exchanged rings. When we kissed, it was the most magical kiss I had ever received. I really did feel like a princess being swept off her feet by her prince charming.

It seemed only like a moment, even though the ceremony lasted about a half an hour. After lighting the unity candle we headed back down the aisle as Mr. and Mrs. Steven James.

I glanced around as we were heading out the door to see who came to honor us today. I stopped short when I saw them. A couple I had never seen before. The man looked a little bit like my father and the woman standing next to him was smiling at him. She looked a little familiar as well, but I couldn't put my finger on where I would have seen her. They must have been visiting one of the families that came. I just shrugged it off, and moved on, but it left the strangest feeling in my heart. I would have to ask Steve about it later.

When we went outside to make pictures. I looked for them again but they were nowhere to be found. Maybe I wanted my parents there so much I just thought I saw them thinking they were my parents.

Waiting outside for me was my friend Billie, sitting in her wheelchair with her mom standing next to her. She looked great except for her casts. She had them rewrapped with purple in honor of my wedding.

"You look awesome!" She cried. "But I knew that you would! And Steve, he cleans up real good, girl, are you lucky or what?"

I gave her a hug and whispered in her ear. "He's mine now, so keep your eyes in your head!" I laughed.

I had the photographer take a picture of Steve and I with Billie, before we moved on to the routine photographs with the wedding party, and Steve's family. I wished my family was there to get pictures with but I pushed that thought away, and concentrated on my new family. If I thought too much about my family not being there, I would start crying again, and I couldn't have that.

The reception was beautiful. My wedding planner was there the whole time and even served the guests so my family, and I wouldn't have to. The centerpieces were awesome. I almost wish I'd chosen artificial ones now so I could keep them forever but then I wouldn't have the delightful fragrance of the lilacs, which is one of the reasons I chose them to start with. I guess pictures of them would have to do, to remember them by. I would take one home with us to enjoy this evening though. It would be pretty with my candlelit evening I had planned for us. I told everyone in my wedding party to take one also when they left.

I looked around the reception hall to see if that strange couple was still here. I wanted to introduce Steve, and myself to them, but they were nowhere to be seen. I guess they just came for the ceremony.

After the reception, we went out of the activity building so the guests could see us off, and blow tiny bubbles at us. At the end of the driveway I turned and threw my bouquet. I heard Billie let out a yell! She had caught it even though she was lower than anyone else seated in a wheel chair.

"Congratulations, Billie." I said. "Any prospects?"

"I'll never tell." She winked.

We changed into our street clothes, and said our goodbyes, and left the party that was still going on.

"Let's escape before they know we're gone!" Steve whispered.

"Good idea." I laughed

We ran to Steve's SUV. There was writing all over the windows with shoe polish and streamers attached to the mirrors and antennas and a ton of tin cans dragging behind, but we moved on out anyway! We just laughed about it all the way home. I'm sure people passing us understood, and thankfully the police didn't try to stop us. I could just imagine them grinning, as we passed by.

It was around six o'clock by the time we got to the apartment. Before we could rest we wanted to unload the SUV, and clean it up. I was looking forward to our time alone. A night we wouldn't have to spend apart, a time that we would be joined the way God had intended, as husband and wife.

After everything was unloaded, and the flowers, and cake were put away, we were finally able to rest, and enjoy our time alone. I lit some candles, and put the lilac centerpiece in the middle of the table. For our supper I had some tossed salad in the refrigerator already made up, and we broiled some steaks. I wasn't really hungry but Steve was famished. We opened a bottle of wine, and ate our supper by candlelight and soaked in the ambiance, and the aroma of lilacs.

Our wedding night was amazing. Steve was so tender and loving, and it felt so good to be in his arms all night. I still couldn't believe I was finally married to this wonderful man.

We decided that we would go to church in the morning, but we would have to leave soon after, though, because we had to drive to Charleston this afternoon to check into our hotel. Our cruise would leave out early Monday morning, so we were spending Sunday night in Charleston.

During the church service, pastor Stewart welcomed us as the newest married couple. We had to stand of course, and every one clapped. It made me feel good to be loved by so many people. Steve's family was there including his brother Jacob, and Kari, and the kids. It made me feel good to see them. I hoped the message would be meaningful to them so they would take another look at their relationship with Christ. I glanced at Kari every so often and she occasionally had tears in her eyes. I knew something was happening in her life as the preacher spoke of the love of the Christian family, and of the Father's forgiveness. The message was of the prodigal son. It couldn't be more appropriate for their situation.

After church, the pastor wanted Steve, and I to stand at the back door so the congregation could greet us as they left. Everyone was so gracious, and kind. I was so grateful for such a loving church. A few people that didn't come to the wedding handed us gift bags, and cards as they left. I made a mental thought to get more thank you cards, when we returned.

I wondered if I would see that couple that was at my wedding again, but they were nowhere in sight. I wondered if I would ever see them again.

When we got home we packed the SUV, and opened our gifts that we just received. We were excited that some people gave us money. That would be helpful during our trip. We pocketed the cash for the trip, loaded up our bags, and headed out on our new adventure.

Neither one of us had ever been on a cruise before so this would be a lot of fun. It would be hot this time of year in the Caribbean, but I was looking forward to soaking up the sun and the beaches. We checked the weather forecast for the area, and luckily no hurricanes were predicted. So it would be smooth sailing.

"It's too bad that we couldn't bring my little brother and sister." I said to Steve.

"Hey, this is our honeymoon." He smiled. "Maybe next summer during our summer break, we can take them on their own adventure."

"Okay." I laughed. "It's a date!"

Chapter 27

The day had finally come! Joanie and Josh were going to live with the Jordans. They finally were given temporary custody through the foster program while they were awaiting their adoption hearing in December.

"Mama Sadie, Daddy Kyle!" They heard the children call as they came running up the steps. Sophie and Peter were lugging their suitcases, slowly walking behind them, and last of all came Ruth. She had some paper work for them to sign for the transition.

They opened the door, and the twins grabbed them around their legs obviously excited to be finally be there.

"We're here, we're finally here!" exclaimed Joanie.

"Will we be staying now, Daddy Kyle, forever and ever?" asked Josh.

"Yes, Lord willing, you will be ours forever. Would you like that?"

"Oh yes!" laughed Joanie

"Me too!" added Josh.

"Sophie and Peter, would you like to see the children's rooms? They are all ready for them and you can meet Snowball and Charlie." They set their bags down and they followed the twins up the stairs.

They went to Joanie's room first. "Look Mama Sophie and Daddy Peter. My room is like a room for a princess!" she said, and then looked under the bed, looking for Snowball. She had to pull her out from under the bed because she was afraid with all the commotion going on.

"Look at my new kitty, her name is Snowball. Isn't she beautiful?"

Sophie hugged Joanie. "She's beautiful, honey! No wonder you couldn't stop talking about her."

Next they went to Josh's room. Joanie still was clutching her kitten when Charlie came scampering out. "Charlie, I'm home!" yelled Josh. Charlie ran and jumped in Josh's arms, and started licking his face. Josh started giggling.

"This is Charlie, he's my dog." Smiled Josh. "And this is my room. I love Star Wars, don't you, Daddy Peter?"

"I do, I remember seeing the first one several years ago." He smiled. "I do like your room. You and your sister are going to be very happy, and comfortable here, I can tell."

"We're going to leave you two to unpack your things in your rooms while we talk with Sophie and Peter and the social worker, okay?" smiled Sadie.

"Okay." They both replied.

Kyle took their suitcases up to their rooms so they could start unpacking, and putting their clothes in their drawers.

All of the adults all went down to the kitchen to drink tea and discuss the next steps in transferring the children. Abby was going to join them later, and as they sat around eating sandwiches, and finger foods along with the tea, she made her appearance.

"Hi, welcome." Sadie greeted her at the door. "We're in the kitchen eating a light lunch, would you like to join us?"

"Sounds good, I haven't eaten yet, and I am a little hungry."

The twins came down when they heard them speaking, and eating. "Can we have a sandwich and some milk?" They asked.

"Sure, just make sure your hands are washed after playing with your pets, okay?"

"Yes ma'am." They said. They rushed off to their bathrooms, and when they returned their lunch was served.

"We are going to have you two sit outside at the picnic table, would you like that? Us grownups have some things we need to talk about."

"That will be fun! Good idea!" they laughed.

"Careful not to let Snowball, and Charlie out!"

"We won't, they are closed up in our rooms." Said Joanie.

After they heard the door slam shut, they got back to business. Abby and Ruth shared the paperwork they had. It was to make the transfer of custody legal. It was a more of a formality at this point. They were theirs on a temporary basis pending the outcome of the hearing in a few months. Neither Ruth nor Abby thought that the adoption would be contested after the facts came out of their relationship with the twins being their niece and nephew, and Jobella's biological relationship with them. The only problem would be is if Jobella would contest the adoption. She had her heart on getting the twins back now that her and Steve were married. When she learns that she has an aunt and uncle she knew nothing of, let alone find out that she is their daughter, they don't know how she will feel about it.

They discussed how they still didn't want Jobella to know about the arrangement or their existence until they met in court in December.

"We took a chance, and went to her wedding. We wanted to see our daughter getting married." Confessed Sadie. "We tried to stay in the background. I don't believe she noticed us."

"It was a beautiful wedding, wasn't it?" exclaimed Ruth.

"Oh it was. Jobella was so beautiful!" Sighed Sadie.

"Abby, you looked so pretty as well!"

"Jobella reminded me of Sadie when we were married." Added Kyle. "She looks a lot like Sadie."

"That she does." Said Ruth. "Must be the red hair."

They chatted a little longer about the wedding and then Ruth and Abby got up to leave. They hugged Peter, and Sophie who had tears in their eyes as they were leaving the children behind for the last time.

"We meant what we said about you visiting us often. The twins need a grandparent's influence, and we both think that you fit the bill. The twins love you, and know you, and I want you to continue to be in their lives." Said Kyle.

Ruth and Abbey both thought that was a wonderful plan.

"Children, come and say goodbye to Mama Sophie, and Daddy Peter. They are leaving now."

"Are you going to come as visit us, Mama Sophie?" asked Joanie.

"We sure are, if you want us to."

"Yes, yes!" added Josh.

"Then it will be a date!" laughed Sophie, wiping a tear from her eye. "Sadie and Kyle will have to invite us first of course."

They only had a few days before they would have to take the twins to their first day of pre-kindergarten. They had taken this week off following the wedding, and the transfer of the kids to them so they could have some time together. Sadie decided she would only work part-time during the hours the twins were in school. Kyle of course, as a doctor would be required to work regular hours, and occasionally would be on call.

Kyle and Sadie spent some time going to the park so the children could ride the rides in the playground, and wade and splash in the fountain pool. When they build their house on their property they decided that they would have to make sure they put in a pool for them since they like to swim so much. They also took a day to go shopping. The twins needed new clothes for school, and they wanted to get them a few educational toys to help them in school.

Another day, they made a short trip to the beach in Wilmington, and went to the aquarium. The children enjoyed watching the nature movies, and touching the animals in the petting pool. After the aquarium, they spent the rest of the day on the beach, playing in the sand and splashing each other in the water.

The Tuesday after Labor Day, Sadie and Kyle took the twins to the pre-kindergarten to get them registered, and introduce them to their new teacher. The school was actually located at their home church, and was part of the children's ministry. They knew some of the kids, and teachers personally that worked in the school. They were happy that the twins were so receptive to going. As a matter of fact, they were very excited to be going to school.

They were glad that the school was in a separate building from the church so they wouldn't get confused when they brought them to Sunday school. The Jordans toured the building, and was able to look around the classroom, and meet their teacher and see where the playground, and recess area was, and of course they also saw where the offices, and cafeteria were. It was well set up, and the staff were every bit as professional and educated as they would have been in a regular public school or pre-school.

School would start the next day for the twins. On the way home they stopped by their favorite McDonald's for a happy meal, and took it to the park to eat to celebrate starting school. They talked about what it was going to be like for them to go to school. Sadie told them she would drop them off on the way to work, and she would also pick them up back up after work.

"We're going to school just like 'Bella!" Exclaimed Joanie

"She was in high school, silly." Corrected Josh. "She wasn't in kindergarten like we are going to."

"Jobella started out in a school, just like the one you're going to. Someday when you are older you'll go to high school, and college just like her." Instructed Sadie.

"When are we going to see 'Bella again, Daddy Kyle? We miss her a lot. She said she was going to come, and get us again." Joanie asked.

"You're are going to see her in a few weeks, when it's almost Christmas. She's going to college now, and won't be able to come back home until then." Kyle answered, hoping they would accept that explanation.

"That will be okay, I guess. It will be forever before Christmas though." Sighed Josh.

"It will be here sooner than you think!" Sadie responded.

Chapter 28

The cruise had been wonderful. We had a luxury suite with a private balcony so even staying in the room part of the day was a vacation in itself. We enjoyed going up on the promenade deck, and watching the sunsets as part of our evening routine. The shows were wonderful, just like being in a Broadway theater. We even danced at the captain's dinner. Something we wouldn't think to do any other time but this was our special time. Everyone else was dancing, and we didn't want to feel left out. Especially since they wanted everyone that was celebrating a wedding or anniversary to get up and dance.

The port-o-calls were great. We went to the Bahamas. We mainly walked around, soaking up the island culture, and ate at some quaint hole-in-the-wall locations, and walked along the beaches enjoying the impossibly blue waters, and surf and of course getting tanned.

But it was over now except for the memories, and the photographs. We had bought some of our portraits that they took during the cruise, and a book to put them in. It would be a great scrapbook to have for our first week of married life. I would have to work on that in my spare time!

It was the Saturday before Labor Day now and only two days before Steve and I would be starting our separate schools. We were already preregistered so all we had to do was pick up our orientation packets, and books when we started on Tuesday.

We were going to our parent's house for a Labor Day picnic. It would be a great time to share our cruise memories, and photos with them. Jacob and Kari left to go back to Washington State on Friday because their kids started back to school on Tuesday as well, and they had to get back to work after their vacation.

Every once in a while I thought about the twins. I wondered if they would be heading off to pre-kindergarten on Tuesday while I headed off to college. At this time of my life it is probably just as well that they are in foster care. It is quite a transition from being home alone with a part time job, and being a new college student, married, and still working part time. It was a juggle to do all three things, and do them all well. Hopefully by December I would have everything down to a routine so adding them to our lives wouldn't be a so much of a problem. I know Steve said he would help where he could, but he also had a part time job, and was a full time student, but with the children in pre-school maybe it wouldn't be too bad.

Our Labor Day barbeque was great! Steven and his dad grilled while his mom and I made the potato salad, baked beans, and a red velvet cake for dessert. After dinner we all sat down and showed everyone our cruise pictures. We got extras of a few of the portraits so we could share them with his parents. It was nice to rehash our trip while it was still fresh in our memory. Like it was something we would forget anytime soon!

Over the next three months things did settle into a kind of routine. We would have our breakfast, kiss goodbye, and leave for our separate schools. I worked three afternoons a week at the law firm after school until five, and Steve had a work scholarship at his school, and he worked in the campus's bookstore. Then it was home for supper, homework, and falling into bed exhausted. We went to church on Sundays, and usually ate at his parent's house afterwards, and then back to our school, and work on Monday. I was scheduled to take my LSAT the week before Thanksgiving, so I had to study for that along with my other classes. My boss let me study for it at work as long as we weren't busy. He felt like it was one step closer to my being able to join their firm in the future.

School was going well for both of us. I was taking my pre-requisites for getting into law school, and Steve was in his second year at the seminary. He was getting a ministerial degree. He would have to make a decision soon on what direction he wanted to go in. He was interested in both youth ministry, and missions and couldn't decide which way to go. With the degree I was working on, I was hoping that we could stay closer to home, but of course it would be determined on what God wanted him to do, so I was open to anything. We always have to be open to God's leading especially in choosing what career path we're on.

Fall had set in, and the days were getting a little cooler. The cool air felt good, and I had a ton of energy. I loved North Carolina Falls. The trees were beautiful at this time of year, and I loved walking through the leaves as I went from one class to another. I enjoyed sitting in the quad, and studying with my fellow students. I tried to do as much studying as I could before going home, so I could spend my evenings with Steve.

Before we knew it, Halloween was here, and we only had a little over a month until our hearing to see if we would qualify to get custody of the twins. I couldn't wait to see them again. I prayed that God would work out that miracle that Zoe talked about when she said that she talked with my mom and dad in heaven.

As I thought about Halloween, I wondered if Joanie and Josh would be celebrating it in a traditional way or if they would bypass it. A lot of churches had Fall Festivals during this holiday so that children would have a Halloween alternative. I wondered if they were going to church, and if this were something they would be doing.

The week before Thanksgiving I took my LSAT. Luckily, they were giving the test at Duke. It took most of the day. It wasn't as bad as I thought it would be. My co-workers did a good job prepping me for it. It would be about a month before I would get the results back, and I would be anxious about it until the results were in. A lot of people fail those kinds of tests on the first go around, but as I usually do before I take a test like that, I give it to the Lord in prayer, and trust him for the outcome. It usually prevents me from getting nervous about a test because I know that the Lord is with me as I take it. I wouldn't be able to start my law courses until I pass it, and I really wanted to start my pre-law courses next semester.

At last! Fall break and Thanksgiving. We needed a few days off to recuperate from the last three months. We had gone non-stop since starting school. It would seem good to have a little time to ourselves. We were going to Steve's parents for Thanksgiving dinner, and then Steve and his dad would watch the football games on television. Steve's dad decided to try and deep fry the turkey this year. Mom and I stayed inside working on the rest of the dinner, and dessert and prayed that his dad knew what he was doing. This was going to be his first attempt at frying a turkey. I would've rather cooked it the traditional way. I always loved the smell of the turkey and dressing roasting in the oven, but we gave into his culinary urges to help with dinner. Besides it got them out from underfoot while we were cooking.

The dinner was wonderful, as I knew it would be. My mom-in-law was a great cook. Even my dad-in-law did a great job on the turkey. I was proud of him and Steve.

After dinner we sat around watching the television. I wanted to watch "It's a Wonderful Life" but the guys won out with the football game. Actually Duke was playing a playoff game, so I didn't mind watching my team on television.

The day after Thanksgiving we went to town, and bought our first Christmas decorations. I didn't know if the twins would be joining us for Christmas so we wanted to make our apartment as festive as possible just in case. We did a little Christmas shopping as well, but I didn't know whether to get anything for the kids or not. We did pick out a few things for our parents and co-workers.

It was fun decorating our home with all the ornaments and nativity scene. We wanted to make sure that Christ was the center of our holiday no matter what else we did. We put the nativity set up first of all and everything else would be decorated around that. I was glad I had a fireplace in my apartment. It would probably be another week or two before we got a tree. We didn't want to get one too early and have it wilt before Christmas.

I found myself thinking about the twins again. If they were decorating for Christmas at the foster parents house. At home we always decorated the weekend after Thanksgiving. I wondered if they thought about me at this time of year as well. I didn't know if they were told about seeing me soon.

❦ Chapter 29 ❦

Our hearing was in two weeks now, and I was getting butterflies just thinking about it. I tried to get something out of Abby, and the other partners to see how things were going but they were hushed about the whole thing. I thought it was rather strange because I figured Abby would want to start prepping me for the contingencies that might arise. I didn't like not knowing anything that was going on.

When I asked her how the plans were going she said she thought it was all going to work out in my favor. All she said was that she, and my Aunt Ruth were working on it, and plans were being made. She did, however, say not to spend too much time or energy working on moving the twins in with us until after the hearing in case it doesn't go the way I want it to. If they did come to stay with us it would be a little while before that happened. Paperwork, was all she said.

I must have worried her with my response. I didn't speak to her the rest of the day. She knew I was mulling over what she said.

That night when I got home, Steve was fixing our supper of Thanksgiving leftovers that his mom sent with us. It still smelled just as good as the first time it was cooked. When I walked in I went straight to our room without saying anything to him.

"Hey, what's up? Why are you so quiet?"

"Abby was implying that we may not get Josh and Joanie anytime soon. She said she thought that things would work out in our favor, but not to prepare to bring them home for a while. I was hoping we'd get them before Christmas!" I cried.

"It's going to be okay. God is going to work out everything in his own time, you'll see. You do have faith that God knows what's best, right?"

"Right, but I guess after being apart for so long I just want it all to be over, and for them to be here with us."

"But for the time being, I've got a nice hot supper I've been slaving over all afternoon for you, so put a smile on your face, and let's enjoy this supper, and our relationship with each other, and with God, okay?" He teased.

"Alright, I'll try to be more patient. I'll keep telling myself, it's going to be fine. We'll see the twins in two weeks. I can hardly wait!"

"Now, that's more like it. Now let's eat, I'm starved!"

As we held hands to pray, we remembered our families, especially his brother, sister-in-law, and their children. We prayed they would become closer to God. I prayed too for the twins that their family was good to them, and was teaching them about God. Then I remembered my three friends. With everything that was going on in my life, I had almost forgotten about them. I would have to remedy that soon. Maybe if I went to see them it would take my mind off my own situation for a few hours.

I told Steve that I really should go and visit with them, and he agreed. He actually said he'd like to see them as well. Maybe he could give them a little spiritual insight, if needed.

As it was getting a little late in the evening, I decided to try to contact them between classes tomorrow from my cell phone. I had all their cell numbers on my phone along with their mother's numbers in case I couldn't reach them.

I don't know what made me think of them during our supper prayer, but now that they were on my mind, I couldn't stop thinking about them. Was God nudging me again, concerning them? He did that before their accident. I hoped that everything was okay now with all of them. I was especially concerned with Eliza. I wanted Steve to be able to talk with her if she still had doubts about being saved.

I slept fitfully that night, tossing and turning, and my dreams were scattered between seeing the twins torn from my arms, and my friends abandoning me. When I couldn't get settled, and was moaning from the bad dreams, Steve woke me up.

"Are you okay? You were crying out in your sleep."

"Hold me, I can't seem to get calmed down. I guess I'm thinking about things too much."

He wrapped his arms around me, and held me and kissed me until I was calm enough to go back to sleep. I thanked God again for Steve, my physical rock.

After resting peacefully the rest of the night in Steve's arms, I was more ready to face what the day had in store. We would go our separate ways to school, and to work and I would make my calls through the day as time allowed. I might even call aunt Ruth to see if she had a different slant on what was happening with the twins, and what if anything, she knew.

"I'll let you know later what I find out. Maybe we can schedule a time in the evenings to visit if that's alright with you." I told Steve.

"That's fine, just let me know. We'll schedule our homework, and other things around it. I'll be home by four on most days, and of course, you know what your schedule is."

After my English class on Tuesday morning, I called Billie first. I didn't know if she was still at her mom's house or not, but I figured most people could be reached on their cells. When the call went to her messages I hung up and tried her mom.

She picked up after the third ring. "Hello."

"Hi, this is Jobella. I was trying to get in touch with Billie."

"She's gone to therapy. She got all her casts off last week, and they have to retrain her different muscle groups. She's walking with a walker now. She still can't use crutches, because it bothers her arms too much. She's getting there slowly, but surely though. Thanks for thinking about her. You can probably reach her after lunch sometime. She would love to hear from you. She's dying to see the pictures from the wedding."

"Have you heard anything from Zoe and Eliza?" I asked tentatively.

"I think Zoe has had some kind of set back, and I'm not sure what's going on with Eliza, you may have to get that information from her or her mom."

"Okay, thanks. I'll try to call Billie later. If you see her let her know I called."

"It was good talking with you. You can come over anytime. Just call, and let us know so we'll be sure to be home."

It was time for my next class so I would have to space my calls out. I was thankful that Billie was okay. I just prayed the same for the other two.

Later in the morning I called Zoe. She was out of the hospital as well, but she was having a lot of problems with her motor skills and speech. She still was in and out of therapy as well.

"Hi Zoe. It's Jobella. I was wondering how you are and if you'd like to come by and see me, or if I could visit with you?"

"I'm okay. Here's Mom.

"Have you heard anything about Eliza? I haven't tried to call her yet."

"That is the saddest thing. She still hasn't gotten movement or feelings back in her arms and legs. The last I heard they were going to put her in a rehab nursing home. They want to do more intensive occupational and physical therapy with her. You probably won't get her on a cell, but you can call her mom. I'm sure she'll let you in on what's going on. Continue to pray for Zoe as well, okay? After you spoke with her in the hospital. She had a small stroke and she lost some of her mobility and memory."

That night I told Steve about Eliza and Zoe. I called her mother and she told us that they were going to only hold Eliza in the hospital for another week or two, but then they would have to discharge her to the nursing home. They felt they have done everything they could do for her after three and a half months, but she was going to have to get long-range therapy and would probably need total care for the rest of her life.

The news brought tears to my eyes as I told Steve. He held me in his arms. We decided to stop, and have a season of prayer for her and her family, as well as our other two friends. We would give the pastor and our church an update on them and start a prayer chain for all of my friends on Facebook. We would each of them and their families and offer our support. This was the least we could do for my dear friends. Sometimes when all else fails, and medical options are used up on someone, there is always God. He can still work miracles, and no matter what else happens we won't give up until the miracles happen, whether it is for a full recovery or for acceptance.

Steve and I decided to visit Eliza in the hospital the next night. We found her in the extended care unit. She was by herself when we entered the room.

"Hi, Eliza. How are you doing?" I asked.

"Well, see for yourself! This is how I'm doing." She replied, and then added when she saw Steve, "Hi, Steve."

"We just wanted to visit for a little bit. Your mom told us about your prospects."

"So, you're here to try to cheer me up, then?"

"Well we did want to see you and pray with you."

"Don't waste your time. If God wanted me to be healed, I would have been healed by now. I don't think I can serve God in my condition anyway, and I don't think He expects me to either. I think He just gave up on me."

"He's not given up on you, Eliza." Said Steve. "He uses people in all kinds of conditions, just as they are. He used people in the past that were blind and some people in their deathbeds to write beautiful hymns. He even used people who were quadriplegics, make beautiful drawings, and paintings, using only their mouths with a pencil or paintbrush, and made them to glorify God. Just look at that Christian lady several years back that broke her neck in a diving accident. She's a famous artist and writer now. Life wasn't easy for her either, and I'm sure she wanted to blame God several times for her accident, but she was able to be used by God because she had faith, and determination to not let her disability get in her way to be a servant of God."

"But she had talent to start with. It was easy for her."

"I believe God has given you a talent also. You just need to tap into the power of God and the talents he's given you. He can make it happen. We also aren't going to give up on the idea of you getting better either."

"Thank you both for coming. You have given me something to think about. I will pray about it, and I want to thank you both for your concern. I have been really depressed over the last three months, and several times I prayed, but it didn't seem like the prayers were going anywhere. I guess because I was too angry with God for doing this to me. Maybe other's prayers for me will do some good as well."

"I would like to pray with you at this time before we go." Steve added and Eliza nodded her assent. "Our Father, be with our sister Eliza. You know her life, and her future. You know what her needs are at this time. We pray for her complete healing, both in her body, and spirit, but especially her spirit. Help her to accept the outcomes, whatever you deem them to be. We will give you the honor, and praise for whatever happens. In Jesus name I pray, amen."

"Thank you, Steve. Your words meant a lot to me. Jobella, you've got a good one here. He's going to be a great minister. By the way, next time you see me, you'd better bring your wedding pictures. I would love to see them."

"We'll be sure to do that."

We left her room, feeling like maybe we cracked a little bit of her hard shell that's keeping God out. Maybe with further meetings, and prayers, maybe God can make a difference in her life.

Chapter 30

The day had finally come at last. As we were getting ready for the hearing later this morning, my stomach was in knots. I would finally get to see the twins after over a year and a half. I think Steve was almost as nervous and excited as I was. He was pacing the floor while he was waiting for me to get ready.

"What do you think is going to happen today? Do you think you'll get custody of your brother and sister? Do you think they'll remember us and know we're married now?"

"You are sure asking a lot of questions. I don't know what is going to happen. Abby hasn't given me any clue about it. I just quit asking her after a while. I just know she's been very secretive about it, though. I think they will remember us. It's not been that long. I don't know if they've been told about us being married."

Later we were in the courtroom waiting for the judge to appear. Abby was sitting next to me, watching me was I was doodling furiously on my yellow pad anxiously awaiting the twins to come in. She said they wouldn't be there until later in the day. They would come in shortly prior to the decision by the judge. Because of their age and vulnerability the judge was afraid their presence would be disruptive to the hearing.

I almost felt as nervous as the last time I was here during uncle Bud's trial.

"Don't worry, it's going to be alright." Abby whispered, patting my hand, trying to reassure me. She noticed how fidgety I was.

"I don't want to lose them to the system. I love them, and want to take care of them." I whispered back.

We were interrupted by the bailiff, "Here ye, here ye, the right honorable Judge Peterson presiding. Please stand."

We all stood as directed, and then sat down after him as per court protocol.

"We are here today to determine the custody of Joanna and Joshua Jordan. We will hear from the social worker assigned to the case, and the officer on duty the night the children were taken into protective custody after being left at the station by their sister. We will also hear from the current foster parents, as well as the previous ones. Then we will evaluate the plea of the sister, Jobella Jordan James, in this case who wants to be granted the privilege of caring for them. After all of the testimony is given a decision will be made whether or not to grant Jobella Jordan James custody, or to make other arrangements for their care."

I was more nervous than ever after he said that. I didn't realize so many people would be involved determining my fate with the children. For the first time, I felt like I was on trial. As Abby looked at me, she was concerned. I had turned pale, and felt faint. Waves of nausea were overflowing in me.

"Ms. Freeman, would you call your first witness?"

"I would like to call Officer Gerald Remy to the stand."

After being sworn in, Officer Remy began his testimony. "I was on duty the night Ms. Jordan brought her brother and sister in to the station. She was visibly shaken, and tearful when we called in a forensic doctor, and later a social worker. The children had signs of abuse. There was no other way to describe the bruises and whelps on their bodies. It was obvious that Ms. Jordan did not abuse them. The children clung to her, and they all three described what happened at the hands of their aunt and uncle."

"So what you are saying is that Ms. Jordan came of her own free will to report her aunt and uncle for abuse."

"That's right. I'm not sure she knew the consequences of her reporting them, and that the children would be taken from her, and the home where they were staying."

"Why do you say that?"

"When the social worker came to take them away, she was fearful for them, and afraid she'd never see them again. She begged us to let her keep them."

"She didn't have her own home or a job at that time, how did she think that she would be able to care for them?"

"I don't know if she thought that far ahead. She just wanted the children to be cared for, preferably by herself."

"I have no more questions for this witness your honor."

"Officer Remy, you may step down. Ms. Freeman, you can call your next witness."

"I would like to call Mrs. Grace Welbourn."

"Mrs. Welbourn, you and I have been on cases together over the years. I know it's been at least twenty years we go back. I appreciate that association very much. You've done a lot of good for people, and have placed a great number of children in foster care under a lot of different circumstances. You've even helped with adoptions from time to time. What makes this case so different?"

"I was called to the police station on the night that the abuse happened, so I first saw them when the wounds were fresh. This particular case tore me up because I thought how awful to have just lost your parents, and home and then having to go live in squalor with abusive and drunk relatives. I know Ms. Jordan wouldn't have chosen that situation if she knew what her aunt and uncle were really like. I believe she just came to the station, kids in tow, to report her aunt and uncle. I don't think she ever thought they would be taken from her. She had already lost so much, and then to lose the twins as well, it had to be hard for her. She appeared to be totally dejected when they were taken away by me, and she turned to leave."

"But you did what you had to do for their well being."

"I know that, and I believe Ms. Jordan knew that as well. The children couldn't stay in that environment. I felt that once Ms. Jordan had her own place, and a job, we could relook at the situation at that time."

"But other events happened then to prevent her seeking employment, and a new home."

"Yes, the court is aware of everything that happened since that time."

"If you were to relook at the situation today, and have to determine if Ms. Jordan would be a fit guardian for the children what in your own professional opinion would you decide."

"Many things have to be looked at when we determine the suitability of a home. Is there a father and mother figure, and are they mature enough to care for the children. Do they have a stable income? Is there love in that home, and is there at least one parent with them at all times when they are not in school. Do they have proper medical insurance in case one of the children gets sick? They need to be able to care for the foster children, as they would their own. They also have to be aware of the responsibility that comes from having children in their homes."

"So what do you think about Jobella's suitability, given these circumstances?"

"I don't know Jobella all that well, but I'm aware that she, and her husband are in school full time, and are working part-time. That doesn't leave a lot of time left to care for the twins. Mr. and Mrs. James do have a home now, and a loving relationship. That is in their favor and I do believe she loves her brother and sister very much. I guess my only concern is the time factor, and juggling too many responsibilities. I'm afraid that she wouldn't be able handle everything that is going on in her life now, and do a good job with everything."

"Thank you for your input, Mrs. Welbourn."

Abby looked over at me, and I was in tears. It wasn't looking great for me after what the social worker said and she was concerned for me.

"Call your next witness, Ms. Freeman."

"I would like to call Ruth Applewhite."

With that I looked up. Shock must have shown on my face, because Abby looked straight at me when she called her. I think she wanted to see what my reaction would be.

Ruth was my aunt and I've seen her around town occasionally, and I knew she finally got her act together, but I had forgotten that she had gone to college and finished her degree in social work of all things. I was shocked when I found out that she was involved in this case.

"Ruth, you've been involved in this case since the very beginning, a year and a half ago, and now you are involved again. Can you tell us what has happened and how you figure into this case, now?"

"I'm ashamed to say that a year and a half ago I was part of the reason, Jobella lost the children to start with. My husband at that time was drunk and abusive, and I was only a little better myself. Since he went to prison, however, I basically turned my life around. I had to serve community service time at the women's shelter, and I got interested in going back to school to finish my degree in social work. I actually only had a few classes left to finish when I married Sam. Well I finished my degree, sold our house, and I got an apartment. I got right with the Lord again, and started back to church. After I finished by degree, I got a job with the county social service department. They trusted me enough to assign the twins to me. I was flabbergasted they would do that, but because of the way I had changed, they felt their welfare would be a good test for me."

"Since they had been placed with Sophie and Peter Dickson, you developed quite a relationship with them."

"Yes, Sophie and Peter were great with the twins. It was a little shaky at first according to their former social worker, Mrs. Welbourn, but by the time I took over the case, they were very close to the twins. Sophie and Peter were kind of like the grandparent's they never knew."

"Were they treated well in this home?"

"Oh yes, the Dicksons were very loving. They were a little strict, but never demanding or abusive."

"I've met Mr. and Mrs. Dickson. They are a lovely couple and from what I've seen, they were very loving to the children." Replied Abby.

"I had a few qualms about the children leaving their care and moving to another home."

Again Abby looked at me to see my reaction to this turn of events. I was a little shocked when I learned that the twins were torn from a home they so easily must have loved. Was this going to make a difference in my being able to get them?

"You've moved them to another home?" asked Abby

"Yes this one was even more suitable. We moved them around the first part of September. It ended up that the couple were actually a part of their family."

"I didn't think the children had any other relatives in the area."

"They didn't live in the area at the time the kids went to live with Mr. and Mrs. Dickson. This couple was missionaries in Java. I knew nothing about them until about six months ago. The Jordan's lost touch with them about nineteen years ago and never heard from them since. So we didn't even think about them."

Oh my gosh! I didn't know anything about this! This day kept getting more and more bizarre. I had relatives that were missionaries? Did they plan to just come back here and set up housekeeping with my brother and sister like nothing had ever happened? I wasn't sure I liked where this was going. It sounded like a plot to keep me from getting the twins. Now I know why Abby wasn't saying much to me. She knew this was happening. Then it hit me. This must have been what the letter from Java was all about. The letter Abby didn't want me to see.

When Abby saw how upset I was getting, she called for a recess. It was close to lunchtime, so we all decided to go, and grab a bite to eat at the courthouse dining room. Steve and his parents joined us.

I was picking over my food and trying to decide if I really wanted to eat, or go to the bathroom, and bawl my eyes out.

When Abby came to the table she sat down beside me. She saw that I was on the verge of tears. "Jobella, you've known me for almost two years now, and you know I only want what's best for you, right?"

"Of course, you've been almost like a mother to me."

"I know that some of the things you're learning about today have been shocking for you, but it's not the end of what you're going to learn today. Trust me, okay? By the end of the day you are going to be a different person, but in a good way!"

With that she put her fork down, and gave me a hug. Poor Steve didn't know what to think. I've been so emotional lately! My stomach was doing flips so I decided that I'd better force myself to eat something, or I would pass out before the day was over.

When we got back into the courtroom, I was still nervous. I just couldn't get over everything I learned this morning. I sure didn't know what to expect from the rest of this day.

They would be bringing the twins in this afternoon, and my heart longed to see them again. No matter what happened, I would see them, and I would still be their sister, and they would always be in my heart.

The judge came in and called the session back to order.

"Mrs. Freeman, please call your next witness."

"I would like to call either Sophie or Peter Dickson to the stand."

Sophie and Peter whispered to each other, and it was decided that Sophie would testify.

"Sophie, can you tell us what it was like to care for the twins starting from the beginning?"

"I just want to say that they are darling children, and they never gave us a bit of trouble. At the beginning they cried a lot though, because they missed their mom and dad, and Jobella, of course, but after a while they got use to us, and we became like their family. We are looking forward very much to continuing to be able to visit with them, which we have done since they moved in with their new family."

"What do you think about the family they moved in with?"

"They are wonderful. I couldn't ask for anyone better to care for them, and the children love them."

"Ms. James is trying to get permanent custody of the twins. That's what this hearing is about. Do you think it is in the best interest of what the twins need, to be turned over to her at this time?"

"That isn't my call to make, ma'am, but the children do need a lot of care, and I know it's going to be hard for Mr. and Mrs. James while they are in school to give them the proper care they need. I hear they are newly married, and while that is wonderful, it can be stressful as well."

Why is Abby doing this to me? Why is she bringing all these people here to tell the judge that I wouldn't be able to handle it? What is going on?

"Thank you, Mrs. Dickson. You may step down now."

"Your honor, I would like to call Jobella Jordan James to the stand now."

I turned and hugged Steve and walked slowly to the podium.

"Jobella, you and I have been great friends and work partners. I have defended you in your trial against your uncle, and have been with you when you were hospitalized, and even was your matron of honor at your wedding, and I continue to be your friend even through this hearing."

"Yes ma'am. Like I said before you've been like a mother to me."

"I know you want to see your brother and sister again, and for them to become a part of your family. This is very important to you. I also know how extremely busy you are with school, and with working at the firm. You are a perfectionist from what I've seen, and I know you'll go far given the right circumstances."

"I want the children, and my heart yearns for them. I will be very disappointed if they are not a part of my life."

"Jobella, the children will be coming into the courtroom in a few minutes, but I want to prepare you for what you are about to see. The children are very happy now, and their new family is great. They will be coming in with this new couple, and this couple is considering adopting them."

"No!" I cried, "They can't do that! They are my brother and sister! I want to adopt them myself!"

"Jobella," she paused and smiled. "The new couple wants to adopt you as well, as their daughter, along with the twins."

What was happening here, what was she telling me? I felt the room spinning then. I was close to passing out, but I had to stay alert. I would be seeing the twins soon, and I didn't want them to see me passed out on the floor.

As I sat there, the doors to the back of the courtroom opened. Joanie and Joshua came running through them toward me, leaving their foster parents behind. The judge let me come down from the stand, where I was sitting. I threw my arms around them, and hugged them so tight they could hardly breathe. I smothered both of them with kisses. I told them I loved them so much, and wanted to be there for them forever and ever.

Then I looked up at the man and woman that wanted to take the twins, and I wanted to hate them. But as I gazed into their eyes I found that I couldn't.

"'Bella, this is Mommy Sadie and Daddy Kyle. They want to adopt us. We have our own rooms, and they even got us each a pet. They even have a room for you and Steve too." Joanie smiled.

"We want to stay there, 'Bella, and we want you to come see us too!" added Joshua. "Please let us stay with them!"

As I looked at the couple, I realized they were the ones who had come to my wedding. Were they at my wedding to take notes on how they could win the hearing, and be able to adopt the kids?

"You were at my wedding. I saw you, and you looked familiar but I couldn't quite place who you were."

"We wanted to come to your wedding, because we missed out on so much of your life, we didn't want to miss our daughter's wedding too."

Steve had to come over and help me into a chair after that comment. If he didn't, I would've passed out for sure.

"Jobella, you are Sadie's and my daughter." Kyle explained. "Kevin was my identical twin brother. I was in med school at the time Sadie got pregnant and because we were getting ready to go the mission field and didn't want the mission board to find out about you, we gave you up for adoption. Your father never mentioned us to you, and you didn't know we existed up until now, because part of the adoption contract was that we were never to have contact with you, but obviously the circumstances have changed.

Sadie added; "We don't ever plan to take your mom and dad's place, but we want to give you and the twins a home and roots to grow with. We have fallen in love with Josh and Joanie already, and we have always been in love with you, our one and only daughter. We just want to spend the rest of our days getting to know all three of you, and your Steve, and any little ones you may have, and by the way, if I'm not mistaken, will happen a few months from now."

That last comment brought me out of my stupor. "What did you say?"

"I was only pregnant once, but I would recognize that look anywhere!" she laughed.

After we sat around, and talked a bit more, the judge grew weary of our chitchat, and called the court back in order. Abby smiled at me then, and I smiled back at her.

"Did you know about what was going to happen today?" I whispered to her.

"Sorry to keep it from you, but I've been keeping things from you for a long time. I was there at your birth, and adoption, the first time. Life has a way of coming full circle, right?"

"You're kidding, right?"

"Not at all. So are you ready for the judges decision?"

"I guess so."

The judge struck his gavel to quiet everyone down.

"After hearing the testimony, and reading over all the documents, and seeing what has been transpiring in my courtroom over the last several minutes, I'm ready to make my final decision on the disposition of custody of Joshua and Joanna Jordan."

It was so quiet in the courtroom, you could literally hear a pin drop.

"Joshua, Joanna, and Jobella, you three have gone through some horrifying ordeals in the last year and a half but hopefully those problems are completely behind you now. Mrs. James, I know your desire is to adopt the little ones, but I believe it is in their best interest to stay at Dr. and Mrs. Jordan's home while their adoption request is being processed. Also as part of the adoption, Dr. and Mrs. Jordan wishes to add you on as their daughter legally, as well, even though you are already their biological daughter."

I sat in tears as the judge handed down the decision, but the tears weren't for what I was losing, but for what I was gaining, a whole new family, including my brother and sister!

"Mrs. James, do you have any comment, or anything further to say to this court?"

"Just that this has been an incredible day. I feel like I finally have my life back. I have my brother and sister again, and I have a mom and dad! A year and a half ago I didn't think that I would ever be able to smile again. I felt like God had deserted me, and he didn't care what happened to me. I was so down I even tried to kill myself. During this past year things did improve, especially after Steven got better, and we were married, but the whole time, I still felt like my life was incomplete, like a piece of the puzzle was missing. I know it was because Josh and Joanie weren't with me. I thought that if I could just get them back, and raise them, it would make the rest of the pain go away. I didn't know what was going to happen today. I wanted the twins so much that I didn't see any other way it was going to be acceptable to me. That is, until I met Kyle and Sadie, well, my new mom and dad." I smiled, looking at them. "Yes, I accept your decision wholeheartedly. I'm looking forward to getting to know them, and letting them take care of the twins and us, and yes, spoiling their grandchildren."

With that he struck the gavel again declaring that Kyle and Sadie would become the adoptive parents of Joshua, Joanna, and Jobella.

Josh, Joanie and I gathered with Steve, Abby, Kyle, and Sadie, and had a season of love and sharing that carried over, after the courtroom drama, then back to their house. They must have had a sense that they would be victorious today because they had a celebration cake, and ice cream waiting to be eaten after a very large dinner they had prepared earlier.

We talked long into the night, even after Steve's parents had gone home, and the twins went to bed. They confessed to us that they were the ones that sent the bouquet of lilacs and calla lilies the week before our wedding. They found out about our wedding plans from Abby.

As the evening turned to night, Steve and I were so tired that we asked if they would mind letting us spend the night, and drive back home in the morning after breakfast.

"Sure! We have your room all made up for you! Welcome, Jobella, to your new home, at least until our new home is built on your old property."

That night I drifted peacefully to sleep in the arms of my beloved Steve. I finally felt complete again, knowing that the twins were happy and safe in the next rooms, loved not only by me, but also by our new mom and dad.

"So the Lord blessed the latter end of Job
more than his beginning . . .
Job 42:12

Epilogue

A year had passed since the hearing, and our adoption by Kyle and Sadie Jordan, my Mom and Dad. Steven is in his third year of Bible school. God has called him to be a missionary, like his father-in-law, and I fully support his decision. I've started taking my law courses at Duke after passing my LSAT last fall. I'm not exactly sure how it will fit in with my plans to be a missionary's wife, but I know that God will work that out in time.

My Mom was right about my being pregnant at the hearing. Baby Grace is three months old now, and is being spoiled rotten by both sets of grandparents, and her little aunt and uncle. Her grandma James watches her for us while we are at school. We are grateful that she is willing to do that for us. Grace is the love of our lives, and we can't wait until the end of each day to bring her home, and smother her with our love.

I still work at the law firm three afternoons a week. The extra money comes in handy when paying for the necessities like rent, bills, and yes, spoiling our daughter. Steven still works part time as well. We try not to touch my inheritance any more than we need to.

Abby and I are still the best of friends as well as co-workers and I designated her to be Grace's Godmother. My boss at work, who gave me away at my wedding, is Grace's Godfather.

Mom and Dad did buy the land that our house used to be on, and I was glad they did because it would've been a long time before we could have afforded to build there. The foundation is being built now. Dad was able to get the blueprint for our house that was there before. He plans to build their new home similar to the one we lost. Joshua and Joanna will get their wish of having their own rooms again, just as I had promised them.

My new Mom and Dad are great. I have grown to love, and appreciate them more and more every day. Dad's physician practice has done remarkably well, and is seeing more patients everyday, thanks in part to his wonderful skills and bedside manner. Mom is still working at the clinic as a nurse while Josh and Joanie are in school. The twins are blossoming with their new mom and dad, and hardly ever think about the tragedy two and a half years ago.

We all go to the same church now. Mom and Dad decided to join the church that Steve and I got married in. Every weekend it's almost like a family reunion with both sides of the family. Our parents have become the best of friends, and we often go out to eat together, or have dinner at each other's house after church. Mom and Dad still occasionally go to their home church, just to keep up with the friends they made there.

Speaking of friends, I am still in touch with them, but now between school, work, and a new baby, I don't see them as much as I'd like. It remains to be seen what will happen to my three friends and their families, but I know that the God that redeemed me, has touched each of their lives, and hearts in their own special way.